Once Upon A Rhyme

Book One

The Itsy Bitsy Liar

Abigail Manning

Once Upon A Rhyme: The Itsy Bitsy Liar
© 2023 Abigail Manning

ISBN: 9798371770202

Cover design by Karri Klawitter

Edited by Silvia Curry

"The itsy bitsy spider crawled up the water spout.

Down came the rain, and washed the spider out.

Out came the sun, and dried up all the rain,

and the itsy bitsy spider went up the spout again."

prologue

"Too slow, Lacey!" Jezebel stuck her tongue out as she darted in front of me, splashing a muddy puddle on my socks. "I thought you said you were going to beat me!" she teased.

"I'm trying!" I huffed, my cheeks puffed up with the humid air. "You have better shoes than me!" I glanced down at my worn leather boots, riddled with more holes than a slice of cheese. The misting rain soaked through the soles, making my feet slide inside the shoes.

Jezebel looked down at her custom stitched boots, completed with embroidered roses and creeping vines, only a touch extravagant considering she still had plenty of growing to do. "You're just making excuses! Now come on; I want to get home early enough that we can swipe some sticky buns from the kitchen!" She whirled back around and dashed down the half-flooded alley.

With the new hope of sticky buns charging my steps, I sprinted after her, this time only a few feet behind her splashes. Jezebel rounded the corner, but when I followed her turn, I nearly slammed straight into her back. She had halted right in front of the gate to her three-story, carved stone manor. I stopped only inches away from slamming my nose into the back of her head.

"Geez, Jezebel. Why did you—"

"Shh! Be quiet! It's our fathers." She grabbed my arm and yanked me behind the stone pillar that supported the manor's iron gate. I pulled my arm loose from her claw-like grip and peered around the stone's edge. My father's dark locks, wrinkled forehead, and tall physique instantly triggered a smile on my face. Standing beside him was Jezebel's father. He was an important, and sometimes scary, man, with emerald-green eyes that looked kind of like the venomous snakes Mother told me to be wary of.

Jezebel tugged on my sleeve. "Look, some of the palace guards are there, too."

I squashed my brows together with a twist of my lips. Jezebel was right; standing a few paces behind her father were three royal guards, dressed in royal-blue uniforms with glittering gold buttons. I looked back at my father and felt my heart stutter for a moment. I hadn't noticed until now, but Father's typically friendly face was replaced with wide eyes and a jaw clenched tight enough to crack stone.

Did something happen between him and Jezebel's dad?

Jezebel's father, Duke Byron, was one of

the most important men in the kingdom of Reclusia—at least, that's what Mother always said. We've always been fortunate that Father was able to work for him, especially since it allowed me to meet and befriend Jezebel. But right now, it looked like Father was feeling anything but fortunate. His hands balled into fists, brushing against a leather sack I'd never seen before, fastened to his hip.

"You... you sent me into a trap," Father growled, approaching the smug-faced noble, but the pair of royal guards stepped forward, blocking his path.

"Why, I did nothing of the sort." Duke Byron shook his head innocently. "All I did was send my messenger out to pick up a magic stone from the jeweler. I must say, Merrit, I was absolutely *appalled* to hear you were secretly attempting to smuggle unrefined magic stones for your black-market dealings." He pressed a fretful hand to his cheek, cocking a sideways glance at the guards, as if ensuring his act was drawing the proper reaction. "I hated to report you to the guard, especially with you being a father and husband, but as an honest and trusted citizen, I simply could not ignore such a dangerous crime."

Jezebel gasped next to me. My breath snagged in my chest, draining the blood from my face as I turned to face her horrified stare. "Y-your father works in the black-market?" Her eyes widened larger than a glass marble, staring at me with what almost felt like betrayal.

I shook my head, flinging water from my dark braids. "No! Of course not. Father would never do something like that!" I snapped my eyes back to the scene at hand, feeling my heart constrict at the sight of the guards closing in on Father.

"You're a liar!" Father's voice cracked as he stumbled back a step from the guards. He looked like a cornered dog. "You're the one who told me to pick up the stones for *your* dealings! I only did it because you promised that you would send Lacey to a proper academy in exchange fo—"

"Oh, Merrit, lying will only make things worse." The duke sighed as he motioned for the guards to apprehend him. The guards swept up along the sides of my father, seizing him by the arms as I choked back a gasp. The duke shook his head. "There were dozens of witnesses who saw you leave the jeweler right after the stones went missing, and if we look right here..." He strolled casually up to Merrit and tugged the leather bag free from his belt. Without even checking its contents, he handed the bag over to a third guard, who lingered a step back.

The burly guard pulled the bag's cords and looked up with a displeased scowl. "These are the missing stones. You're going to need to come with us, sir." He signaled toward his men, but Father pulled back in resistance.

"No, please! You can't do this." Father's pupils were as wide as a polished onyx platter, shifting his desperate gaze between the duke and the guard. "My family needs me. If I'm imprisoned, then who will provide for them!? Please, Duke Byron, I have been nothing but loyal to you! I beg of you, as a fellow father, please don't entrap my family in your lies."

The duke's face hardened, cracking his smooth façade into a deep frown that creased his chin. "You had best watch your tongue," he snapped, flicking his tongue like a lunging serpent. "I'm not the one who was smuggling deadly stones. You should have considered your precious little family before you did something so foolish." His eyes glinted wickedly as a hidden smile twitched his lips.

No... Father's not a bad person! He can't go to jail!

Father stared at him agape as the duke's betrayal slowly infected his fiery gaze. "You viper! You know perfectly well that I only did this *because* of my family!" Moisture glassed over his eyes, and I leaned out a step from the pillar. I couldn't just hide and watch Father be accused like this. The duke's anger had stiffened, frosted over like a mute chunk of ice that was impermeable to Father's heated stare. "I won't stay quiet about this... my family won't withhold the truth! I will fight to expose your lies. You may have the king's favor, but there are others who possess more."

The slightest crack formed in the duke's unbothered shell as a flush of crimson crept up his neck. Jezebel's eyes followed me as I slipped through the gap in the iron fence, but she didn't say a word to stop me. The duke approached Father with slow heavy steps, narrowing his gaze with every inch like a ravenous predator. "Don't fool yourself, Merrit. No one will listen to the fibs of a desperate thief." His sharp hiss cut through the pattering rain.

"They'll listen to me!" I called out across the manor grounds. The shock of the group was reflected by a crack of brilliant lightning. "I know my father's not a liar! I'll tell everyone the truth!"

Father pulled against the guards. "Lacey! What are you doing here!? Go home at once!"

I winced under his sharp command, but my feet were too sunk into the mud to move. "But, Father... I don't want to leave you." Tears welled up in my eyes, sliding down my cheeks, mixing with the drops of rain that streaked my face. "You didn't do anything wrong. I heard everything. The duke is the one who's lying!"

"Lacey! That's enough!" Father's eyes were frantic. "Go home! Now!"

"But, Father!" I screamed against a roll of thunder. I turned my tear-stained cheeks to the guard, pleading with them to let him go. "I need you!"

I glanced over at the duke, seeing an

irritated flush rise up to the edge of his trimmed beard. He gritted his teeth as he watched the smallest touch of sympathy begin to swell on the guards' faces. He took in a breath that sounded more like an inhaled growl, swelling his chest like a roaring beast. Another crescendo of thunder seemed to rise with his frustration, until his poised demeanor was replaced with a tight-fisted stance that flickered an ominous silhouette behind a flash of white lightning. He swept over to the confiscated sack of gems.

"Hey what are you—" The guard reached out to halt the duke, but froze at the sight of his piercing glare, sharp enough to puncture armor.

"Silence." He sneered at the guard. "Remember who filled those pockets of yours." He snapped his attention to the other two guards with a gritted nod of warning. "Remember who you truly need to fear."

The men shared a silent look—one that didn't sit well in my stomach—then remained obediently silent as the duke fished through the leather pouch with a cotton-gloved hand. The blood drained from Father's face as he watched the duke extract a single white gem from the pouch, examining it with a wicked glint in his eye.

An unrefined stone...

"W-what is that? It looks like..." Father's breath hitched as the duke's focus turned to me. His looming shadow trapped me where I stood, freezing me in fear as he slowly crossed the muddy grounds with a devilish grin. I couldn't move, couldn't breathe, my entire being frozen under his terrifying presence. Father's eyes dilated and he choked on a humid gulp of air. "B-byron, wait! What are you doing!? She's only five, Byron! Don't touch her!"

The duke didn't even flinch at his pleas, waving them off like a pesky insect. I snapped back to my senses and stumbled back, tripping in the mud and fumbling over my worn shoes. I felt like I was moving in slow motion, with the bars of the iron gate growing farther and farther away. When I finally reached the gate, I stopped to squeeze through, but was halted when Jezebel stepped in front of me, eyes sharp and narrowed.

"Jezebel, move!" I pleaded, trying to force my way past her.

She didn't budge; her once friendly smile replaced with a heart-shattering scowl. "I don't help criminals." She sneered.

The sting of her words left me entirely speechless. *Jezebel thought I was a criminal... or she didn't want her father to be caught as one instead.* I spun around with a pounding heart, just in time to see the duke eye me down with a skin-crawling smile. He gently rubbed his fingers across the stone's rigid, unpolished surface, causing sharp sparks of black and silver to jump beneath its surface.

I could barely see Father struggle against

the guards through the blaring rain. He was thrashing and screaming at the duke to show mercy, his veins bulging out of his neck and forehead as he nearly unhinged his jaw with the depth of his shouts. I went as stiff as a block of uncarved marble. I made a meek attempt to back away, but stumbled against my stiffened ankles, falling back against the iron gates with a cry.

The glittering stone was nearly vibrating to life with all the energy stirring inside it. The unrefined power sparked chaotically beneath its sheer surface. Duke Byron glanced down at the stone, inspecting the power's potential as he monitored the rising glow. "Looks like there's enough for a single, life-long curse," he mumbled darkly, casting his venomous gaze down on me. He glanced at my thrashing father from the corner of his eye, allowing the touch of a twisted smile to spread over his thin lips. His body seemed to relax almost pleasurably as he absorbed the horrific look on his contorted features. "It seems only fitting that the daughter of a liar should take after her father."

"No!" Father's scream overpowered a vicious crack of thunder, right as the duke thrust the stone against my forehead with a chaotic snap of light. I screamed, as white-hot pain flooded through my every vein, burning me from the inside out. The stone drained its power into me in a nerve-splitting instant, causing the seizing light within it to fade. My entire body trembled and I collapsed into the mud, watching the duke drop the stone next to me, which was now as black and clouded as a lump of dusty coal. He pulled off his singed glove, still glowing with orange sparks around the char of the fingers and dropped it into the mud with a gentle stamp of his boot. Wordlessly, he turned away from me, every inch of his skin glowing with the satisfaction of his crimes.

I couldn't speak or even cry. My tongue still felt like it was burning, heating from the inside out and strained by some sort of chain that kept it bound in place.

Father's body crumpled under the guard's hold, his knees bending like the snap of fragile twigs as they splashed in the mud. "W-what did you do to her?" His voice was feeble and shallow, barely audible, as his eyes never turned away from me.

The duke's cloak flowed regally across the sopping puddles as he left for the manor, no longer bothering to entertain Father's babbles. Instead, he turned his attention to the head guard, who had remained stark and mute throughout the entire ordeal. "Today you and your men caught a thief in the act of stealing illegal, unrefined magic stones. One of the stones was already used when you caught him, but you have no idea what it was used for. Do you understand?" The duke's voice was almost as tight as his suffocating glare, clearly communicating his unspoken threat.

The guard nodded stiffly. "Yes, sir."

A nauseating smile pulled at the duke's lips, revealing his polished white teeth that gleamed like a ghoul against the white flashes of lightning. He placed a hand on the guard's shoulder, gripping firmly. "Excellent." He flashed one final glance at my crumpled form, taking in the image like a fine piece of artwork before settling his victorious sneer onto Father. "We'll see who listens to your *truth* now."

chapter one

Twelve years later...

"Lacey, dear. Can you pass me that spoon?" Mother pointed her elbow at the thick wooden ladle as she haphazardly swirled the bubbling pot of porridge by the iron handle, padding the heat with a worn rag.

"Of course not," I said politely, reaching across the narrow space for the ladle and sliding it into Mother's palm. "I can't reach it, and I'm going to be early if I leave now." I hurried across the petite servant's house, racing to stuff on my slippers and tie on my frilly white apron with a snug bow.

"Oh goodness, I wasn't even looking at the time." Mother hastily spooned out a bowl of steaming porridge and placed it on the square table. The thick grainy smell swirled around the house, rousing my stomach with the hearty scent. "Will you have time to eat? I'd hate to make you late again." She turned away from the firewood stove, wiping her hands against her cotton skirts. Sticky clusters of porridge smeared the light gray skirts, which matched the olive oil stain below it.

I smiled at Mother, giving her a peck on her round cheek before grabbing a scrap of crusty bread off the table from yesterday's dinner. "I'll have a few bites of porridge before I get to the manor." I swung the door open as I stuffed a bite of stale crust into my mouth. "I'll see you when work begins. I hate you!" Crumbs coated my tongue and lined my smile, muffling words as I waved through the doorway. Mother's warm smile beamed back at me like the warm rays of dawn, crinkling the corners of her chocolate-brown eyes.

"I hate you too, my love. Have a good day!" She waved me off with a chuckle, and I hurried down the familiar path.

The air was crisp and moist, with the fresh scent of spring dewdrops clinging to the tree leaves. A cherry-red cardinal fluttered in front of my path, sweetening the air with a spritely song. I typically enjoyed the long daily stroll, but on the days I was running late, it was a little less than desired. I ran through the wooded path at a light jog, attempting not to burn up all my energy before a long day of work. A puddle splashed underneath my slipper, dampening the stocking against my toes.

"Oh, wonderful," I mumbled to myself, feeling a slight swell of joy that my true feelings were spoken aloud.

It wasn't often that it happened.

I grimaced as the dampness spread between my toes, chafing the soft in between as I dodged another stray puddle.

Perhaps there will be time to change stockings before the mistress awakes?

The idea sounded nice, but I knew perfectly well that Evie would likely be bright-eyed and bushy-tailed before I even walked into her room. I tried to push aside the discomfort in my slipper to consider a possible excuse if I truly did walk in late.

I tripped on my way to work? No, I didn't need sympathy. How about, I got distracted by a rabbit? No, then she'll want to ask me about it.

I groaned, hiking up my skirts as I leapt over a fallen branch. It would be so simple to tell Evie the truth—that I was up late working on my loom weaving and overslept. It was really that simple, but at the same time, it wasn't... Evie was a fair and kind mistress, so it pained me to fib to her when the truth wasn't something she would be offended by, but I wasn't allowed to tell the truth—hadn't been able to since I was five.

A long sigh parted my lips, which came out more as a pant, as I spun around a tight bend. My lungs protested the morning jog, but I didn't have the luxury of slowing down. If I was late, I would need to explain why, and I didn't want to lie to Evie, not again.

I'd been serving her for a few years now, and I still hadn't managed to make her despise me—likely because I didn't do much talking in her presence. Sure, she'd heard me lie, but she only thought that my quirky fibs were entertaining, especially when they were so obviously an untruth. No one knew the truth behind my twisted words; well, except for my mother and father.

My heart constricted at the thought of Father. For a brief moment, I closed my eyes and imagined his plump smile, jade-green eyes, and scraggly beard. As his face formulated in the forefront of my mind, the loud clatter of iron bars smashed through my thoughts, shadowing his smile behind the cold metal. I opened my eyes with a tight-throated sigh, trying to push the painful thoughts far away.

Only three more years... then I can see him again.

My aching lungs rejoiced within my chest as I caught sight of the lord's manor between the blossoming dogwood trees. A brush of wind showered the white petals across the path, filling the air with their intoxicatingly sweet scent. I slowed my jog to a heavy-footed walk as I crossed onto the lord's property, attempting to regain my composure before anyone saw me arrive from the window. My eyes darted anxiously to the sundial that rested eloquently in the center of the garden.

Not late. Well, not yet.

My walk grew brisker, and my heart

pattered anxiously as I passed Dedra, the head housekeeper, on my way to the servants' entrance. The woman glared at me down her slender nose with a perceptive squint, almost as if she could see the word 'late' tattooed across my forehead. I gave her an easy smile, trying to hide the twitch in my eye as I watched her huff at her pocket watch.

"Good morning, Lacey," she said a little less stiffly than I had anticipated. Perhaps she was acknowledging that I might still arrive on time. "How are you today?"

I flinched, something I always did whenever I was asked a direct question, but fortunately, this one would be easy.

"I'm doing wonderful, thank you. I had a lovely night's rest." I smiled brightly, attempting to showcase the energy of a girl who didn't only sleep for a few hours in a hardback chair. "How are you today?"

She gave me a polite nod, then turned her attention back toward the garden. "I'm fine, thank you. You had best hurry to the mistress's room. I'd hate to hear that she was waiting for too long after she awoke."

I gulped at the unspoken warning, then darted inside the manor while releasing a relieved breath. *That sounded normal enough.* I hurried up the servants' stairwell, replaying the conversation in my mind over and over, as I often did when conversing with anyone other than

Mother.

Ever since I was cursed, my mother taught me to be careful of what I said. It was easy to excuse the lies of a child, but as I grew older, Mother feared others would discover my curse if I didn't watch my tongue. Despite being forced to tell only lies, I had always felt myself to be a fairly honest person—though my words could never reflect that. If my curse had become common knowledge, it would have been nearly impossible to find respectable work. And it had taken me long enough to find this job... After all, who would want to hire a servant whose words they could never trust? It was a difficult sell.

Once I had reached the manor's second floor, I scurried around the corner across the polished floors, careful not to slip on the fresh wax. When I reached Evie's door, I paused for a moment to compose myself—brushing the stray dark hairs from my sweat-glistened brow and adjusting my frilly handmaiden apron over my petite form. I took a breath and gently clicked the latch open, opening the tall oak door with slow movements to prevent any squeaking.

"Lacey? Is that you?" Evie's sweet voice pierced through the quiet I was attempting to uphold, causing me to wince in shame.

Well, so much for getting here before she woke up...

I pushed the door open the rest of the way and slipped inside with a proper curtsy. "Pardon my lateness, milady. I thought you might sleep late this morning, so I didn't wish to wake you." My stomach churned as the white lie tainted my lips. It had gotten so easy to find replacements for the truth that begged to burst free. No matter how many lies I told, I still despised the way they overran me.

"Now where did you get a silly idea like that?" Evie laughed shrilly. I rose from my bow to meet her bright blue eyes and instantly, I felt a wash of ease pass through me as I noticed her playful smile. "You know perfectly well that I rise with the sun." She stretched her arms upward with a refreshed yawn. Despite being awake, she was still sitting in the center of her luscious four-post bed, half-buried by the silk sheets and hand-stitched quilts. She looked so small in the center of the massive bed, like a tiny porcelain doll tucked in by a child. As a matter of fact, all her features were doll-like to some extent. She had big eyes, long dark lashes, and a small heart-shaped mouth that dotted her smooth complexion. At only seventeen, she was already everything a proper young lady could dream to be.

I gave another apologetic bow before briskly walking over to the heavy blush-colored drapes. "My apologies, Miss Evie. I suppose your morning habits didn't cross my mind today." I tugged the drape's cord, letting in the most enchanting blaze of golden sunlight. The warm glow washed the frilly room in its light, earning a slight squint from Evie.

"Is that so?" She tossed her coverlet aside, giving me a pondering look as she evacuated the mass of cushions and sheets. "So, you mean to tell me that you neglected to arrive early on my greatest day of need?" she gasped dramatically, clutching a hand to her heart as she tossed her bare toes over the side of the tall mattress.

"Are you referring to your visit to the Reclusia palace?" I asked with a knowing tilt of my brow, a jesting smile tugging at my lips. Evie was always enjoyable to talk to because she loved when I asked her questions. Questions weren't capable of lying since they were directed toward another person, so my curse didn't filter my words whenever I asked one.

"Yes..." She drew out the word with a tart hiss as I turned away from her to select a day dress from her wardrobe. "I've tried everything! But Mother and Father insist that I compete in the prince's ridiculous competition. They say that if I reject the invitation, it will reflect poorly on the *family*." She rolled her eyes as she groaned. "Of course, they only care about appearances, not their daughter's happiness and well-being. Some ladies might swoon over the chance to wed a prince, but I want nothing to do with him or any other royalty." She folded her arms with a huff, sticking her chin in the air with an unladylike pout.

"Why don't you simply fail the competitions?" I asked as Evie stepped in front of me, allowing me to aid her out of her nightgown. "Only the loser has to marry the prince, after all."

Evie flicked me a quizzical glare as she stepped out of the soft silk slip. "You mean, the winner?"

I flinched. *Drat.* "Did I say that?" I widened my eyes innocently, trying to look equally lost.

Fortunately, she didn't look too concerned about my slip up and instead, she let out a soft giggle as she stepped into her teal day dress. "Don't go losing your mind on me yet, Lacey," she teased as I pulled the skirt atop her petticoat. The shimmery fabric shifted between teal and silver against the dancing light as I helped her slip it over her shoulders and began fastening her laces. "And to answer your question, I would love nothing more than to make a mess out of the prince's pompous game and flunk every challenge, but I'm afraid Mother and Father already threatened me to drop the idea. Apparently, failing the competition would bring even greater shame than ignoring the invitation. They won't be joining me in Reclusia's capital—too much business to oversee—but they warned me that they would arrange a visit if they received word that I was performing exceptionally poorly." She let out an exasperated sigh as I finished off the last of her laces, tying the bottom into a neat bow. "Isn't that ridiculous? They treat me like a child, while simultaneously expecting me to become a queen. They don't care a bit about whether or not I want to spend my life in a stuffy castle."

She sat in front of her vanity with a huff. I gave her a sympathetic smile as I opened a small silver ornament box atop the vanity, scooping a handful of hairpins to tuck between my lips before setting to work on Evie's golden locks. "That's terrible," I mumbled between pinched lips.

Terrible that you have the opportunity to become a princess...

The prince's bride competition was an age-long tradition that had followed the kingdom of Reclusia since it was formed. Reclusia was built on the foundation that intellect shall always be valued above all, and therefore, any heirs shall only marry the wisest candidate found. That way, our kingdom will continue to grow in knowledge forever more. It was a rather tired tradition at this point, but for the sake of ceremony, it continued on. All the noble ladies and eligible neighboring royals were invited to participate for a chance to win the prince's hand, and I'm sure many of them saw the competition as a grand opportunity, but not Lady Genevieve Rayelle Palleep.

I removed the final pin from my mouth as I tucked it discreetly behind a perfect curl. She always looked beautiful, but today, her usual joyful shine was slightly duller than normal. She rotated her head in the mirror, inspecting the hairstyle with glittering eyes. "My goodness, Lacey. It's a good thing you're staying at the manor, because if you were to style my hair like this for the prince, I'm certain he would call off the entire competition the moment he saw how adorable I looked." She giggled girlishly as she rose from her seat, spinning on her heel to meet my gaze and snag my hands. "Though I do wish that you could come. It will be so boring without someone I actually enjoy talking to."

I couldn't prevent the smile from passing my lips as her sweet words sank in. Evie may have been far above my station, but she was one of the easiest people in my life to talk to. I did believe she was a being a tad childish for neglecting the importance of such an opportunity, but a touch of me also pitied her for having to go through such an endeavor alone.

I gave her hands a reassuring squeeze before dropping them to fetch her satin gloves. "There's no need to be so fretful, Miss Evie. I'm sure you'll have a wonderful time at the palace."

She scrunched her nose up at me, as if she could smell the flowered lie. "I appreciate the optimism, but I must admit, I'm highly doubtful." She tugged on her gloves, then followed me as I approached the hall door to hold it open for her. She stopped before making her way toward the morning meal and gave me one final glance, with a mischievous glint in her sapphire eyes. "Maybe I'll just have to fail after all. If it forces Mother and Father to visit me, then at least they'll have to endure the boredom alongside me." She giggled, then departed the suite, striding gracefully through the hallway.

I rolled my eyes with a chuckle as I closed the door behind her, turning my attention to the wardrobe and empty travel cases that lined the wall. One by one, I lined the cases and trunks across Evie's bed and filled them with various ballgowns, day dresses, and hairpieces. Once the first trunk had been neatly filled, I found my mind filtering with curiosities about the royal palace. My thoughts swirled as I envisioned the elaborate ballrooms, tantalizing feasts, and blossoming gardens. Evie may not be interested in becoming a princess, but she was definitely neglecting to recognize how incredible the palace could be on its own.

I pulled a stunning violet gown from the wardrobe, imagining its flowing tulle dancing across the palace floors. My gaze caught the edge of Evie's elongated mirror, and I couldn't help but hold the dress up to my shoulders and imagine the gown on my plain figure. It was definitely disappointing that I wasn't chosen to accompany Evie on her trip. Though, all in all, it was a good thing I was staying behind. I had grown comfortable in my work here and had learned how to communicate through my curse among the other staff. Placing me in a whole new environment and expecting me to perform my tasks while juggling Evie's stressed chats would only be a recipe for disaster.

No one could find out about my curse, not again...

The dress skirted elegantly across the floor as I performed a girly twirl in the mirror. Halfway through my spin, I halted stiffly, forcing my tongue to swallow back a gasp as I stared up at Dedra. Her pointed glare raked over me suspiciously, cocking a brow at the violet gown I still held tacked to my shoulders. I quickly shook out of my petrified state and bunched up the gown in my arms, attempting to pretend I was simply folding the garment.

"Lacey." Dedra's gaze briefly followed the wadded gown with a suspicious incline of her brow before turning a far more focused look toward me.

"Yes?" I squeaked. My cheeks blazed with heat after being caught in my moment of daydreaming.

"I came to inform you that Miss Elaine has fallen ill and will no longer be able to serve Lady Genevieve during her visit to the palace."

My mouth fell open as I slowly processed her words. *If Elaine can't go, then that would mean...*

"I know it's short notice, but I'll be sending you in her place. Since you're already packing,

27

go ahead and add an extra trunk for your belongings. You'll depart with Lady Genevieve at sunrise." Without waiting for me to even shape my lips into forming a proper reply, she spun back on her heel and strode toward the door.

Fear and excitement raked over my heart. *This is my chance to see the palace, but at the same time, how will I be able to control my lying around so many new people?* Tension clamped around my lungs as I imagined lies spilling out of my mouth, causing rumors of the cursed peasant to spread from the center of the kingdom.

No... not again. No one can know about my lies. Not if I ever want to see Father freed.

"Madam Dedra, I can absolutely go!" I sucked in a sharp breath the moment I called out to her, pressing my fingers to my lips as if I could undo my mistake. It was always in my moments of distress that I let the curse win. "I mean, I would love to go! No, not that... I'm really not busy at all, so I'll have to—" I bit my tongue, my cheeks flaring as I dug my teeth into the troublesome muscle.

No, no, no!

Dedra stopped in the doorway, giving me a puzzled look as she tried to make sense of my absurd babbling. "I understand that you're excited, Lacey, but you really should try to relax. Just be grateful you were given the opportunity and smile quietly." Her voice trailed off as she turned back out of the doorway, leaving me alone with my stirring thoughts.

I sighed, turning my eyes to the now wrinkled dress in my arms. "Yes, I'm ever so grateful."

chapter two

"Oh, Lacey, I just heard the news!" Evie burst through the bedroom doors with a massive smile, nearly causing me to drop the box of hair pins I was holding. Evie twirled like the dancer in a music box, until she flopped across her voluminous bed, perfectly threading her petite form between the multitude of trunks that littered the top of it. "Oh, you should have seen the look on my face when Dedra told me that stuffy old Elaine couldn't make it. I nearly spit out my tea!" She rolled over onto her back, tussling the elaborate hairdo I had given her against the fluffy coverlet. She stared at me with a giddy, upside-down grin. "Aren't you excited? This boring trip of decorum just turned into a whole trip with one of my dearest friends! And no parents, either! Oh, I do hope you're looking forward to it."

Her unrestrained joy created a pull against my heart. I wanted to be excited for her, but I was too worried about the probability of my curse slipping out. Despite my fears, I gave Evie one of my perfectly practiced false smiles. "I couldn't be happier."

Evie's grin broadened, and she let out an excited squeal before sitting back up atop the bed. "Wonderful! The trip should be far more bearable now that I'll have you in my company. Have you packed yet? You'll want to bring your finest dresses to the palace. Oh! This will be your first time in the capital, won't it?"

I maintained my cheerful smile, but felt my eye give a slight twitch at the question. "Yes, it will."

More excitement bubbled up from Evie as she monologued her experiences in the city; but my festering mind blurred it all out as my memories replayed images of my time in Reclusia. Flashes of shadowed alleys, clusters of homeless commoners, and dinner plates sparsely filled with decaying food haunted my mind. I reflexively scratched the back of my head, still able to recall the feeling of spiderwebs clinging to my scalp after sleeping beside their webs.

"Lacey? Are you alright?"

I jumped, readjusting my focus on a worrisome look that gripped Evie's sweet features. *Had my thoughts leaked into my expression?* I feigned a natural smile. "Yes, I'm wonderful... just lost in thought, daydreaming about the palace." I swallowed anxiously, holding my breath until I was certain Evie had fallen for my words.

"It is beautiful, I suppose." She sighed, newly distracted by her emotions. I let out my held breath. *Just relax. As long as I keep a clear head, I'm sure I can make it through this trip unnoticed.* "I've only seen the exterior of the palace, but I'm sure the inside is just as grand. I'd love to explore while we're there, but I doubt I'll have the time between the ridiculous challenges and dinners with the *prince*." She faked a gag.

"Do you really despise the prince that much?" I'd known Evie for almost ten years now, and despite having zero interest in becoming a princess, she was still known to be a hopeless romantic. I couldn't understand why she wouldn't be swooning over the chance to marry a literal prince charming.

"I don't *despise* him necessarily. I'll have to meet him first to do that." She flitted over to the pre-packed trunks, popping the latch off the largest to inspect the contents. "I simply dislike the idea that he believes he is entitled to marry the 'brightest mind in Reclusia.' Honestly, he'll never truly marry the smartest girl, because the wisest noble will be smart enough not to compete in the first place."

I folded my arms with a teasing smile. "Ah, so is that why you don't want to attend? To prove that you're the wisest lady without even lifting a finger?"

Evie flicked her curls at me with a flamboyant grin. "What does it matter if I am? The prince isn't smart enough to catch up with my ingenious ways of thinking anyway. He would have never even known what he was missing." Dramatically, she sashayed across the plush carpet, posing against the drapes as she reached the end of the room.

"The poor prince will never be able to find someone as perfect as you, milady," I teased, sharing a small laugh with Evie as she ceased her posing.

"Ugh, I had better hope he finds someone better than me," she groaned between fading giggles. "I couldn't imagine being forced to spend my life held to the expectations of a royal. I scarcely have any freedom as a low-ranked noble. Being a princess must be a nightmare, don't you think?" She flicked her vibrant blue eyes at me as she posed the question.

The warmth of my previous laughter was still fading inside me as I pondered the question for a brief moment. *Be a princess? I can't imagine anything worse for a girl cursed to only tell lies.*

"I think being a princess would be a dream come true." I shrugged as my truth twisted across my tongue. There was no harm in pretending that I dreamed of being royalty. I'm sure every normal girl did at some point in their life—just not girls who are attempting to hide a curse. Instead of a crown that made everyone look at me, I only wanted to go unseen, at least until my father's sentence was complete.

Evie's expression turned startled. "Really? You think so?" Her eyes went wild with thought. It was the same look she had when she was preparing to do something mischievous.

"Yes, of course. Doesn't every girl want to be a princess someday?" I gave her an innocent smile, but her pondering expression never faded.

"I'm sure I did as a child, but certainly not anymore." She tapped a dainty finger to her chin, sneaking glances up at me through her dark lashes. "Tell me, Lacey. How badly do you actually want to be a princess?"

Not one bit.

"Oh, desperately so." The curse tensed around my throat, forcing a touch of swoon into my tone. It always affected my tone whenever I was adamantly against the lie I was speaking.

A spark flickered across Evie's face, and for a moment I felt a touch of unease settle in my stomach.

"Is that so…?" She paced the floors, scuffing her slippers against the rug in perfect rhythm with her clicking tongue. I nervously watched as an idea spread to life across her curling lips.

Her eyes latched onto mine with an almost predatory look, and I took an involuntary step backward at the pinning glare. "Evie? What are you thinking?" I'm not sure why, but a layer of nerves wove and twisted within me almost as if it was prepping for a far larger intake of stress.

"Oh, Lacey, I've just had the most inspired

idea." Her eyes glittered with eagerness as she switched from pacing to circling me like a greedy vulture.

I spun around to try to catch up with her orbiting until I had a lock on her face. "What kind of idea? What are you planning?" The nerves strung together across my chest, much like the first weave that went across a circular loom, preparing itself for a larger picture.

Evie stopped her circles to reach out and snag me by the hands, her nails digging into my palms with unrequited excitement as she nearly vibrated with the bursting thoughts. "Why don't you take my place in the bride competition!?"

My jaw dropped to the floor, and the string of nerves tightened from a hard pull. "P-pardon?" My mouth went dry as cotton as I gaped at the absurdity that lit Evie from the inside out.

"Think about it, Lace. This could be perfect!" She released my hands with a flick of her arms, twirling across the room in bliss. "You've always wanted to be a princess, and I want to avoid the competition at all costs. If we switch places at the palace, then you'll have a chance at marrying the prince, and I'll be free to explore during the festivities."

It took all my brain power to absorb the preposterous idea. *I can't possibly take Evie's place in the competition. Curse aside, I know nothing about how to perform in front of nobility, not to mention that we look nothing alike.* I glanced over at the mirror, comparing my straight, dark locks and warm brown eyes to her sapphire gaze and golden curls. We had the same heart-shaped face, and my nose was almost as small as hers, but she was still a good four inches taller than me and wasn't lacking in curves like I was.

"What about our appearances?" I asked through a tight throat. The curse was getting angry at me for asking so many questions. It was sadistic in the way it demanded control over my words, because staining my truth was never enough for it.

Evie waved a gloved hand in dismissal. "That won't be a problem." She sounded as calm as a lady discussing the amount of sugar in their tea. "No one at the palace knows what the real Lady Genevieve looks like. I'm not ranked high enough in nobility to attend court and neither are my parents, so for all they know, Lady Genevieve could be a man." She giggled at the thought, but her confidence did little to reassure the twisting strands of nerves that clung across my chest. "Besides, my family isn't attending... As long as you don't miserably fail any of the challenges, they'll have no reason to travel over and scold me... I mean, you."

Oh, is that all? I simply have to pass for nobility, perform challenges at their level, and avoid being caught as an imposter... Wait, isn't there a law against posing as nobility?

The building web of nerves hugged against

my chest, suffocating me as I fought my constricting throat to utter another question. "What if we get caught?" My voice was weak and breathless as the curse now restricted air from assisting my voice. I'll need to lie before I can ask anything more.

"Why would we?" Evie said nonchalantly, popping the latch of another trunk open. It took me a moment to realize that this time it was *my* trunk she was digging through. She picked up one of my handmaiden dresses and held it up to herself in the mirror. "Goodness, don't I look cute! Lacey, you should try on some of my dresses to see which suits you most."

This is getting out of hand. I need to stop this absurdity at once.

"Evie, I really think that this is—" My tongue thrashed in my mouth, fighting me as I tried to force it into submission. "A *great* idea."

No... The constriction in my throat instantly eased, revealing the curse was satisfied by my lie.

Evie beamed in my direction. "I'm so glad you think so, too!" She tossed the handmaiden dress back into the trunk and ran up to give me a tight squeeze. I didn't return the embrace, but instead, remained as stiff as stone while I wracked my brain for any clues to talk my way out of the situation. Evie must have noticed my lack of contact, because she pulled away to gawk at me, taking in the terror that eclipsed my features. "Are you alright, Lacey? You look a little pale." She pulled back from the embrace, looking genuinely worried about my well-being.

I ached to tell her the truth. She wasn't the type of person to force me into this. If only I could tell her that I was terrified.

"I'm a little excited," I mumbled weakly, my stiffness still unchanged.

A sweet smile brushed Evie's lips. "Ah, I understand now. You're nervous, aren't you?" Her calming voice almost soothed the binding nerves in my chest, but not enough to cut the ties entirely. "I can understand your worries, but I really think we can do this. This might be your chance to marry a prince, of all things! If I can give you the opportunity to fulfill your dreams, I don't want you to miss out on it."

It was almost painful to see how earnest she was being. *She's only trying to be a good friend...*

"But I won't force you if you're too scared." She took my hands in hers again, giving them a gentle squeeze. "So, tell me, do you want to do this with me? Will you take my place in the competition and let me take yours as a handmaiden? You can say no; I won't be upset with you if you decide you can't handle it."

The curse had hurt me many times over my life, but never as much as it did now. Evie's kind and caring eyes searched mine for honesty, *pleaded* with me for sincerity, and as much as I wanted to give it to her, there wasn't an ounce to be found. I didn't want to do this; I couldn't possibly survive as a noble, but no matter how terribly I wanted to confide in my friend about my fears of being exposed, there was only one thing I could say.

"I'd love to."

chapter three

I placed the final trunk in front of the carriage, watching with a tense heart as the coachman casually hoisted it over his shoulder to fasten atop the cabin. My eyes followed the trunk that contained my belongings, wondering if they would ever be mine again after this trip. It had been impossible to sleep last night with all the pressing worries that scraped at my brain. When I tried to explain to Mother that I was attending the competition with Evie, she also seemed a touch worried about my curse being exposed, but had remained kindly optimistic. I wanted to tell her the extent of my fears, but my twisted tongue made it too difficult to explain Evie's plans, so I ended up withholding the fine details.

Maybe I can still find a way to talk Evie out of it. We still have a little time.

My heart pattered roughly inside my strained chest, making it difficult to focus on my duties. I entered the carriage to try to prep the cabin for our travel, stashing our lunches beneath the bench seat and fluffing the cushions on the bench. Anything that could help distract me from my tension was more than welcome. After a few minutes of flittering about, Evie exited the manor, followed by her stoic-faced parents. Her expression matched her hardened parents', clearly trying to showcase her disagreement toward the journey. It was odd to see such a taut frown on Evie's typically cheerful face, especially when it contrasted with the vivid yellow dress and gaudy, floral-brimmed hat she wore. The three of them approached the carriage, and I took my place beside the footman, standing at attention with a quiet smile.

"Have a safe journey, dear." Lady Palleep gave her daughter an awkward hug, as Evie remained stiff as a board. "We'll be certain to stay up to date on your ranking in the competition." She pulled back from Evie, giving her a look of warning as she pressed her lips into a tight line.

Evie didn't say anything, and I sensed that she was fighting hard to hold back a less than respectful retort.

Lord Palleep placed a firm hand on Evie's shoulder. "Go make us proud, darling," he said with an expectant nod. "Remember when you're at the palace, you're representing the entirety of the Palleep family name, not just yourself. So be certain to maintain the optimal image of who we are."

I bit my cheek anxiously as I noticed Evie's back tense at her father's *encouragement.* She raised her skewering gaze toward her parents and gave them a gritted smile. "Yes, Mother. Yes, Father. I'll do my best to uphold the true image of our family." Her voice was lathered in sickly sweetness, simply oozing with concealed sarcasm that her family either completely missed or chose to ignore.

"I'm glad to hear it, dear." her mother said primly, already motioning for the coachman to open the cabin door. "Be sure to write us. We'd love to hear about your interactions with the royal family."

Evie turned toward the cabin door, and once her face was hidden from her parents, she rolled her eyes. She waved a casual goodbye from over her shoulder, not even bothering to turn around as she stepped into the coach's cabin. "Of course. Farewell, I'll see you in a few weeks."

I cast her parent's one final glance, taking in the lack of care in their expressions, before they too, turned away to head inside. Once it was clear that they were done seeing their daughter off, I climbed into the cabin behind Evie, taking my seat on the opposing bench. Evie was already staring out the window when I settled against the cushions, glaring at the glass with a fuming red enveloping her cheeks as she rested her palm stiffly under her chin.

Is she really that angry with them?

For a few minutes we lingered in the awkward silence as the coachman and footman finalized the last few checks on the carriage and horses, before closing the cabin door on us and taking their positions on the box seat. Evie continued to glare ferociously out the window as we slowly began to roll away from the manor grounds and pass through the iron gates that separated the front of the property from the main road. I was beginning to wonder if Evie would remain silent for the entire duration of the trip, until a sudden outburst from her nearly sent me tumbling off the bench.

"Do you think they bought it!?" She snapped her eyes to me with a complete one-eighty as her angered-red eyes vanished with a single blink.

My heart stuttered in bewilderment as I gaped at her shocking change. She seamlessly transitioned from a brooding sulk to her chipper smile. "B-bought what?"

"My disappointment, of course!" She settled back into the cushions of her bench with an eager squirm. "I couldn't possibly let them see I was suddenly looking forward to the trip. They would have gotten suspicious and sent an extra chaperone or something. Therefore, I had to put on a display of complete and utter displeasure." She pressed a theatrical hand to her forehead, feigning a tragic swoon.

"Oh, of course. I knew that." I tried to keep my voice level, attempting to mask the surprise that still lingered in my tone. Evie was a surprisingly talented actress. "So, you're looking forward to the trip now?" A bubble rose up in my throat as I asked, not fully wanting to speak the question I didn't want to hear the answer to.

"Well, of course," she said giddily. "I get an entire trip to the capital, free from propriety, and you get the opportunity to win the heart of a prince! Aren't you excited?"

My stomach lurched as we hit a rather sharp bump. *There has to be something I can say to convince her to drop this whole scheme... Come on, think.*

"Actually, I'm not feeling very well at the moment." A slight wind of tension released from my chest as I internally celebrated that the lie was permissible by the curse. "I'm worried I might be growing ill. Maybe the switch isn't such a good idea after all." I pressed a thumb to my forehead, attempting to fake a headache.

It always pained me to lie intentionally, but I didn't have any other option in this instance. If Evie and I switched places, it would only be a matter of time before my lies got us caught and got us both into major trouble. I might even end up joining my father in the dungeons... or worse. The slight uneasiness in my stomach festered into an actual feeling of nausea as I considered the potential punishments for posing as nobility during such an important event.

Evie's brows knit together with worry as

she studied my pale complexion with concern. "Oh no, are you alright?" She pressed a gentle hand to my forehead, checking for fever. "You don't feel warm. Do you feel sick?"

"No, I feel fine now." My eyes bulged for a moment as I caught onto the twist in my words. *I actually feel sick now, so my lie about feeling ill is now true. Drat.* "I mean... I feel great. No... I just." I sighed, burrowing my face into my palms.

I'm doomed.

To my surprise, Evie actually giggled at my verbal war. "Goodness, you really are nervous." I peeked up at her through my fingers and noticed a relieved expression fill her sweet features. "You worry too much, Lacey. I'm sure you'll do great in the competition, and the prince is certain to notice you. I mean, look at you! You're already stunning enough to be a princess."

I blinked at her in confusion, wondering if my lying curse had somehow spread to her as well. "Don't you think the prince will notice that I don't act like a noble?" I tried to layer my tone with uncertainty, hoping she would catch on to my deeper fears.

"He won't notice, not after I give you a few lessons in etiquette." She winked at me. "We should have this afternoon to ourselves, so I'll give you a crash-course on all the important bits." She stretched back against the seat, pulling off her frilly sunhat to set next to her.

The churning in my stomach intensified.

How am I supposed to learn a lifetime of etiquette in a single afternoon? She can't possibly believe that will be enough to fool everyone. "Do you think that will be enough time?" I asked skeptically, hoping once again to trigger some form of concern in her.

"Definitely!" My heart sank as her stubborn optimism eclipsed my already dwindling hope. "Nobles are boring and simplistic. Copying them is as simple as nodding and agreeing to everything they say."

But what if I don't even understand what they're saying?

"That's reassuring." I sighed under my breath, feeling the weight of my encroaching new reality crush into my shoulders. *This is going to end horribly.*

"That's the spirit!" Evie said brightly, jumping up from her seat while wobbling with the sway of the carriage. "All we have to do now is make the switch. I've worked it all out. We're going to be swapping carriages at the edge of town, so we'll need to switch before then." She turned back to the bench and picked up her gaudy hat, holding it out to me with a grin. "The only people we really have to fool are the coachman and footman, which should be fairly easy underneath a big, distracting hat. I packed a servant's bonnet for me to wear as well, that way they won't notice my hair. Once we've switched carriages, we'll officially be away from everyone who knows our true identities, and then the ruse can officially commence." She dropped the hat onto my lap, and I felt it hit me like a load of bricks.

I stared down at the contrast between the frilly accessory and my plain servant's skirt it rested upon. *Is this it? Is this really the only option I have?* I could always simply refuse to swap clothes and not give an explanation for why, but what would Evie think if I did? Despite everything she was putting me through, she wasn't trying to be malicious. I didn't want to make her hate me by simply shutting my mouth and refusing with my actions. Would losing Evie as a friend be worse than exposing the truth behind my curse? Or would shunning Evie end up causing her to deduct that my silence was caused by something other than my own will? My head spun wildly as I tried to pick apart all the possible escape routes. No matter how I turned it over in my head, I couldn't think up a single way this would end without damage.

"Are you sure you want to do this?" My throat tensed around the question, causing it to come out just as feeble as I felt.

Evie pulled a folded bonnet out of her pocket, sprawling it out on her lap to mirror the sunhat in mine. She gave me a firm nod.

"Yes." Her sapphire eyes glittered with determination, piercing my hope of escape with a shattering blow. "You may be my handmaiden, but you're also my friend. If this gives you the chance to live out your dream, then I'm elated to give you that opportunity."

Why Evie... Why did you have to make this so hard...?

"Besides, I'm getting a pretty good end of the deal as well! I can't wait to wear a dress that isn't made out of twenty pounds of satin." She giggled, then laced her fingers around the bonnet, as if it were the quill to a contract we were ready to forge. "Sorry, I'm getting ahead of myself. I'll admit, I'm excited, but this isn't just about me." She raised her gaze to meet mine, her eyes hungry with the anticipation. "What about you, Lacey? Are you sure you want to do this?"

Her question rattled in my ears like an unfair, twisted joke. I opened my mouth to redirect the conversation with another question, but the sadistic curse closed my throat, preventing me from skittering around its rules any longer. My heart hammered against my ribcage, quickening even further as my gaze fell onto the hat that rested atop my lap.

I'm sorry, Father. I'll do my best to stay hidden, I promise. I'll do everything I can to keep your name from being tarnished any further.

I looked up at Evie, feeling a slim gloss of tears coat over my brown eyes. "I'm sure."

chapter four

My body moved almost involuntarily as I switched into Evie's vibrant yellow gown. The smooth silk felt foreign against my skin, acting as a constant reminder that I was already wearing a mask. Evie looked radiant in the plain handmaiden outfit, babbling on and on about how fabulously deep the pockets were and how light the material felt. She used the reflection in the carriage window to pin her hair up into a tight bun and camouflage her shiny blonde locks.

What if the coachman notices our switch? Would he say anything to Evie? Or would he simply tattle on us to Lord Palleep?

Fear ticked against my brain as I imagined the look of disappointment on my mother's face as I told her I was dismissed from the lord's service. *I can't lose this job, and I definitely can't allow word of my curse to spread. I'll just have to perform... perfectly.*

I clutched the smooth yellow silk, wrinkling the skirt in small, fist-sized patches. My heart skipped a beat as I looked down at the unattractive crinkles, wondering if I had already failed the first test of propriety. I desperately raked my hands over the fabric, my sweaty palms only succeeding in dampening the silk.

"Look, we're approaching the royal carriage!" Evie pressed her eyes against the window, but I was far too tense to follow her gaze.

This will be my first test. Will I pass? Or will this charade end before it even begins?

A piece of me secretly hoped our little switch would fail early, because in that scenario, the worst result would be me losing my position. If the switch succeeded and I was caught at the palace, the punishment could be far more severe... I gulped at the thought as the carriage slowly pulled to a stop.

"Alright, here we go." Evie adjusted her bonnet snuggly against her scalp, tucking away her giddy smile with an emotionless façade. "All we have to do is cross from one carriage to the other. Keep your head low and don't make eye contact with the coachman or footman. Are you ready?"

No...

"Yes." The word was bitter in my mouth. Anxiety strung across my chest, adding another layer to the web of nerves that had already taken refuge within my pulsing heart.

"Perfect." She gave me a final wink, then shifted toward the door in preparation to exit, then stopped abruptly. "Whoops, you need to go first, not me." She shimmied back, offering for me to move in front of her like a true lady should.

I stared at the closed door, terrified of the simple act of walking out before my mistress. *They will be looking at me first. It's my job to fool them.* My lungs clamped shut as I heard the footman clatter down from the box seat, making his way toward the door. The cabin still felt like it was moving, and I felt a slight twist in my vision. The world spun briefly as the web in my heart stretched to my lungs, siphoning all the oxygen from me in a blurring moment. The door clicked open and I nearly gasped as the fresh air brushed against my senses.

I can do this. Just walk from one carriage to the other.

My legs felt like lead as I shakily approached the carriage steps. The footman had his head bowed low to the ground, giving me the slightest touch of relief that his vision was averted from my face. I took the steps one at a time, keeping my eyes fixated on the shiny black carriage with the royal crest painted prominently on the door, a mere ten paces away. When my feet touched the pebbly road, a nervous pulse swept through my system as I noticed our coachman conversing with the royal coachman. My steps halted for a moment as I fought the urge to turn and dart back inside the cabin with Evie.

Don't panic. He's distracted, just keep your

head down and walk.

I lowered my eyes to the gray pebbles that scuffed the bottom of my slippers. The wide-brimmed hat Evie had brought did a remarkable job of hiding my face, but unfortunately, it also blinded my vision. I did my best to walk straight as my ears pricked up at the sound of Evie exiting the carriage behind me. It took all of my willpower not to turn around and see how she was upholding her own act.

A lady wouldn't look back at her servant. Just keep walking.

When I finally reached the royal carriage, a mixture of relief and crippling terror fastened around my mind.

This is it. There's no going back once I step in this carriage, not until the competition ends.

The royal footman must have noticed me pause at the carriage steps, because he offered his hand with a pleasant smile. "Do you require assistance, my lady?" His polite use of my borrowed title flooded me with unease. *Will I ever get used to such formalities?*

Feeling the eyes of the other footman on the back of my neck, I managed the calmest smile possible for a girl on the verge of a heart attack and took the footman's gloved hand with the most graceful touch I could muster. Thankfully, his gloved hand shielded his fingers from the dampness of my slickened palms as I carefully ascended the two daunting steps. When I had made it inside the cabin, I sat with stiff, stuttering movements, overcompensating for my usually poor posture but forgoing comfort entirely. Not even a moment later, Evie stepped into the carriage behind me, with the most perfect collected composure I had ever seen. The footman didn't even bat an eye as he closed the carriage door and left the cabin's side to assist the other men in loading our trunks.

Evie's gaze remained fixated on the window, glancing away each time one of the men turned in our direction. It baffled me how relaxed she was when we were literally in the process of committing an identity crime. The following minutes felt endless as the men loaded the carriage one trunk at a time. When the final trunk was securely fastened, the men bid farewells and returned to their respective carriages. I nearly melted into the cushioned bench when the wheels finally rattled across the coarse road.

Evie let out a soft sigh, showing her first sign of tension throughout this entire charade. "We did it." She giggled softly, gently pumping her fist in victory. "It will only be a few hours until we reach the palace."

My stomach curdled at the thought. "Only a few hours?" My voice slurred as the curse debated whether my words were a statement or a question, but there was no tension at my throat, so it seemed to be deemed passable.

"Yup, the carriage was meant to meet us halfway, so all the ladies arrived in the same fashion. That way, the prince won't be able to determine any of the ladies' ranks. Apparently, station is not permitted to be discussed, since the only important factor in the competition is how well each lady performs."

The strings of tension that crisscrossed my chest forced a tight breath from me. "Is that so?" I breathed. "Are there any other unspoken rules I need to know about before we arrive?" I bit my cheek, trying not to allow the irritation festering within me to break free. *What else has she neglected to share before I unwillingly agreed to this?*

She tapped a thoughtful finger to her chin. "I can't recall." She shrugged, sending a ripple of anxiety through me. "I'm sure they'll explain the rules once we get there. I honestly quite like the fact that the ranks are kept secret. It allows people like *Lady Genevieve* and the infamous blood princess of Sarnold to compete on even terms."

"The blood princess will be there!?" My voice tried to elevate to match my terror, but the curse snagged around my throat from my overuse of questions, minimizing my alarm to more of a squeal.

Evie tilted her head at me, clearly unsure of what to make out of my odd vocal inflection. "Yes, of course. All the eligible royalty will be attending."

I dug my fingers into my skirt, giving up on the idea of keeping the fabric smooth. *The blood princess is going to be there?* I fought back a shudder as I recalled the stories that had filtered through the kingdom. The blood princess was the only surviving daughter of King Hans of Sarnold. The king, queen, and his eldest son had perished during a horrid attack nearly eight years ago, but the princess was left unharmed. Her uncle has taken over as king until she comes of age, but no one truly knows what happened to her family that night. The princess was only ten years old when it happened, but was rumored to have a sword in her hand when found after the attack. Some theorize that she held the sword in self-defense, while others believe she had slain her brother in order to be first in line for the throne.

What will she do if she learns she's competing with a commoner? I can only imagine how insulted she will be...

Evie tried to fill me in on the basics of the etiquette expected by a lady of her—I mean, *my*—standing for the rest of the trip. I tried to take in as much information as I could, but in the end, it felt as if her lessons were landing on deaf ears.

I can't possibly turn into a noble throughout the duration of a single carriage ride...

My mind festered with doubts and worries as we clattered through the cobblestone road that parted the royal gardens.

"Oh, look. We're here!" Evie pressed her face eagerly against the window, lightly fogging the glass before settling back into her seat and smoothing out her skirts with a more respectable posture. "Aren't you excited?" Her giggle seeped through her relaxed demeanor before she swallowed back the laugh and calmly folded her hands in her lap.

I tried to think of any last way to escape this mess before I was officially trapped in my new identity, but it was too late. The carriage was rolling up the palace steps, and I was dressed as Lady Genevieve. There was no time to switch back even if I could find the words to convince Evie. If I didn't want to end up in the dungeons, I needed to stop being Lacey, at least for a little while.

"I can't wait." I smiled at Evie just as the carriage pulled to a stop. The footman hopped down from the box seat and hurried politely over to the door, creaking it open with a deep bow.

This is it. When I exit this carriage, I will no longer be Lacey, the cursed handmaiden. I need to become Lady Genevieve, no matter what it takes.

My lungs remained void of all air as I stepped down from the carriage. My heart pounded so aggressively that I feared the footman might take notice as I slowly turned my gaze up to the castle steps. The palace was absolutely beautiful. Tall marble turrets surrounded a more rustic stone frame, which towered high beyond the trees. Lush gardens blossomed from every corner, filling the air with the sweet scent of roses and lilies. Directly in front of us, a larger fountain gurgled peacefully at the base of the palace steps, singing with the croaks of toads and a buzzing dragonfly. At the base of the steps, a tall, rounded man, with a prim smile and rosy cheeks, gave me a low bow as he watched me look curiously around the palace's entrance.

"Welcome, Lady Genevieve Rayelle Palleep of Reclusia." He rose smoothly from his perfectly executed bow, smiling warmly. "We are honored to have you in attendance. I am the head steward, Sir Franklin. If you and your servant would kindly follow me, I would be more than happy to direct you to your suite."

My legs turned to jelly, refusing to move when Sir Franklin held out his arm in invitation. I risked a glance back at Evie who was once again completely immersed in the role of a servant, even going so far as to avert her eyes from me when not being spoken to. I gulped, turning back to the steward with a forced smile.

"I would love that. Thank you, Sir Franklin," I said, slow and clear, trying to ensure my enunciation was on point. After speaking, my spine began to bend into a bow, the way I always did when addressing someone above my station, but halfway down, I recognized my error and stiffened straight as a board. Panic seized my chest, twisting another strand into the web that entangled my heart. Not even a full five minutes as Evie, and I already made an error.

Did he notice?

I bit the inside of my cheek as I cast my gaze anxiously back up to the steward, who thankfully wasn't shouting the word *imposter* yet. I let out a tight breath, gathering my sunny yellow skirts in my hands before ascending the steps to fall behind the steward.

You can do this. Just be like Evie and don't talk too much. Although the only thing Evie ever does is talk... Oh dear.

When we entered the palace, my panic was eclipsed by awe as I gaped at the stunning foyer. Tall velvet curtains adorned the elongated windows, casting rectangular beams of light across the striking floor. A mosaic of gemstones glittered underneath our feet, creating a perfect image of the Reclusia royal crest.

"They're magic stones," the steward said proudly, following my gaze to the extravagant floor. "They bless the castle with security and good fortune. Many of our citizens enjoy stepping over the stones to feel a touch of their power. Would you like to give it a try?"

My breath caught. *Magic stones?* I glanced back down at the vivid mosaic and quickly recognized that the stones were perfectly cut and polished, indicating that they had been refined.

My chest ached in warning as I looked wearily over at the stones. The curse I carried was from the power of an unrefined stone, meaning I couldn't risk coming in contact with a refined stone. The clashing power between processed and unprocessed magic was similar to that of opposing magnets. The powers rejected each other and often had... explosive results.

I gulped. "I think I'll try it another time. I'm rather tired and don't think I can stay awake a moment longer. May I visit my suite first?" I asked sweetly, trying not to let the panic lace through my tone.

The steward gave me an understanding nod. "Of course, my lady. Right this way."

A wave of relief swept over me and I followed the steward with a much more cautious step. *Are there stones hiding in other places? What will happen if I cross over one?* I tried to silence my thoughts and not allow my worries to override me before we even arrived at the suite.

I'd only ever touched a refined stone once, when Mother and I were still scraping by in the capital. A street vendor was selling lockets with chips of joy stones set in the chain. He was letting the children try the chain on so they could grow joyful about the product and sway their parents into buying it. Things were tough back then, and despite knowing perfectly well that Mother could never afford such a valuable trinket, I wanted to at least have a taste of what the magic's joy could offer. That was the day I learned that I wasn't only cursed by an unrefined stone, but that its entire essence had been drained into me.

My neck itched as memories of the burning pain resurfaced across my skin. *I'll need to keep a close eye out.* As we walked, I held my chin high, the way I knew a noble should, but kept my eyes focused on the floor, darting my gaze at the detailed granite and stone in search of any other tucked away magic. We ascended a few flights of stairs until we reached the third floor, where I deemed the rest of the space safe enough. The flooring switched to thick carpet, so I lifted my eyes to the rows of elegant mahogany doors until we stopped in front of one.

"Here we are, my lady." The steward opened the door with a sweep of his arm, stepping aside for me to pass him. My eyes widened as I took in the pure extravagance of the suite. The space was large enough to house at least three families, with a plush settee, a full fireplace, and a bed that even dwarfed Evie's. A servant's bunk lined the far wall, with a thin, gray, privacy curtain fastened at the top and a set of drawers beneath it. Two floor-to-ceiling windows stood prominently with a set of glass doors in-between, which appeared to open up to a small balcony. It was absolutely beautiful, yet seeing it disgusted me. Pretending that any of this belonged to me felt like a greater lie than one that could be spoken. Maybe under different circumstances I would do anything to claim a room like this as my own, but not today, not like this.

"I do hope you find the accommodations to your liking." The steward stepped aside, allowing a bustle of servants to funnel into the room with all our various trunks in their arms. "Please take this time to rest from your travels until the festivities begin this evening. I'll send up a pair of meal trays from the kitchen for you and your maid while you settle in. Please be sure to arrive at the dining hall no later than seven o'clock sharp for tonight's dinner. Any of our staff will be happy to show you the way."

This evening? The competition is really starting so soon?

The steward gave a final flourished bow, bending perfectly at the waist. "Is there anything else I can assist you with, my lady?"

A thousand questions burned in my mind —about the competition, the gemstones, and whether they had a rope ladder stashed out on the balcony. "No, that will be all." I gave him a tired smile, and he seemed to take the hint of my weariness.

"Then I shall take my leave. Welcome to the palace, Lady Genevieve." He spun around on his polished heel and calmly ushered the other servants out with him as they finished lining our trunks up against the far wall.

The moment they left, I felt as if a pressure had released from my chest. I turned around to glance at Evie, who was now cheerfully moving to unload our trunks into the wardrobe. My mouth fell open as I watched her slowly begin to unpack each garment, organizing them into neat piles.

"Evie, you don't ha—" My tongue thrashed in my mouth trying to convert my words, but I swallowed before the lie could fill in the rest.

Evie turned to me with a relaxed smile, a bundle of nightgowns folded neatly in her arms. "What's the matter, Lady Genevieve? Would you prefer I hang your ballgowns first?"

Goodness, she's really committed to this whole servant image.

I took a slow breath, testing my throat before I tried to voice any further thoughts. "Can I help you unpack?" A touch of longing clung to my voice as I guiltily looked over at the massive number of trunks.

This should be my job, not hers.

She set the bundle down to fold her arms at me with a stern lift of her brow. "Now, Evie. What type of maid would I be if I let you hang your own clothes? You should rest; you have a big night ahead of you." She winked at me playfully, and despite knowing she was only playing a role, I couldn't help but feel as if I had already robbed her of her true self.

I fiddled with my fingers, trying to find the

words that would allow the Lacey inside me to come back to life for a brief moment. "Please? I want to show you the proper way to handle the garments before I relinquish the task to you."

She pursed her lips for a brief moment, then dropped her arms with a defeated sigh. "Alright, fine, but only because I have no idea what I'm doing." She gave me a guilty smile, then reached out a wrinkled petticoat to me. I smiled broadly, taking the garment in my hand like it was a security blanket that gifted me a piece of my former self. Evie noticed my smile and her face turned stern again. "But this is the only time. After we unpack, you need to stop acting like Lacey. For the next month you're Evie and I'm your handmaiden. We wouldn't want to risk getting caught now that it's too late to switch back."

My fingers dug into the petticoat, unwilling to let go of the remnant of my identity I had just secured. "Well, it's not completely too late to switch back. We could always trade before the dinner tonight." I almost gasped as I realized my intended words were actually what passed my lips. That could only mean that I already knew what I was saying couldn't be true...

"Well, that would be foolish." Evie laughed. "You haven't even gotten to meet the prince yet! It's alright to be nervous, but don't forget why you wanted to do this in the first place." She dropped the dress in her arms and let it flutter across the floor as she tiptoed through the sprawled garments to place her hands firmly atop my shoulders. "This will be wonderful, you'll see. Now, next time we leave this room, Lacey is nothing more than me, your quiet handmaiden. So, who are you?"

My shoulders stiffened. Evie was right, there was no avoiding it now. I was committed to whatever this competition had in store for me, and if I didn't want to be discovered as either an imposter or a liar, I needed to stop fighting and embrace the lies that so desperately wanted to consume me. If Lacey wanted to survive, she would need to use Evie as a shield.

"My name is Genevieve Rayelle Palleep," I stated with the first breath of boldness I'd felt all day. "And I'm a born and raised noble."

chapter five

Just as the steward had said, a pair of lunch trays were delivered to our suite only a few minutes after we had finished unpacking. My stomach was in far too many knots to consider eating, but the jewel-toned fresh berry tartlets and the savory vegetable soup swayed the knots to unravel just enough to make room for a few bites. The warm broth eased my waves of nausea and helped clear my head in preparation for tonight's competition. I paced the room in nervous circles, trying to determine the best approach to this evening's events, while Evie flitted around the room in search of the perfect gown for me.

I definitely couldn't try to actually win the competition. If by the off chance I won, Evie's parents would be informed of their *daughter's* victory and would quickly discover that we had switched places. *That would be a guaranteed trip to the dungeon for me, or maybe even the gallows...* I tensed my shoulders to prevent a shudder from rolling down my spine. Thinking about being caught would only make me appear more nervous, and right now what I needed was to be calm and collected. If I couldn't win the competition, then I would simply have to lose. Although... I couldn't do too poorly, otherwise Evie's family would assume she's failing intentionally and visit the palace. *There's a second recipe for getting caught...* The only way I could make it through this event in one piece, is if I simply performed average.

That shouldn't be too difficult, right? I'm great at being average.

My head spun with deeper worries as I barely noticed a blur of Evie flutter behind me and start playing with my hair. She mumbled something about me sitting down for her and I wordlessly complied, allowing her to lead me to a vanity where I sank down in front of the mirror. As she worked, I found my thoughts drifting back to the competition, this time centering around the challenges that would occur.

They were meant to test intellect, weren't they?

The web of tightening anxieties seized around my lungs, causing me to swallow back a nervous gulp. I knew how to read and write, but only because my mother taught me. I had never received a formal education or studied anything beyond the proper way to serve tea. Would I be able to avoid staying at the bottom of the score sheet? Just how difficult would these challenges be?

The rest of the afternoon went by in a haze, filled with hairpins, petticoats, and at least three different gowns for me to try on before Evie settled on a deep blue ballgown with black lace sleeves and a purple rose embellishment at the waist. When I finally inspected her work in the mirror, I couldn't help but gasp at the dramatic change.

"I don't even recognize myself." I gaped, blinking back at the familiar brown eyes in the glass that served as the only confirmation that Lacey still existed behind all the finery.

"You look stunning, La— I mean, Evie." She giggled. "You look as if you had been meant to wear ballgowns your entire life!" She gave me an approving nod, looking up and down at my outfit to admire her handiwork.

"Well, of course I do." I gave her a teasing smirk, picking up my skirts with a dramatic twirl. "I was simply born to be a princess." I gave her a flourished bow, enjoying the opportunity to release a little tension before I attended the most stressful dinner of my life.

"Now, that's a lie."

I froze halfway up from my bow, feeling paralyzed as I noticed Evie's tone rid itself of jest. *Has she caught on to my lying so soon?*

"You weren't born to be a princess." She took a step closer toward my frozen, hunched form and pressed a finger under my chin. With a confident smile, she lifted my chin higher and higher until my head was held tall. "You were born to be a *queen.*"

I released a tight breath of relief. *Why do you insist on giving me daily heart attacks, Evie...?* I managed a soft smile. "Do you really think so?"

Her sapphire eyes brightened. "Yep!" She unhooked my chin and took a proud step backward, admiring me as if I were her daughter about to make her first societal debut. "The prince isn't going to know what hit him when he sees you! Even if you don't win all the challenges, he might just have to bend the rules a touch." She winked.

"I wouldn't mind that." I laughed back as my chest tightened in response to the potential of such a twinge in the rules occurring. *Maybe I need to convince Evie that the prince is attracted to plainly dressed women...*

A soft knock directed our gazes to the door, signaling that it was time for me to depart to the dining hall. My heart pattered inside me, tangling the web of nerves and doubts as I looked at the door with full reluctance.

"Well, that's your cue." Evie grinned, giving me one final look before tweezing a loose thread from my skirt. "Are you ready?"

My lips moved unsteadily into a stuttered, fake smile. "I'm ready."

• •

The palace hallways seemed far eerier in the fading light of dusk. The diamond-paned windows glistened warmly with the dwindling sun, but the elongated shadows made my anxious fear feel equally eclipsed by its fading hope of morning.

What if I get caught right away? What if Evie was wrong about nobody knowing her here, and there's someone who recognizes me as a fake? Will I be able to avoid getting last place in the first challenge? What if my failure is a dead giveaway that I'm a commoner?

With each step through the ornate halls, I felt my worries grow grimmer, no longer able to keep the rustling fears at bay. *Stop it, Lace— I mean, Evie. I need to keep it together. Don't let yourself get entangled in the worries. Not yet, at least...*

When we arrived at the dining hall, my knees locked in place as I waited for the footman to pull the grand doors open. My heart hammered in my ears, sending floods of adrenaline through my muscles in case I felt the need to turn and run. As the doors widened enough for me to glimpse inside, my gaze fell on at least a dozen women, all staring at me. The nerves I had felt before this moment were nothing compared to the crippling suffocation that enveloped me now. I fought my lungs to remember to breathe as the ladies each glossed their scornful gazes over me with unmasked judgment.

They were all beautiful, dressed in the

absolute finest of apparel, with vivid gowns, artful makeup, and glittering jewels woven into their hair. I remained completely frozen, unable to do more than barely inflate my lungs as the footman cleared his throat to silence the already muted room.

"Lady Genevieve Rayelle Palleep of Reclusia." He spoke the name so regally, that for a moment, I forgot that the title was meant to be Evie's—or mine, or whoever it belonged to now. He stepped aside for me to enter, but I couldn't persuade my feet to move. The dozens of eyes that latched onto me gripped me in place, seizing my muscles despite how much adrenaline coursed through them for me to flee. Blood rushed coldly through my veins, numbing my fingertips before they could scrunch up my skirts.

"Lady Genevieve?"

I nearly jumped at the voice as I turned to a kind-faced servant who was giving me a guiding point. "Your seat is located between Lady Jezebel of Reclusia and Princess Lyra of Bellatring. This way, please."

Wait a minute, did he say Jezebel?

I followed the direction of his hand and noticed the empty seat he was referring to, nestled between an unrealistically beautiful dark-haired woman, and a stern-faced blonde with a set frown. *Jezebel? It couldn't possibly be...* My muscles loosened the slightest amount, allowing my jaw to unlock with another fake smile. "Thank you. I thought that was meant to be mine but wasn't certain." I gave him a polite nod, tensing my legs before they could instinctually bend into a curtsy. The servant smiled back at me, following behind me as I approached my new seat. He briefly stepped in front of me, pulling out my chair and then later pushing me gently up to the table.

The grand dining room felt far too large even for a full table of guests. Tall, arched windows lined the exterior wall, allowing the soft embrace of dusk to glisten off the crystal goblets and polished silverware. An elaborate chandelier strung with pearls and rubies dangled above the center of the enormous table, accenting the detailed wall sconces that illuminated the far side of the room. My gaze lowered from the glistening lighting onto the complicated display of fine dishware that terrorized me with its ridiculous number of forks, spoons, and glasses.

Evie never went over dining etiquette. How am I supposed to know what utensil to use?

For the first time since taking my seat, I cast a wary glance over at my table neighbor, the one the servant referred to as Princess Lyra. She was even more stunning up close; her portrait-perfect figure was elegantly poised, highlighting her strong jawline and perfectly squared shoulders. Long, dark hair cascaded regally down her shoulder in a twisted braid, dotted with woven pearls and sapphires that glinted like stars against her almost ebony locks. Despite the warm season, she wore a long-sleeved ivory gown, covered in embroidered lilacs.

Were all princesses this… perfect?

I shifted my eyes back to the table, suddenly remembering there was supposedly another princess at this table who wouldn't likely be so charming. *I wonder which of these girls is the infamous blood princess?* I fought the urge to glance around the table and cast judgment, instead shifting my attention to Princess Lyra's place setting to see if it matched mine. My muscles stiffened for a brief moment as I noticed that there was already something different between the two places.

Her napkin! Where is her napkin?

My gaze darted around the table until it finally locked onto the simple linen cloth that rested flat atop her lap. It only took a moment more for me to realize that everyone else had already placed their linens on their lap, so I hastily unfolded mine as well, doing my best to look like I hadn't just cheated off my neighbor. My pattering heart settled the slightest amount as I confirmed that my place now matched every other lady in the room. I may have even relaxed if I hadn't felt a pair of piercing blue eyes tunnel through my mask.

With slow movements, I turned my

attention to my other table neighbor, a pale-faced blonde with a taut expression and an upturned nose. When I gave her my attention, I had half-expected her to shy away from me after I noticed her staring. However, she didn't back off even the slightest; instead, she only narrowed her icy eyes onto me, sending a chill down my spine.

"Pleasure to meet you, Lady Genevieve," she said tartly, still raking her gaze across me as if still deciding whether she wanted to befriend me or eat me for dinner. I swallowed dryly.

Does she already suspect me as a fake? The napkin incident couldn't have been that apparent... could it?

"It's nice to meet you as well." I smiled through the discomfort, trying to focus on appeasing whatever doubts she may have been harboring. "I actually prefer to go by Evie, if you will. You'll have to forgive me, but I can't seem to recall your name." I tried to sound as polite as I could. In actuality, I could never forget Lady Jezebel's name, not when it was the same name as—

"It's Lady Jezebel Gannet of Reclusia." She smiled stiffly. My stomach dropped, and like a thirsty predator, her smile drained every drop of blood from my ashen face.

Jezebel Gannet? It couldn't possibly be...

"You wouldn't happen to be Duke Byron's daughter, would you?" My tongue felt like lead in my mouth, unwilling to ask the question I already knew the undeniable answer to.

How could I have forgotten those scathing eyes?

"Why, yes. I'm pleased to hear you've heard of him." She brightened a touch, beaming with a prim pride that sickened me. "We're quite well-known in Reclusia, since my father is amongst the highest-ranking nobility in the kingdom. I believe I've heard of your family as well. Palleep, was it? I'm sure they're notable enough since you received an invitation." Her shrill voice held the slightest rasp to it, making every word feel as if it had a touch of bite behind it. "It must be exhilarating for some of the *humbler* nobility, such as yourself, to be here."

She cocked a thinly plucked brow at me, as if testing my reply to her use of *humbler*. My chest squeezed as I fought the urge to cower under her venomous glare. For a moment, I considered averting my gaze from her, in case she suddenly recognized me from her childhood. Although, it seemed as if her interests were only aligned with knocking Evie down a few pegs, and not exposing Lacey. She must not have recognized me with all the finery and the new title.

Why does it have to be her of all people? The daughter of the man who imprisoned my father, the friend who betrayed me with no remorse, and the one who first exposed my curse to the world.

"Yes, I'm rather excited to have been

chosen to attend." I smiled smoothly, pressing the surfacing memories of my last interaction with Jezebel as far down as I could.

"She's a cursed little liar!"

"Don't go near her; her lies might be contagious!"

"I bet she gets it from her father. He lied so much that he went to prison!"

A slight sneer tugged at Jezebel's lips, reinventing my horrific memories of her with an older image. "As you should be." Her lips twisted in self-satisfaction. "Just don't forget the presence of those you compete against. Most of the women here were practically bred to marry a prince. We wouldn't want to disrespect anyone by standing in their way, now would we?" Her red-painted lips dripped with venom as she craftily passed on her warning.

Only five minutes into dinner and I've already received my first threat... Though honestly, I'd expect nothing less from Jezebel.

I straightened my shoulders, squaring up to my childhood villain with the falsified confidence of the real Evie. *We aren't children anymore, and as long as I carry Evie's name, I carry her status, too.* I gave her an overly sweet smile, steepling my fingers gently atop the table. "I wouldn't dare disrespect any of the other families, especially yours." My smile deepened as the lie sank sweetly into my tongue like a delectable nectar. *I suppose not every lie is painful...*

Jezebel's brows knit slightly, crinkling her forehead as she continued to plaster on her manipulative smile. She looked as if she was trying to determine whether my cheerful complacency was a ploy or not. She pressed her lips together into a fine line before folding her hand's discreetly into her lap.

"Good." The staccato syllable oozed with dissatisfaction as she turned her attention toward the opening doors. "I hope to see that your *respect* is appropriately displayed."

A stir of irritation and icy fear fought for dominance within my mind. She always knew just how to ruffle a person, while simultaneously playing on their insecurities or fears. While she didn't know I was fearful of being outed as an imposter, she still managed to establish her self-imposed dominance before I could even make it through the first course.

Heat seared through my fingertips as my gaze followed the servers who poured in through the open doors. In perfect unison, the servers swiftly moved behind each seated lady and delicately placed a steaming bowl of soup in front of our places. I remained still for a moment as I carefully observed Princess Lyra to see which spoon she selected for the starter course.

The one on the outside, got it.

I selected what I hoped was the appropriate utensil and gingerly scooped up my first spoonful of the creamed soup, being extra careful not to slurp. The rich flavor nearly caused me to swoon as I felt my eyes' urge to roll back into my head. At least this stress came with the reward of incredible meals. As we ate, I took the opportunity to investigate my fellow competitors. There were sixteen of us in total, and most looked to be anywhere between sixteen years old to their early twenties. As I observed them, I was relieved to see that a few of the younger girls looked almost as nervous as I was. Even Princess Lyra, who seemed to be the most poised of all, kept sneaking tense glances down to the end of the table. I followed her eyes once, and nearly jumped when I saw who she was looking at.

The blood princess...

While I had no proof it was her, it only made sense considering how many of the girls were averting their gazes from her. She had beautiful dark auburn hair, tanned skin, and striking gold eyes. But what must have once been a princess-perfect face was covered by a long ugly scar that crossed from over her eye to her cheek. A shiver coursed through me as I watched her golden gaze flick toward mine. I redirected my attention on my nearly empty soup bowl, desperately hoping I hadn't already made two enemies in one dinner.

As the first course concluded, and an array of fresh salads were swapped out for our soup bowls, a few of the ladies began to question the whereabouts of the prince. There was still an empty chair at the head of the table, likely intended for His Highness, but no signs that he intended to join us.

Didn't he want to meet the girls he could potentially wed?

As the meal carried on, I continued to mirror Princess Lyra's etiquette all the way down to washing my hands in the finger bowl at the end of the dinner. My stomach rejoiced at the feeling of being filled with such delectable foods, flooding my body with drowsiness that I knew I couldn't cave to quite yet.

I still have to compete tonight.

No sooner than the thought had filtered through my brain, Sir Franklin, the steward from earlier, approached the head of the table and cleared his throat. "Welcome, esteemed guests of Prince Carlex of Reclusia. As you know, you have all been invited for the purpose of competing in the prince's bride competition, an age-long tradition where our heir selects the most intelligent candidate to rule by his side." A few of the girls straightened in their chairs as he spoke, as if correct posture would give them points for intelligence. "As I'm sure you've noticed, Prince Carlex was unable to join you all for the evening meal, but I can assure you that you'll still get a chance to see him this evening. The question is, who will find him first?"

A hush swept through the room as Sir Franklin paused to fold his gloved hands in front of him with a pleased smirk.

Find him first? Is that meant to be a clue or something? But we don't even know what the challenge is yet?

The web of nerves stretched across my chest once more, fighting to restrain me from thinking clearly.

"Now, if you'll all follow me to the ballroom," Sir Franklin continued. "It's time for the first game to begin."

chapter six

The ballroom overwhelmed me the instant I shuffled in behind Lyra. The domed ceiling glittered with elegant chandeliers, dripping in crystals and gold chains. A large platform shrouded by cobalt curtains marked off what must have been some type of stage, while the rest of the room was left empty for dancing. The dazzling light illuminated the crowd before us in vivid detail, displaying a collection of well-dressed gentlemen, all patiently standing along the edges of the room. Whispers circulated around the girls as we all clustered into the middle of the room, eyeing the attractive men with curious glances.

"Why are there only men?" one of the older girls murmured.

"Which one is the prince? Is he the tall one in the center?" another chimed in.

"No, that can't be him; his hair is much too dark. Prince Carlex is blond, right?"

The soft whispers escalated into unfiltered chatter as the group's collective curiosity grew. I looked around at the men who encircled us, examining their clean attire and perfect smiles. There wasn't a single one I would doubt could be a prince. They didn't look alike, but they all possessed the physical charms that would be expected of a future king. I had only joined the ranks of nobility a few hours ago, so naturally, I had no clue which of these young men was Prince Carlex, but I didn't expect the other girls not to recognize him as well. Had they never seen him before, either? Sir Franklin's words were beginning to make more sense as the evening carried on.

Is this what he meant by finding the prince?

Before we could theorize any further, a small tapping drew our attention to the curtained stage in the corner of the room. Standing at the center of the stage was a young steward dressed in attire that was only slightly more formal than the rest of the staff. Atop his pressed tailcoat he wore a fluffy white ascot with a brooch resembling the royal crest pinned to the top.

"Greetings, and welcome to the first event of Prince Carlex's bride competition." The steward's voice was strong and clear, instantly hushing the girls who hadn't noticed him earlier. "Throughout this competition, I shall be your official host and will provide you with instructions prior to each of the five events. As for the competition as a whole, there are only three rules. Once the competition has begun, each participant must commit to the full tournament. No matter a participant's rank or status, all participants shall be judged on equal grounds. And third, participants are forbidden from sabotaging each other unless an event's rules state otherwise."

The hairs on my arms rose as shivers trickled down them. *Was it common for the competitions to involve sabotage?*

A few of the other girls seemed to mirror my unease, but we all remained quiet as our new host continued, "With the rules officially spoken, and the first event being upon us, you are all now subjected to the first rule. No one may be dismissed from the competition until it has reached completion."

He flashed a smile that looked almost mischievous as he watched each of our reactions with a close eye. *Are we already being judged?*

"Now, without further ado, please allow me to explain the rules of our first event."

My chest wound tight into a tangled knot as I took in a fortifying breath. *This is it. Just do your best and hopefully, you won't end up in last place. It couldn't possibly be that difficult... could it?*

"As I'm sure you've all guessed, Prince Carlex is somewhere in this room..." He paused, allowing us to give one final glance around the dozens of men who encircled us. "For the first event, your task is simple; you must determine which of the men in this ballroom is the prince."

I darted my eyes around the various gentlemen with a new suspicion in my gaze. They all looked regal enough to be a prince... How was I supposed to guess which one was the real Prince Carlex? *I hope the other girls are just as worried...* The rich food in my stomach churned as I fought the urge to chew my nails. What if this was a test to weed out any imposters? Surely any true noble would be able to pick out a prince from a crowd... What if I was the only person to guess wrong?

"To aid in your search, you will be provided with a riddle," the host continued. "Once this riddle is spoken, you will have one hour to dance and socialize with the other gentlemen. After the allotted time has passed, you will be instructed to approach the man you believe to be the prince. Each lady who guesses correctly shall be gifted points for today's events. Scores shall be announced throughout the kingdom each day that follows an event. Now, before we begin, are there any questions?"

He glossed his eyes over us with an almost humorous light in his eyes, causing me to wonder if he enjoyed watching us squirm with nerves.

"No? Excellent. In that case, allow me to read off our riddle."

He unfolded a small yellowing parchment from his coat pocket, smoothing out the crinkles painfully slowly as we all watched with greedy eyes.

He cleared his throat. "Cloaked in blue and announced with pride, the prince you seek currently hides. You have seen his face and have learned his place. If this evening you wish to score, stand by him in an hour more."

I stared blankly at the host's curling smile, trying to repeat the words in my mind before they were lost behind the pounding in my brain. *Cloaked in blue?* My gaze instantly gravitated to all the men wearing blue coats and sashes. The other girls seemed to have the same idea, because their eyes instantly latched onto the men in blue. Atop the bubbling pressure within me, a touch of relief surfaced as I noticed the girl's' frenzied eyes.

They don't seem to know the answer yet, either. Maybe I still have a chance to blend into the scores.

"Your time starts now. Happy hunting." The host gave a flourished bow, then stepped back behind the curtain right as a collection of musicians stepped forward, claiming the stage with the beginnings of a beautiful waltz.

All at once, the girls scattered, each blazing for a dance partner to claim and interrogate. For a dazed moment, I remained in the center of the dance floor, still trying to digest the information we had just been dumped with. The ballroom felt like it was swallowing me whole as blurs of ballgowns and bowing gentleman entered the dancefloor, swirling around me like encroaching vultures. I snapped back to my senses only a moment before a twirling couple, who had already engaged in the first dance, collided into me.

My grip tightened around my skirts as I hurried off the dance floor, trying my absolute best to look slightly coordinated as I rushed to the edges of the room. Once I was a safe distance away from the chaos, I took a moment to inspect everyone's partners. To no surprise, every single lady was dancing with a man who wore at least a morsel of blue. I bit my lip, wondering if I had already missed my chance to scope out the prince before getting lost in the web of dancers.

No, don't give up yet, Lacey. There's still plenty of time; I just need to find someone to dance with.

I gave myself a self-assured nod as I looked around at the remaining gentlemen. A few of them were chatting amongst themselves in small clusters, while others were engaged in chats with the other ladies. As I raked my gaze over the crowd, I found my focus snagging on a pair of green eyes that caught me back. The man smiled at me from across the dance floor, holding his hand up to his companions to pause their conversation before crossing the room to me.

I tried to feign a sweet smile as he approached, but my twisting nerves caused my eye to twitch in an unattractive manner.

He wasn't wearing any obvious blue, but he certainly was handsome enough to be Prince Carlex. He had smooth brown hair, dashing green eyes, and a charming smile that could easily make a debutant swoon. When he stopped in front of me, he took my hand with an alluring grin, then leaned down to bestow a kiss on the back of my hand.

"Good evening, my lady," he greeted warmly, sending a slight flutter through my chest. *Evie... you never taught me how to flirt. Is flirting required for nobility? Goodness, I hope not...* "Unfortunately, I am unable to share my name with you due to the constraints of the competition, but may I be so bold as to ask yours?"

His dazzling eyes glittered with all the enchantment I had expected from a handsome prince. My mouth felt like cotton as I pried it open to answer his question. "My name is Evie." The lie slid smoothly off my dry tongue. The curse truly seemed to love the charade Evie had concocted.

The gentleman smiled, flashing the most perfect row of pearly teeth. "It's a pleasure to meet you, Miss Evie." His voice was smooth and honeyed, swaying me even more to believe that he may actually be the true Prince Carlex. *He isn't wearing blue, though...* "Would you care to dance?"

My heart actually fluttered at his request.

Despite not having a clue how to properly waltz, a fester of excitement whirled inside me as I reached out to accept his outstretched hand. *I've never been asked to dance before...* Perhaps Evie was right about me enjoying parts of the switch. After all, when else would I get the opportunity to dance in a ballroom with a charming gentleman?

Maybe it's alright if I enjoy just one moment. Then I can focus on the competition...

A shy smile spread up my face as I gingerly rested my hand in his. "I would hate to dance with you."

Oh, drat.

My almost-partner's face instantly flushed red as he snaked his hand away from me. The blood drained from me entirely as I pressed a hand to my mouth, wishing I could retract the words with my gasping air.

"Well, then," he huffed indignantly, adjusting his lapel before turning his back to me with a sneer. "I suppose I'll step aside so you can seek a new dance partner to offend."

"Wait, I—" I caught myself from uttering an apology, unsure what dreadful insult my curse would twist it into instead. He briefly turned around to flick me an aggravated grimace, but then carried onward when I remained silent. My palms slickened as I watched him return to his companions, likely spouting about the disrespect he'd just endured. I pressed a thumb to my brow with a groan.

Nice going, Lacey... Now none of the men will want to dance with me, or even talk with me, for that matter. Why did I have to get so wrapped up in the idea of dancing in a palace?

As redundant as it was, I cursed my own curse, feeling slightly eased after finding a worthy place to pin the blame for my embarrassment. Judgmental gazes swept over me from across the dancefloor, until soon, even some of the ladies were looking at me with distaste. I stepped back toward the edges of the room, trying my best to sink into the shadows and avoid their gazes. It was only the first event, and my curse had already placed me on everyone's hit list...

What should I do? I can't be the only one to fail the event. Evie's parents will visit the moment the scores come out, and then I'll be in heaps of trouble. I have to do at least moderately well, but how can I find the real prince if I can't speak with any of the men?

A small chair called to me from the corner of the room, and I sank into it as my thoughts tripped over each other in a tangle. The weight of the heavy satin skirt eased tremendously, allowing a brief moment of relief on my waist. The chair was dug fairly deep into the corner, but I could still see a majority of the ballroom. Perhaps I could still take a guess by simply observing their mannerisms and deducting clues from the riddle? It wasn't the most efficient strategy, but it certainly couldn't be as harmful as trying to open my mouth again.

I watched the men with a careful eye for the next few minutes. When exiting the dance floor, some bent at the waist, while others bent at the spine. Some led the dance on instinct, while others let the ladies make the first sway. There were certainly clear differences between how they all moved and presented themselves, but no matter how many observations I made, it didn't matter if I couldn't deduct what any of it meant. The dress and borrowed title may proclaim me as a noble, but in truth, I was a lowly commoner who didn't know anything about the proper way for a Reclusian prince to bow or dance.

This is hopeless...

I leaned back against the chair, resting my head against the cool stone wall, fighting my brain for any further ideas. Weariness from the day was beginning to seep into me, causing a yawn to split my lips. My lashes drooped with my heavy eyelids, urging me to rest despite being in the middle of a royal event. I gave into the desire only momentarily, hoping that a small sense of rest would help me remember all the elements of the riddle.

"My word... she must be joking!"

I jumped in my seat, nearly scraping my scalp against the stone I was resting against as I turned to see the gawking expression of Jezebel and two other competitors. My skin instantly crawled at the sight, filling my tired bones with spastic adrenaline.

"What in the kingdoms is the matter with you?" Jezebel snapped her fingers an inch away from my face. I flinched at the rude gesture, earning a belittling laugh from Jezebel's followers.

"Look at her, she was really almost asleep!" One of the girls snorted behind her—an older one with jet-black hair and tanned skin. "She must not even want to find the prince."

"That or she's cocky enough to believe she can win without even trying." Jezebel's tone grew icy. She folded her arms with a tilted chin, staring down at me with a challenging sneer. "Evie, was it? What makes you think you're so special that you can be rude to the king's guests, and then insult his event by taking a nap in the midst of a challenge?"

Oh dear... How am I going to clean this up?

I scrambled out of my seat, hoping to display some form of dignity as I addressed their questions. My heart drummed inside me, forcing my blood to run like lightning as I fought to come up with words that wouldn't be reversed into a bigger dilemma.

I need to blend in, so I need to convince them that I'm not a major competitor but that I'm not a pushover, either.

"Well?" Jezebel edged, raising her plucked

brow impatiently.

"I was only taking a break from dancing," I said plainly.

The third girl, a bright-eyed redhead, furrowed her brow. "What dancing? Jezebel, Lydia and I haven't seen you on the floor once."

The three girls narrowed their eyes at me with heightened suspicion, cornering me in my lie.

Drat.

"Well... I actually don't need to dance." I fiddled with my fingers as I averted my gaze, desperately trying to translate my curse in my head before speaking it into words.

"And why not?" Jezebel questioned tartly. "Do you honestly believe you can find the prince without dancing with him?" Her piercing blue eyes gnawed at me with suspicion.

She can't possibly suspect my lying curse, can she?

I bit my cheek hard. I couldn't allow Jezebel to recognize me... I'll need to take a different approach.

"Yes, I do," I said, crossing my arms with forged confidence. The girl's faces twisted into appalled gapes as I fought a wave of nausea that swayed my legs.

"What makes you so confident?" Lydia, the dark-haired girl, scowled with festering irritation.

"I already know who the prince is," I

smirked proudly while internally screaming at myself.

Lacey! No! Why would you say that!?

"Oh, really?" Jezebel's suspicion seeped into her tone. She looked like she was contemplating murder for a moment, but then in the blink of an eye she spread a pearly smile across her lips with an unsettling grin. "If that's the case, then I look forward to seeing if your prediction is correct or not." Her jaw looked tight, as if she was biting back a far less friendly comment. "You seem to know what you're doing, so we'll go ahead and return to *our* competition."

I gave her a friendly smile that held just about as much internal resentment as hers did. "I wish you all the best of luck," I said sweetly, my stomach souring.

"And you as well," she said tautly, turning back to the other two girls. "Come along, Lydia, Maren. We need to inform the others that sweet Genevieve has already solved the riddle. That way no one else will come disturb her as she *rests*." She flashed me a wicked smile from over her shoulder as the trio turned back to the dance floor.

I managed a polite wave before nearly crumbling back into the chair with an exasperated breath. Nerves drilled into my core, spreading the web of anxiety throughout my body like an internal cage was beginning to consume me from the inside out.

How am I going to get out of this? If I don't guess the prince correctly, then Jezebel will know for certain that I'm a liar. And will that be enough for her to remember who I am?

I buried my face in my hands, balling my hands into fists, pounding softly against my skull.

Think, Lacey, think! The answer has to be here somewhere... How did that riddle start again?

"Cloaked in blue and announced with pride..."

I looked up from my hands to scan the ballroom once more, and most of the girls seemed to have clung to their suspected prince by now. All of them were wearing some sort of blue on their apparel, but what about the other part of the riddle—*announced with pride...* Did that refer to the prince's temperament? Was he loud and outgoing?

I looked across the room again to try to see if I could gauge any of the men's personalities from afar, but they all seemed to smile the same from where I sat.

What about the rest of the riddle? "The prince you seek currently hides..."?

My nails dug into my satin skirts as I furrowed my brow in thought. At first assumption, it seemed like the riddle was referring to the prince hiding in plain sight, but what if he's not... What if he was legitimately hiding...?

I pressed a finger to my chin, allowing the thought to fully develop as I glanced around the room with a new set of eyes. Instead of investigating the clusters of young men, I searched the ballroom for hiding spots or corners similar to the one I had taken refuge in. I rose from my chair, stepping farther out into the room to get a better view of my surroundings.

Cloaked in blue and announced with pride... It couldn't be...

My gaze drifted toward the musicians who had taken over the stage, my eyes fixated on their set-up. The beautiful music was airy and quick-paced, mirroring the rhythm of my heart as I felt it speed up as the clues slowly came together in my mind.

You have seen his face and learned his place... That's it! It has to be!

The excitement that poured through me blinded me to the point that I didn't even notice a group of ladies approach me from behind. I spun around when I heard their slippers click across the polished floors, a smile plastered to my face.

"Hello there, Evie, was it?" One of the girls spoke up, flicking her fan above her nose as she eyed me with distaste. "My name is Victoria of Bellatring. I'm sorry to interrupt your evening, I just wanted to ask if what Jezebel has been saying is true. Do you actually believe you know who the prince is after hiding in the corner all evening?"

The ladies who lingered behind her also held ornamental fans to their faces, clearly hiding their mocking smiles. *Jezebel certainly works fast...* Despite their rude confrontation, my smile never faltered. Jezebel could ridicule me all she wanted, but at least for tonight, I had her outplayed.

"No actually," I beamed, brightening my smile, "I have no idea where he is."

chapter seven

"Time is up." Our host stepped out from the curtain, swapping back out with the musicians as they lulled the final chords to a stop. "Gentlemen, if you would please return to the edges of the room and ladies, please gather in the center."

My legs still wobbled slightly as I stepped away from my cozy little corner. I felt confident in my answer now, but at the same time, I felt the web within my chest tighten with fear.

This will be absolutely humiliating if I'm wrong...

Jezebel's ice-blue stare drifted in my direction, smirking at me with her own flourishing confidence. *Had she put together the clues, too?* Honestly, that would be the best-case scenario for me. After digging my grave while speaking with Jezebel, I had no other option but to succeed in this event in order to avoid her suspecting me of my curse. However, I also couldn't be the only one to succeed. Otherwise, I would be in danger of actually *winning* the event, and that would be just as destructive as failing.

I just need to blend in somewhere in the middle. The clue was pretty obvious once you put the pieces together, so I'm sure there will be others who caught on. Either that or I was wrong, and the aforementioned humiliation would take place...

This may very well end poorly...

As we gathered in front of the stage, I noticed the other girls latch their gazes onto various men across the room, as if waiting to pounce and claim them as their prince before anyone else could. My nerves heightened as I slowly recognized that no one seemed to be looking in the direction of where *I* believed the prince to be.

Did I interpret the clue incorrectly? Or were the others just trying to throw each other off? Oh dear...

I chewed the inside of my cheek, fighting the festering anxiety that burned at the back of my throat as I kept my gaze fastened on the host.

"Excellent," the host proclaimed, eyeing the collection of ladies as they all adjusted their attention back to the stage. "I hope you all have completed your investigations, because the time has come to give your answers."

My heart thumped against my ribs, fighting against the entanglement of fears that twisted around the organ as it tried to break free. *I can do this. Don't pay attention to what the other girls' answers are, just stick with your gut.* My stomach churned in response to my thoughts, making it clear that not even my gut could be trusted at this time.

One of the musicians stepped forward alongside the host, carrying a dainty silver bell in the air. "The time has come to select your prince," the host proclaimed. "When the bell rings, please approach the gentleman you believe to be the real Prince Carlex. Once every lady has made their selection, the prince will reveal himself and points will be awarded accordingly. Now is everyone ready?"

No...

The beating in my chest intensified as doubts sifted through my mind. *What if I'm wrong? Will Jezebel recognize me from my lies? Will Evie's parents burst through the palace tomorrow and send me to the dungeon?* My limbs stiffened, paralyzing even my breaths as I felt my confidence sway with each passing moment.

"Wonderful," the host continued, flashing a wide smile down at us. "Then let the selection begin."

The tiny ring of the silver bell felt deafening, causing the ringing to repeat in my ears while a blur of ballgowns bustled around me in a rush to claim their choices. My leaden limbs remained planted, hoping that if I lingered for a moment, I wouldn't be the first person to approach the man I believed was Carlex. When the initial rush ceased, I glanced around with my breath held, watching all the girls flock to various gentlemen in blue coats.

Did none of them think...?

I locked eyes with Jezebel for a brief moment, who was smirking victoriously at me as she clung to the arm of a jaw-droppingly handsome blonde with a blue sash prominently displayed across his chest. A few of the other ladies gathered around him as well, and I felt the dam of doubts that had been building reach its full capacity. My head waged war with the web of nerves as they urged me to follow the majority and stand beside the attractive blonde. I made a half step in their direction, but froze before I could let the tangled web envelope my thoughts entirely.

No, you know that's not the right answer. If I'm going to protect myself from being exposed, then I need to be true to my instincts, not follow the temptation of the lie my nerves want me to believe.

With a fortifying breath, I turned away from Jezebel and her chosen suitor, my eyes fixated on the stage. Since I had waited to make my selection, all eyes on the room now fell on me as I slowly urged my legs to move without stumbling. My heartbeat thundered in my ears, but I tuned it out, focusing on the three short steps that led me to the top of the stage. Every bit of Lacey that still lingered within detested looking up into the crowd, but the Evie I had invited inside lifted her chin high as I met the warm brown eyes of our host, Prince Carlex.

A boyish grin tugged at his lips, showcasing a slight dimple on his right cheek. He wasn't as devilishly handsome as all the men who encircled the ballroom, but he was charming in his own way. His dark hair was combed back in the clean manner that most servants usually wore, but I imagined, if let loose, it would frame his face attractively. He had a strong jaw that softened beneath his dazzling white smile and a tall frame that towered at least a half foot over me as I stopped beside him.

Whispers fluttered across the ballroom, muttering who knows what kind of rumors about my brash boldness or humiliating mistake. Despite the whirling emotions spinning inside me, I did everything I could to stand tall and calm as I proudly displayed my decision.

If I'm wrong, then at least I'll be confidently wrong...

The host's brown eyes glittered at me in intrigue, folding his arms across his chest with a pleased lift of his chin. "Well, well, well... it would appear that we have a winner."

My entire body went numb as I nearly fainted from relief. *Thank goodness...*

"It's a pleasure to meet you, my dear. My name is Prince Carlex." All the oxygen vanished from the room in a single moment as every single lady gasped in disbelief.

Red filled my cheeks as I felt the envious

glare of nearly every girl burn into me. Nausea greeted me with a painful cramp as the realization dawned on me that I had actually won the first event. And that meant I was in the lead to marry the—

"What's your name?" Prince Carlex reached out his hand to take mine with elegant poise. My heart leapt at the contact, and I silently cursed it for being so easily swayed.

What am I doing? I wasn't supposed to win...

"Genevieve Palleep," I squeaked, my throat tighter than the first weave of a loom. "But I go by Evie. Oh! Your Highness." I made a rough attempt at a curtsy, stumbling only slightly underneath my jelly legs.

"Well, congratulations, Miss Evie." Prince Carlex gave the back of my hand a gentle stroke, and I could have sworn I heard Jezebel swear somewhere from behind me. *Oh dear...* "It would seem you were the only one who deciphered the riddle."

Unfortunately, yes...

"I'm honored to have been victorious." I smiled sweetly. His soft pets sent a ripple of ease through my arm, but I could hardly appreciate the sweet gesture when under the scrutiny of fifteen women who were plotting my demise.

Carlex seemed completely oblivious to the death stares I was receiving, keeping his warm chocolate gaze focused on me. "May I ask how you deciphered the riddle?" He dropped my hand, allowing me to take the full stage to explain my process.

Drat. How am I supposed to explain my thought process through lies...?

My fingers fidgeted nervously as I stepped away from the edge of the stage, approaching the cobalt blue curtain that hung along the back of the platform. "Weren't you hiding behind here throughout the ball, Your Highness?" I gestured at the curtain, hoping that redirecting the answer onto him would clear me from explaining in full.

His eyes lit up with satisfaction. "That's correct, Evie. I suppose you could say I was... *cloaked in blue.*" A cheeky smile twisted his lips as he watched the realization sweep across the faces of the other competitors. Jezebel in particular looked a touch red, and I couldn't help but feel a smidge of satisfaction at the sight.

At least she won't have any reason to suspect I'm a liar now. She'll only think I'm a pompous brat. Which isn't great... but definitely an improvement!

"You were also announced with pride, c-correct?" I coughed as my throat squeezed around the question I had tacked onto my statement. The curse definitely did not approve of my methods, but I couldn't let it take full control while I was standing in front of an entire audience.

"I do admit, I take a bit of pride in my hosting abilities." He chuckled, turning his attention back to the crowd. "The riddle was meant to challenge you to look beyond what was in front of you, and I'm pleased to see that at least one of you succeeded in this task."

He flicked me a quick smile and I felt my cheeks grow warm under his gaze. I cursed the blood that reddened my face, desperately trying to remind myself I had no place flirting with a prince.

"For the rest of you, I hope tonight served as a great insight to the challenges that lie ahead. I greatly look forward to seeing each of your gifts shine over the next few weeks, and I hope that somewhere among you lies the future queen of Reclusia."

Jealous gazes pierced me at the mention of the word queen, and I instantly felt the regret for my victory triple. *Maybe I should have followed Jezebel after all...* A deep pit formed in my stomach, increasing with every threatening stare that pinned my shoes in place. Foolishly, my gaze drifted over to the blood princess, and I flinched when my eyes met her golden glare. She seemed entirely unmoved by the event, without even a flicker of emotion burning behind her stone façade. Directly next to her, Jezebel reflected the exact opposite reaction, holding her arms tightly against her chest with a fuming scowl plastered across her features.

"With that said, tonight's event has officially concluded," Prince Carlex announced, snapping me back into the moment. "Scores will be announced throughout the kingdom first thing in the morning, and our next event shall take place in three days' time. Please take this time to rest and enjoy your time in the palace. I promise, from here on out, I will no longer hide and instead, I will make the effort to meet with each of you individually." He turned back in my direction, his tall form shielding my view from the fuming crowd of ladies. "Starting with our winner."

With his back turned to the crowd, he gave me a slight wink, sending another blush through me. A flutter of nerves scattered throughout my system, leaving me mute as I attempted to process this overwhelming predicament.

The prince wants to spend one on one time with me... The cursed liar, who is masquerading as her overconfident, noble best friend. Evie, if I survive this, I might just have to kill you.

"Good night, ladies. I look forward to speaking with you all soon. And thank you for your participation." With the prince's parting words, the servants began to direct the crowds back out of the ballroom.

I eagerly started to follow, anxious to get off the stage, before a slight brush against my hand halted me in place.

"Hold on a moment, Evie." The prince reached out for me, but pulled back when he noticed the haste in my expression. "I'm sorry to keep you, I just wanted to express my congratulations." He ran a hand through his slicked back hair, shuffling the neat style with a light tussle.

I paused, taking him in a little more closely now that my vision wasn't blurred with tension. He didn't look nearly as prince-like as the other gentlemen who had filled the room, but that almost made him look more appealing in my eyes. He looked... normal. Like the kind of man a lowly handmaiden could approach.

Except he's definitely not the type of man I should approach. He's the type of man I was meant to be invisible around...

His fixated gaze made it beyond clear that I was anything *but* invisible to him at this moment.

"Honestly, I'm rather impressed you managed to solve the riddle." He stuffed his hands into his jacket pockets. Rocking his weight back on his heels as his eyes shied away from mine.

Wait a moment... Is he actually nervous to talk to me?

I watched closely as I noticed a slight bounce in his leg and the fidgeting fingers inside his pockets. A boyish smile pulled at his lips as he coyly looked up at me with a softness I hadn't expected to see in a crown prince.

"Most people hold an unspoken expectation for what they expect a prince to be.

I thought it would be insightful to see if anyone was capable of searching behind the fineries." He took a hesitant step in my direction, his hands still buried in his pockets. "So, what I guess I'm trying to say is... thanks for noticing me, Evie."

His warm brown eyes seeped into me, rippling a strange sensation of ease through me. He appreciated that *I* noticed *him?* Oh, if only he could understand the sheer amount of irony that revolved around that epiphany.

I nervously rubbed my hand up my arm, attempting to warm the goosebumps that prickled down my skin. "I'm just glad I was given the opportunity to compete." I shrugged casually, then stiffened directly after. *Is it rude to shrug in front of royalty? Goodness, I have no idea...* I straightened my posture, reminding myself that I was meant to be a lady and not a slumping servant.

"The riddle wasn't really that hard, anyway. I pretty much had it figured out from the start." I scratched at the back of my neck, trying to scrape away the awkward tingles that had burrowed beneath my skin.

"Is that so?" Prince Carlex tilted his head, observing my lying quirks with a suspicious gleam in his eye. *Am I that obvious? Hopefully so... If he thinks I'm pompous, then maybe he'll lose interest.* "Nevertheless, you were correct and for that, I congratulate you. It's nice to know there are competitors willing to look beyond the surface of a riddle." A slight inflection in his tone sent a wave of sympathy through me.

I understand now... He is hoping to find a potential bride who will care about more than just his title or finesse. Well, this certainly will be disappointing for him.

"May I walk you back to your suite? I know it isn't much of a reward for being the only victor tonight, but I wouldn't mind getting the opportunity to speak with you more." His slight touch of shyness was surprisingly adorable, emphasis on surprising. Were princes usually this gentle-natured?

He's so sweet... But I can't possibly walk with him. The more time we spend speaking, the bigger risk there is that my curse or identity will be exposed. I'm sorry, Prince Carlex, but I can't.

"That would be wonderful."

Well, drat. Didn't think that one through.

His expression swelled with a cheerful glow that I actually felt guilty for causing. "Great, shall we be off then?" He extended his arm to me in a chivalrous manner, his leg still bouncing slightly with excited nerves.

Evie, if I break the prince's heart, I'm blaming you.

I accepted his arm with a weary smile. "I'd love to."

chapter eight

My arm felt as stiff as a board as it rested around Prince Carlex's. I'd never been treated like a proper lady until today; therefore, I had never been guided by the arm of a gentleman until now, either. It felt both natural and completely awkward considering I wasn't even sure if I was gripping his arm properly.

Is he comfortable? Am I holding him too tightly? Or perhaps too loosely?

A sharp shoot of pain nearly caused my steps to falter as I felt the back of my heel rub raw into a blister. Evie and I may have been a similar enough dress size where we could cinch in the corset appropriately, but it was becoming apparent that her shoe size was much smaller than mine. Prince Carlex led me down a long back hallway, away from the hustle of the other girls. It was a beautiful route to take, with plush red carpets and dazzling windows that glittered with the glow of the moonlight, but the long path looked like torture as I felt the first drop of blood trickle into my shoe.

"So, have you enjoyed your time at the

palace so far?" Prince Carlex's pale skin looked almost luminescent in the silver light that scattered through the glass.

I gave him a gritted smile, trying to bite back my discomfort as each step grew more challenging. "Definitely. I don't believe there has been a moment I haven't enjoyed." A fresh sting pricked at my other foot, alerting me that now both heels possessed growing wounds.

Why does my suite have to be so far...?

"Have you enjoyed the competition so far, Your Highness?" I asked with a forged smile. Perhaps the talking would distract me from my swelling feet.

The prince gave an almost sad smile, followed by a short laugh. "I suppose I've enjoyed it as much as I can." His arm tensed beneath my touch, but his smile remained perfectly in place. *Is his fake, too?*

My senses dulled to the pain in my feet as I found myself studying him more closely. At first glance, he seemed entirely normal, but under the moonlight, I could see the tension in his jaw, the wrinkle in his brow, and the shadows under his eyes. He wore his smile in the same way I wore mine... as a mask.

"Is something troubling you, Your Highness?" I asked cautiously. It probably wasn't appropriate for me to badger a prince about his mental state, but I couldn't help but feel compelled to at least check in on him. It was hard to smile like that for so long.

He gave me a perplexed look, almost as if he was startled I had noticed something was amiss. "Why do you ask?"

I couldn't tell him what I had noticed, even if I wanted to, so I simply shrugged. "I don't know." A slight twinge of guilt tugged inside me as I watched his false smile return.

"Well, I appreciate your concern, but I can assure you that I'm doing fine." He sounded so sure of himself, but I'd told enough lies in my life to know he wasn't being honest.

I sighed, unsure of how to continue a conversation with my uncooperative tongue. The pain in my heels slowly resurfaced in my mind, causing my steps to grow stiff and rigid. My grip around the prince's arm tightened the smallest amount in an attempt to keep my steps steady, but my increase of pressure didn't seem to go unnoticed.

Prince Carlex's eyes drifted to where I clutched him, a small twitch of interest flickering in his moonlit eyes. "May I ask you something, Miss Evie?" His eyes met mine with widened interest, much like the curiosity of a child who desired to learn more about their world. "Why did you choose to participate in the tournament?"

I paused before answering, contemplating any response that was better than, *"My best friend wanted me to take her place and now you're escorting a compulsive liar."* Technically, I meant to be mirroring Evie, so I suppose the best option would be to use her truth as my lies.

"My parents made me attend," I said. "My family never really listens to what I want to do, and instead, only does what they believe is best for the *family*." It was discomforting how easy it was to meld into Evie's mind. We had spent so much time together over the years that using her truth in place of my lies almost felt natural.

"Oh, I see." His head lowered a touch, drifting his eyes to the floor. "So, you never wanted to participate on your own accord then?"

My breath hitched. I was so wrapped up in telling a clean lie that I didn't even consider how rude I was coming off as.

"No! That's not what I meant to say. I definitely wanted to participate," I added hastily, attempting to repair the damage I'd already made. *Can I be arrested for offending the prince?* "My parents made me come, but I also wanted to try my hand in the competition."

The prince let out a soft breath, leading us down a new hall that greeted us with the first set of stairs. "Well, I'm glad you still wanted to come." His arm tensed once more under my grip—a movement I was far more acute to now that I was forced to hold him so tightly. "I can understand how difficult it can be when parents expect us to do things we don't feel capable of."

Just then, a slight patter of rain washed

against the windows. The soft moonlight that had bathed the halls quickly became cloaked in clouds, leaving only the flicker of the burning wall sconces to light our steps. The soft drizzle of raindrops filled the quiet hall with a comforting white noise, tempting me to fall asleep while standing up.

"Does your family put a lot of pressure on y—" A yawn interrupted my question, causing me to fly my hand to my lips with a blush. I wasn't sure if it was from the curse rebelling against my questions or my crippling exhaustion.

Prince Carlex actually chuckled at my yawn, causing my cheeks to flush hot enough to burn crimson.

"My apologies, Miss Evie. I'm sure you're rather exhausted after such an eventful day. Perhaps we can carry on our conversation after you're more well-rested?" He glanced at me from the side with the beginnings of a real smile. It was like the one he first showed me when I won the event, the one that showcased his sweet dimple.

The stinging in my feet and the weariness in my bones wanted to cave to his idea, but at the same time, I didn't feel satisfied leaving our conversation where it stood. "I'm not that tired." I gave him a slight smile, hoping my yawn hadn't already ruined my chances at further conversation.

"Is that so?" He chuckled once more, turning his head to meet my gaze with a humored rise of his brow. "You'll have to pardon me for being so accusing, but didn't I see you napping in the corner of the ballroom earlier this evening?"

Oh... He saw that? He must have been peeking at the event from behind the curtain... Drat.

"Hmm? That couldn't possibly have been me..." I said coyly, drifting my gaze to the water-dotted panes of glass.

"Couldn't possibly, hmm?" His suspicion rose, and an accusatory smile curled his lips. "So, I suppose there must have been another beautiful woman in a dark blue gown with dark hair, resting her head against the wall for a quick doze?" He gave me a playful nudge that I pretended not to notice.

"Must have been," I said assuredly. "I would *never* be so careless as to fall asleep during such an important event..." I dragged out the words dramatically, grateful that the prince seemed amused by my sarcasm instead of appalled by my unladylike behavior.

He laughed warmly, a sound that sweetly contrasted the cold patter of rain. "Then I beg your pardon for being so assuming. Next time I'll be certain to get the name of the girls I find snoozing in the midst of a competition."

"Why? So, you can subtract points from their score?" I laughed a little hopefully. *If I lose a*

*few points, then maybe the other girls will get off my
back a touch.*

"No, so I could ask her to dance." He
smirked, causing me to turn to him in surprise.

"To dance?" I gaped at him in disbelief, but
the amusement in his eyes only twinkled more
in the burning glow of the sconces.

"Well, of course." He grinned, leading me
up the first flight of stairs. I bit my tongue as
the blisters on my feet screamed in pain with
the ascent. "It's my duty as prince to ensure
that each of my guests are enjoying themselves."
He flashed me a dallying smile that sent a
flutter through our touch. "Besides, I want to
get to know any woman who can be herself
in the middle of a ballroom. Propriety is great
at training young ladies into dawning a perfect
mask, but if I'm going to select a queen over these
next few weeks, I need to find someone who can
show me her true self as well."

Her true self...

"Well, I'm truly just Evie." I smiled guiltily,
feeling nearly like a traitor to the crown for
deceiving the prince so easily.

"It's been a pleasure to meet you, Evie."
His face was rich with vulnerability that I felt
no right to be exposed to. My heart pattered
in rhythm to the rain, feeling equally drowned
under the pressure of the mask the prince had
unknowingly identified in me.

What am I doing...?

My gaze remained fixated on his, so much so that I missed the next step in the dim lighting, causing my slipper to slide off the edge into a fumble. I dug my nails into the prince's arm for support, seething in pain as my heel scraped deeper into the edge of my slipper, warming my skin with a fresh stream of blood. Prince Carlex didn't even hesitate to wrap his arm around my waist and hold me steady. He must have noticed my wincing because his eyes instantly studied me with a worried look.

"Evie, are you alright? Are you hurt?" His voice was loaded with concern, his arm tightening around my waist as he noticed me sway once again with uneven steps.

My arms stiffened around his, both afraid of falling down the steps and clinging too closely to a prince I still had no idea how to offend. "N-no, I'm alright," I hissed unconvincingly through another shot of pain as my feet recentered themselves on the step.

His brow wrinkled sternly. "No, you're not alright. You're clearly in pain somehow."

His grip on me softened, but he still held me close. My fingers were still dug into the arms of his coat, the two of us locked in an odd embrace in the middle of a dark staircase. My heart sped up without permission, and his stern gaze eased when he noticed the encroaching red on my face. He loosened his grip on my waist until his arm was barely hovering above my skirt, guarding me from another fall.

"Please, may I help?" he asked gently.

Odd sensations of warmth flooded through me as my heart continued to pound relentlessly. I didn't trust my words to convey anything appropriate, so I simply bit my tongue and nodded mutely. Thankfully, he accepted my wordless response and carefully guided me into a sit. The throbbing in my heels rushed with relief as the weight of my frail body and massive gown vanished from them. Once I was seated, the prince descended a few steps and kneeled at where my toes poked out from my skirt. His eyes followed to where I was glancing at my concealed injury and he paused before making any moves to touch me.

"May I?" he asked tenderly, patiently waiting for my nod of permission before he gingerly picked up my outstretched ankle.

I winced as he placed his hand on the back of my heel, directly where the wound had sprouted. He seemed to respond to my painful outburst immediately, and carefully, he turned my foot over to inspect the injury.

"Goodness, Evie. How long have you been walking like this?" He looked up at me apologetically, almost as if he felt guilty for not noticing my pain sooner.

"I'm not sure." I shrugged, recalling the exact moment the blister had worn through in the hall. "I barely even noticed it."

He gave me a skeptical look, which I avoided with a shy glance at the floor. "I find that a little hard to believe," he mused doubtfully, gingerly removing the blood-stained slipper from my foot. "It's no wonder your feet got so badly pinched; these slippers seem much too small for you." He placed the shoe atop the step before slipping off the second to place beside it.

"They didn't seem that small when I first put them on." I tried to sound nonchalant, but the sweet relief that flooded my swollen feet made me want to sing for joy. Most of the pain subsided the instant the slippers were removed, but there were still raw patches of skin where the shoes had dug into my feet. Embarrassment swelled inside me as I slowly realized that the prince of Reclusia was currently sitting directly in front of my scratched-up feet.

Could I have failed any grander at being a noble?

I shyly slid my feet back under my billowing skirts, and Prince Carlex cleared his throat with an awkward tug of his collar, a red tinge creeping up his own neck. "Well, you certainly can't continue walking in these." He picked up my bloodied shoes, tucking them under his arm as he extended his hand to me. I watched him in bewilderment as he, a prince, carried my soiled slippers as if it were the most normal occurrence. "Can you stand? Or shall I fetch a physician?"

My heart drummed in my chest as I looked up at his considerate gaze. *What is he doing? He shouldn't have to cater to me like this; he's a prince and I'm just... a liar.*

"I'm alright, thank you." I accepted his hand graciously, feeling anything but *alright* as my heart threatened to pound a hole through my chest. The soft trickle of rain serenaded the roof of the dark stairwell, leaving the room both filled with sound and deafening quiet at the same time. "Would you like me to carry those for you, Your Highness?" I gestured toward the filthy slippers that belonged anywhere but in the hands of a prince.

"No, that's alright. I'll take them with me so I can instruct the cobbler to make you a larger size." He gave me a sympathetic smile, sending another ripple of odd warmth through my twisted webbed core. "We can't have you hobbling around the ballroom in future competitions; otherwise, I might find you sitting in a corner again." He gave me a playful smile, once again surprising me with how real he could be for someone who was meant to be a prince.

I never imagined Prince Carlex to be so... sweet.

"That wasn't me who fell asleep," I chided softly, looking up at him playfully through my lashes. "How could I fall asleep when there was a prince waiting to meet me?"

He gave a slight laugh, reaching his arm out to me as a crutch. I accepted it a little nervously, feeling slightly more conscious of the amount of weight I had to lean on him. "You're right; what ever was I thinking?" He snickered, leading me up the steps far more cautiously now, being certain to keep up with the pace I set.

One by one, we made our way up the steps, with Carlex pausing to check on me every flight or so. The third floor felt miles away when I was forced to use the prince as a cane, but he didn't seem to mind one bit. My heels felt far better now that the blasted shoes had been removed, but they still ached under the pressure of my weight after such a long day of wear. When we finally approached the door to my suite, I felt as if I might collapse with exhaustion the moment I entered.

"Are you sure you don't need me to send a physician to your suite? Those cuts looked rather deep," he asked with a concerned knit in his brow. "It's really no trouble."

Honestly, a fresh bandage would have been wonderful, but there was no chance that the curse would let me convey the need. "Thank you, Your Highness, but I don't think it's necessary." I gave him my most convincing smile.

"Very well then." He sighed reluctantly. "Thank you for allowing me to escort you, Miss Evie." He picked up my hand, raising the back to his lips before giving it a gentle kiss. Heat warmed underneath where his lips brushed my skin, wandering into my heart, uninvited. "I hope to spend more time with you throughout these next few weeks. You have been wonderful company." He gave me a sweet smile, displaying his dimple one final time before releasing my hand.

"I hope to spend more time with you as well." I smiled back, but felt a twinge in my jaw that tightened around my words—as if the curse couldn't decide if my words were a lie or not.

I enjoyed the prince more than I had expected, but I still can't risk spending more time with him, especially when I know I can't win the competition. Perhaps the curse is just as confused as I am...

Prince Carlex turned down the hall, leaving me alone with my bustling, exhausted thoughts for a brief moment before I turned to open the suite door. A yawn overtook me, forcing my eyes closed as I stepped blindly into the suite with a tired stretch. When I finally blinked my eyes open, I nearly fell over as I caught sight of a bright-eyed Evie staring at me with bursting excitement.

"You're back!" She hurried up beside me, practically vibrating with energy that I couldn't possibly fathom at such a late hour. "I already heard the news! The servant gossip around here spreads like wildfire! Oh, Lacey! I can't believe you won! Well, not that I *can't* believe it, I always knew you were capable, but I can't believe you outwitted everyone else!"

My head spun as she flitted around me like a rabid squirrel, picking pins out of my hair and untying my laces faster than I would have deemed humanly possible. "I didn't really outwit everyone." I yawned again, opening my eyes to find a soft powder blue nightgown being thrust over my head.

"Oh, don't be so modest!" Evie giggled, half-guiding, half-shoving me toward the massive pillowy bed. "You did amazing! I want to hear everything about it, but I'm sure you're exhausted, so I just need you to tell me one teeny-weeny detail first." She paused to take in a breath, likely the first one since I'd walked in. "How was the prince?"

She pressed a hand to her chin with a dreamy flutter in her eyes, sitting on the edge of the bed with her knees curled into her chest.

I paused to collect my thoughts, my world still spinning from the events of the day.

How was the prince?

I sighed, letting out a tight breath that felt as if it had been trapped all day before meeting Evie's eager eyes. "He was everything I expected him to be."

chapter nine

And the winner is... Genevieve Rayelle Palleep!

The palace ballroom flooded with roaring applause as every eye turned directly onto me. My blood turned to ice as I felt the scathing eyes of all the other participants sear into me from the corners of my vision.

No... This can't be happening, I can't win.

The crowd split, directing me to the head of the room where the faceless king and queen of Reclusia stood proudly behind their son. Prince Carlex's kind gaze met me with excitement, but the look I returned to him was loaded with horror.

No... I'm not your winner, I can't be.

"Congratulations, Evie." The name dripped like venom off his smiling lips as he slowly closed the distance between us.

My heart pounded relentlessly, tightening the web of collected fears into a tight noose that latched around my lungs, suffocating the breath from me. I opened my mouth to try to explain that this was all a mistake, that I was never Evie at all, but my mouth was dry and not even a sound was permitted to pass over my strangled tongue.

Please, choose someone else. I can't win. I'm not who you think I am.

An earsplitting screech caused the entire crowd to turn their eyes toward the entrance. My stomach plummeted, filling me with nausea and panic as I looked over to see Lord and Lady Palleep gape at me with horrified expressions.

"That's not my daughter!" Lady Palleep wailed furiously.

"She's an imposter! A mere handmaiden!" Lord Palleep pointed toward my chest, holding me paralyzed beneath his accusing gaze.

I felt trapped, cornered on all angles with no way of escape, like a fly caught in the center of a perfectly crafted web of lies. Desperately, I looked over to the prince, hoping to plead some form of forgiveness, but the previous light that had filled his eyes was completely voided, now flushed with anger.

"You dare deceive me?" he growled. His kind features were entirely absent now, swallowed in unrestrained rage.

No, it wasn't my fault! I didn't mean to!

"Yes." My tongue acted on its own accord, condemning me with a single word.

The audience gasped and the prince's fury rose, signaling to the guard with a flick of his hand. "Then you shall face the consequences for your crimes. Commoners must be punished for masquerading as nobility."

Guards swept up along all sides of me, circling like preying sharks before striking with abrasive grabs to my arms and shoulders.

Carlex's eyes darkened, his face grim and pained. "Send her to the gallows."

"No!" I sat up in bed with a panicked start. My breaths came short and raspy, and my skin was slickened with sweat. I clawed at the thick duvet, desperate to touch something real that wasn't tainted by the horrors of my nightmare.

It had felt so real... probably because it could become real.

I wiped the sweat from my brow, pressing a hand to my heart as I felt the beats begin to steady. The drapes were still closed, but I could still tell that it was late. Pitch-black enveloped the room except for the smoldering embers that remained in the fireplace. Rain still drizzled atop the balcony beyond the glass doors, making the darkness feel even more claustrophobic somehow. I glanced over at Evie's bed, hoping to see the privacy curtain still drawn over her bunk, but the curtains were wide open, and two sleepy blue eyes were blinking at me through the dark.

Oh no, I must have woken her.

"Lacey?" She yawned, leaning over to twist on the oil lamp that rested on the shelf beside her. "Are you alright? I thought I heard you yell something?"

Before I could even think of a proper explanation for my outburst, she was already climbing down from her bunk with the lamp in hand. Her loose blonde curls framed her face with frizzy askew circlets that poked out atop her head. She yawned once more, walking sleepily over to join me in the voluminous bed.

"I-it was nothing, I'm alright." I wiped at my arms, trying to dry the feverish sweat before it glistened off the light of her lamp.

Evie crawled onto the bed, placing the lamp in the center as she sat cross-legged next to my feet. When the light finally illuminated me, her tired eyes furrowed. "Lacey, you're trembling." She tucked a wild curl back behind her ear as she shifted an inch closer, inspecting me with concern.

"No, I'm not. I-I'm just cold." I tucked my knees to my chest, squeezing them as tightly as I could to hold back their shaking.

Evie didn't look convinced, and instead, crawled farther up the bed until she was sitting directly beside me. "Lacey, what's the matter? You look like you've seen a ghost." Her calm voice contrasted with the chaotic splashes of rain that splattered against the windows and balcony. "You know you can tell me anything, Lacey. I'm your friend." She smiled warmly at me, causing her kindness to eat at me with regret.

That's the problem, Evie; I can't tell you. No matter how badly I wish I could.

"I don't want to talk about it," I squeaked, my heart heavy as stone as I looked away from what I knew would be disappointment.

I'm sorry, Evie.

"Alright then, you don't have to tell me," she said quietly, tucking her legs to her chest to rest her chin on her knees. "But know that I'm always here to listen." She turned her head on its side, resting her cheek on her kneecaps so she could look at me. "Because you've always been such a great listener for me, Lacey. I know most days I talk enough for the both of us, but I want you to know I really do appreciate how you're always willing to lend me an ear. My family prefers that I live the lifestyle of being seen and not heard, so it's nice to have a friend that I know will always listen."

She gave me a grateful smile, causing my heart to seize with guilt. I wanted to tell her everything; if she could trust me to vent her struggles, then I should have been able to do the same. But this blasted curse... Why did it have to ruin the only real friendship I had ever forged? Why couldn't I just have one person to lean on other than my mother?

There has to be a way to tell her...

"Evie, I—" I stopped, my face twisting in thought as I struggled to form the words that I wanted so desperately to convey. Evie lifted her head from her knees, watching me curiously as I took in a fortifying breath. "W-what if I couldn't tell you the truth?" The question burned in my throat, serving as a warning that I was encroaching on dangerous boundaries with the curse.

She crinkled her brow. "You mean, like... you were lying to me?"

I shook my head fiercely. "Yes, w-wait, I mean—" My tongue went limp, preventing me from finishing my thought. I pressed my hands into my forehead with an aggravated groan.

"So, not like lying then?" She sounded profusely puzzled, and I couldn't blame her one bit.

I sighed, lifting my head from my palms to face her with a stronger sense of determination. *There has to be a way to explain this...*

"Evie, I can only tell the truth." My eyes gripped hers fiercely as my heart hammered in my chest.

What if she can't understand me?

"What? That's not true, I've heard you lie plenty of times." She raised her hand to press it against my forehead, checking for fever. "Are you sure you're feeling alright? Maybe the competition is stressing you out a little too much."

I shook my head once more, my expression pleading. "Evie, please, listen to me. I can only tell the *truth*." I drew out the word, biting my tongue afterward as the nerves resurfaced in my stomach.

I'd never tried to tell anyone about my curse before; instead, I'd always done everything in my power to hide it. But right now, I wanted Evie to know, more than anything. I wanted to confide in her the way she did in me.

Evie's expression remained thoughtful for a moment, confusion still sweeping over her big blue eyes, but almost in slow motion, her mouth fell open and her eyes widened with slow realization. "You're... lying to me right now, aren't you?" she asked breathlessly, leaning forward with growing shock.

Yes!

"No." I grinned as an overwhelming flood of relief melted into me as I felt the burden of my secret slowly lift from my shoulders.

Evie blinked, biting her lip with another puzzled look. "You're not? But I thought... *Oh!* I get it!" Her face lit back up again, and I actually laughed at her stages of understanding. "So, you just lied again? But why? Is it a game or something?" She shifted to sit up on her knees, her face filled with bursting questions.

I shook my head. "I don't know why. I only know that I'm not cursed." I lifted my brow at her, giving her a knowing look.

She bit her lip once more, attempting to decipher my twisted words. "So... you *are* cursed, then?"

I gave her a sad smile, nodding slowly as I watched her face drop.

"Oh, my goodness... Lacey, I had no idea. Was it from a magic stone?" Before I could attempt to answer, her hands flew to her mouth with a gasp. "Oh my kingdoms, of course it was!

The palace mosaic, the one you didn't want to walk across... Not to mention all those times you claimed you were untrained in handling jewelry with magic stones. Oh, Lacey! Why didn't I see it sooner? You were cursed by an unrefined truth stone, weren't you?"

So many emotions flooded inside me as the words I had longed to voice for years spilled out of my best friend's mouth. Tears clustered in the corners of my eyes as a broken smile spread across my face. I nodded slowly, the first tear trickling down my cheek. The saddest look of guilt overtook Evie's face, causing tears to swell up in her eyes as well. She swept me into a tight hug and allowed me to cry for a few moments before I managed to croak out a reply.

"I never wanted you to know." I sniffed.

The lie surprised me. All this time, I thought I wanted to keep my true self tucked away; that if I wanted to be accepted, I needed to prove I could go through life unnoticed. But by telling Evie I never wanted her to know, the truth became clear to me. I'd *always* wanted to confide in someone, even if I couldn't admit it to myself, and now that I had, I felt like, for the first time in my life, I wasn't trapped under a mask.

Evie gasped once more, pulling away from the embrace and holding me stiffly at arms-length in a petrified manner. "Lacey, if you've only been lying to me all this time, then that means—" She didn't finish, her quivering lip overtaking her words until she only managed a mere whisper. "The competition..."

My chest tightened. It wasn't Evie's fault that I was involved in this mess, but that didn't mean I could protect her from the guilt I knew was inevitable. "I have to win the competition, Evie. If I win, then my curse will remain a secret."

She nodded slowly, translating my lies as she slowly chewed on her fingernails. "You're right... What have I done?"

My heart constricted. She shouldn't blame herself for what my curse forced her to believe.

"I'm so sorry, Lacey. I truly believed you wanted a chance to marry the prince." She blinked at me apologetically, her doll-like lashes dotted with crystal tears.

"It's all your fault, Evie." I tried to give her a reassuring smile, but even though she knew the words were a lie, I could still see her wince.

"Still, I should have been more thoughtful." She rocked back onto the pillows, sinking into them with a defeated sigh. "It's such a shame too, you really could have become a princess. How wonderful would that have been?" She glanced over at me with her dreamy expression and I bit back a sigh.

She hadn't seemed to grasp the part where I lied about wanting to marry the prince.

"Evie, what would happen if I won the competition?" I questioned with a far more serious tone.

She didn't seem to grasp the gravity of my question and instead, let out a whimsical sigh. "Live happily ever after as a princess, instead of working as a handmaiden. But I suppose the curse would make things difficult for you once crowned."

I shook my head, trying to showcase that I was implicating something different. "Do you think they will crown a handmaiden?"

She gave me a perplexed look, sitting up from the pillows to try to study my words more closely. "Well, no, of course not. That's why you're disguised as m—" She froze, her mouth still open with a half-formed thought.

"How long did you really think I could pretend to be you?" I asked grimly, my throat beginning to burn from the questions.

"I-I don't know," she stuttered, her breaths shortening in a slight panic. "I guess I just assumed that... Oh goodness, Lacey, what have I done?" She buried her face in her palms, and I reached out to squeeze her hands.

"It's okay, Evie. Everything will be fine—" My breath caught, cutting my voice off too late before the lie had escaped me.

"No, it won't be fine," Evie said hoarsely. "I've placed you in a royal event under a false name for a competition of intelligence when you can only lie." She raised her face to meet mine, her eyes now rimmed red. "This is all my fault, and I'm going to find a way to get you out of this."

I blinked at her, squeezing her hand with a puzzled frown. "How?"

She wiped at her eyes, straightening her posture with a new look of determination holding her steady. "It's too late to switch back, so I can't take your place. Instead, I'll just have to make sure you don't win." She managed a small smile. "I'll teach you everything you *don't* need to know."

chapter ten

For the next two days, Evie drilled every ounce of knowledge she could into my aching head, then instructed me to forget half of it. Now that she knew the secret behind my curse, she had made it her personal mission to squeeze every bit of information out of the palace staff about the next event. Since she was still playing the role of a handmaiden, it wasn't proper for us to be seen together outside of our suite, so we decided to divide and conquer. While Evie went snooping around the staff quarters for gossip, she sent me to the palace library with an enormous reading list.

My spine mirrored the broken spine of the thick book on Reclusian foreign affairs, feeling bent entirely out of shape after spending so many hours hunched over a desk. My head throbbed, fighting me to expel the excess of information on Reclusia's silk trading and their alliance with the kingdom of Ebonair. It was all dreadfully boring, but Evie insisted that I at least familiarize myself with the knowledge in case I get pinned in an unexpected conversation.

It was actually quite astonishing how quickly she had concocted a plan once she learned my secret. It was a shame she never wanted to compete in the competition herself —she was easily intelligent enough to win. Although, I suppose she never wanted to be a princess in the first place—can't say I blame her considering I couldn't imagine being one, either.

A round of girlish laughter fluttered in from outside the library doors, sending a flash of panic through me. I quickly shoved the volume on foreign affairs aside and picked up the romance novel I had stashed in my lap, flipping to a random page. The laughing grew louder, echoing into the cozy library as the doors widened to let in a cluster of my fellow competitors. My heart pattered anxiously as I attempted a casual glance up from the pages.

There's Princess Lyra, Lady Sasha, and I think the last one is... Ellen?

I let out a quiet sigh, feeling the tension release after confirming that Jezebel wasn't among their party. She'd only strolled by a few times since yesterday, but I was beginning to catch the sense that she was wary of me. After this next event, I would need to limit my time in the library—I could only play the role of dedicated bookworm for so long before she started catching on to what I was really up to.

"Genevieve? Is that you?" Princess Lyra caught my eyes as I poked my gaze over the edge of my book. The other girls turned their heads curiously, inspecting my cozy reading corner with puzzled eyes.

"Hello, ladies, how lovely to see you all." I smiled primly while placing my novel on my lap. *I really don't have time for this...*

"So, is this where you've been hiding all this time?" Sasha asked in a soft-spoken voice. In the three dinners we'd shared together, she'd always seemed rather timid. In fact, I think this is the first time I'd seen her speak to someone directly.

I lifted my brow. "Hiding? Well, I can assure you that was never my intention." I pressed my hand to my lips to muffle a dainty giggle. *Lesson number fifteen, when in doubt, giggle.* "I've simply been indulging in some of the palace's riveting stories. I didn't mean to go so unnoticed." I gave them my most innocent smile, tapping my nails lightly atop the cover of my book with nervous energy.

"I see." Lyra returned my smile with a gentle one of her own. "Well, we do hope you'll come join us in the guest parlors sometime. It would be lovely to get to know you while we're all confined to the palace until the end of the month." She motioned gracefully to the other two girls, who both nodded in agreement.

Faking my way through an afternoon of conversation with at least three other noblewomen...? No, thanks.

"That would be wonderful," I said cheerfully. "Perhaps once I finish my current read, I'll come join you all." I lifted the novel with a slight wiggle.

Sasha tilted her head with a puzzled brow. "Were you reading that upside down?" she asked quietly, raising a finger to her lip with a curious nibble.

My blood froze, and I flipped the book around to view the cover, which was quite obviously upside down. *Drat.*

"Oh, how silly of me." I laughed nervously. "I thought that last chapter read a little funny..." My heart pounded stiffly against the web of entangled lies that encompassed my heart.

The girls shared a lost look between each other until Lyra broke the silence with a dainty laugh. "You have a funny sense of humor," she said sweetly. Her eased response sent a slight pulse of relief through me. "You'll really have to join us soon so we all might enjoy a little comedic reprieve from all this competition stress."

I managed a twitchy smile, my own stress insurmountable. "I can't wait."

The trio waved a few polite farewells, and then, just as quickly as they arrived, they slipped back out the doors. Once I was certain they were beyond the doors, I let out a long sigh of relief.

That was close. Now I just need to think up an excuse of how to steer clear of the guest parlors...

A headache prodded at my temples,

causing me to rub my thumbs deep into my skull. Most of the other competitors seemed fairly nice, but that didn't mean I could spend time with them. Even if I truly was a noble and we had dozens of things in common, I would still have to lie to them, and lies add up after a while if you're not careful.

And clearly, I'm very careful... How else would I have ended up masquerading as a lady in a royal competition?

A groan welled up in my throat as I glanced over at the book of foreign affairs I had cast aside. My head throbbed with so much excess information that it actually pained me to even consider reading another word. While Mother made sure I knew how to read and write, I never actually received a formal education; therefore, long studying sessions were practically foreign to me.

Why did nobles have to retain so much useless information, anyway?

I leaned my head back against the soft armchair, tussling the ornate hairdo Evie had spent nearly an hour on this morning. Hairpins pricked at my scalp as I pressed my head deeper into the upholstery. I tried to ignore the painful stings and instead focused on clearing my brain of everything that had left it sore and overused. As I nestled into the chair, a warm streak of sunlight slowly drifted onto my face, bathing me in its golden warmth. For the briefest moment, I shut my eyes and imagined I was sitting at home, dozing in my chair after spending hours weaving a new pattern on my loom. My fingers twitched at the thought, anxious to feel the wooden hoop in my grasp.

Memories of selling my woven creations on the street corner fluttered through my mind with tinged joy. It was always hard to think back to the days when Mother and I were on the streets of the capital, but at the same time, there were still moments of my childhood that I tried to cherish. It was always so rewarding when I could return to Mother with enough money to buy bread for the day, and it was thanks to my meager earnings that Mother was able to afford a suitable dress, which helped get her the position at the Palleep estate. Everything got better after that. Maybe that was why I still enjoyed weaving so much. Perhaps I associated weaving with the crafting of a new future. A small smile warmed my face as I allowed my fingers to mimic the movements of the first web of stiches.

Wouldn't it be nice if I could weave a new future right now?

"Feeling tired again, Miss Evie?"

My eyes jolted open and I nearly tumbled out of my seat as I laid eyes on my traumatizer. Prince Carlex's lips twitched in amusement as he took a respectful step back from my blundering limbs. Blood rushed through my cheeks, sending my heart into overdrive as I locked onto his chocolate brown eyes.

"Your Highness," I gasped sharply. "Goodness, you scared me to death." I placed a flustered hand on my chest, half-surprised that my words weren't actually true when I noticed the sporadic beats of my heart.

"My apologies, I didn't think I would frighten you so badly." He tried to bite back a chuckle, but he wasn't very good at hiding it. "Lyra told me I might find you here, but I hadn't expected you to be dozing again. Although, I must admit, a library is a fine choice for a catnap when compared to a ballroom." He gave me a teasing smile, and I glared at him in return.

Why was he asking Lyra where to find me? Shouldn't he be spending time with the other girls?

"I was reading, not napping." I puffed, snagging the decoy novel once more and this time, ensuring it was right side up before flaunting it.

"Reading... with your eyes closed?" He lifted his brow in challenge, leaning back on his heel with a rather cocky smile.

"Why yes, haven't you ever tried it?" I asked snidely, crossing my legs with an indignant tilt of my nose the way Evie had taught me. According to her, men disliked women who were confrontational and openly spoke their mind, hence why she herself has never had a proper courtship.

To my dismay, Carlex's expression only

grew more entertained. "Well, no actually, I can't say that I have." He stepped forward, snatching the book from my grasp and opening it to a random page.

"Hey, what are y—"

"Ah, yes!" He chuckled, holding the book in front of his squeezed eyes. "I see what you mean. The book is far more fascinating this way. I don't know why I ever doubted you." He peeked his eyes back open, taking in my flustered glare before handing the book back to me.

"Neither do I." I took it with a sharp flick of my wrist, hoping I was balancing the line of being unlikable but not offensive to our future king.

Evie said in order to be unlikable I need to gloat, even though I know he is better off than I am.

"You must understand that everything I say is frankly a truer fact than even a prince would know," I added coyly, pressing my tongue to my cheek to ward off the need to laugh at such a vast untruth.

"Is that so?" He tapped a finger to his chin while leaning against the table I'd been using to stockpile my books. "That sounds like quite the interesting talent. Perhaps you could enlighten me with some of your extraordinary knowledge on a walk through the gardens?"

Oh, drat. Now what have I gotten myself into?

"You want me to go on a walk with you?"

My voice squeaked a bit as I spoke. *Why me!? Why now!?*

"Of course." He nodded and his warm brown gaze softened shyly. "That is, if you would like to. I know we already spent a little time together after the first event, but from what I recall you were morbidly exhausted and in a great deal of pain at the time. So, if you're interested, I'd love to try again." He extended his hand out to me, his expression hopeful and earnest.

No! Ugh, Carlex, if only you understood! I can't get close to you like the other girls can, and I definitely can't win. A walk is a terrible *idea.*

"That sounds wonderful." My teeth gritted as I accepted his hand with a tense smile.

He aided me from my seat, then frowned as he took a fresh look at my expression. "Are you sure? I won't make you come if you don't fancy it. You're allowed to deny my request."

He must have noticed my reluctance, oh dear...

I stiffened for a moment, my hand going limp in his. For the first time in a while, I felt as if I had been caught in one of my lies, but the feeling of guilt was different in Carlex's presence than it had been with Evie or anyone else.

"Yes, I'm sure." I tried to say more convincingly. "I would love to join you for a stroll." I gave him my practiced smile, attempting to flutter my lashes the way Evie had demonstrated over breakfast.

He smiled back, but it didn't reach his eyes. "Thank you, Miss Evie. I promise, I won't take up too much of your time." He offered his arm out to me, and I accepted it graciously as he led us out of the library.

An odd tension lingered in the air between us as we traversed the halls. It wasn't necessarily awkwardness, more like restraint, as if we both were biting back things we wished to speak into the silence. I knew that on my end, I was desperate to explain that I wasn't actually interested in winning the competition and becoming his wife, but there was no way I could voice that without getting Evie reprimanded by her parents or me caught as a lying imposter. As for the prince, I wasn't sure what he was withholding, though it seemed clear that something was on his mind.

When we stepped through the palace doors, the fresh air instantly grazed my skin with a blissful coolness. The air smelled clean and crisp, the way it always did after a fresh spring rain. Prince Carlex led us into the maze of budding rose bushes and overhanging cherry blossoms. Fresh petals showered down across the path when another breeze rustled past us, littering the ground with dots of darling pink.

"Do you enjoy the rainy season?" Prince Carlex asked, noticing my eyes drift across the scattering petals.

I do. I love spring and all the new beginnings it symbolizes.

"I'm not sure, do you?" I turned to meet his eyes, but they were distracted by the same blossoms that had enchanted me.

"I do," he breathed, holding out his hand to catch a falling blossom as it drifted from its branch. "There's just something beautiful about starting fresh, don't you think?" My heart lurched oddly as I watched the blossom settle atop his hand.

Starting fresh...

"I wouldn't know; my life hasn't really had the opportunity for fresh starts." I kept my eyes fixated on the blossom, trying not to let the unspoken truth in my eyes give me away.

All I'd ever done is start over. Again and again...

"I suppose that's a fair point," Carlex agreed softly, watching the blossom flutter from his hand with another breeze. "Those in our station don't often get too many opportunities to stray from the paths chosen for us." He drifted his gaze back to the path, taking each step slower than the last.

"Are you hoping that this competition will bring a fresh start for you?" I implored. It seemed too odd to think that a prince would crave something new when they already had the kingdom at their fingertips, but maybe it was lonelier on a pedestal than I had imagined.

Carlex stopped, his expression searching mine as if the answer he was looking for was written across my cheek. A soft warmth formed a blush on my skin as I shied under his gaze. *Why is he looking at me like that? Do I have something on my face?*

"Yes, I suppose I am," he admitted with a slight laugh. "But I'm not certain the competition will crown a winner who will grant me my hopes."

I pondered his words for a moment, scrunching my brows together in thought. "So, you're worried the winner won't be what you're looking for?" A slight tingle prickled at my throat, warning me that the curse was unhappy.

Carlex pursed his lips, his fingers now tapping where they were laced around my arm. "In a manner of speaking, yes. But it's not really that simple." He guided us behind a hedge of cleanly trimmed bushes, his eyes once again fixated on the ground.

He's probably right. Royal politics and marriage alliances were far too complex for my understanding, but even so...

"Actually, it's very simple," I stated frankly. His head whipped around in my direction, his eyes burning with curiosity. "What is it that you're looking for? If you can answer that, then you know where to start searching."

I knew it was foolish of me to encourage the prince with a lie, especially considering we both knew he didn't get much of, if any, choice in his bride. But there was something about the way he looked at me that urged me to try to give him a touch of hope.

"You make it sound so easy." He chuckled, brushing his fingertips over the tops of the leafy hedges.

"Well, it is," I said proudly, tilting my chin with a curled smile. "Just find what you want, and aim for it. The rest can be dealt with another time."

Carlex actually laughed—a rather warm sound, the type that filled your heart after a heavy rain. "You seem to forget that my destiny is in the hands of a competition, one that *you* are rather involved in as well." He gave me a testing glare and I merely shrugged.

"I'd hardly say I'm involved," I tittered nonchalantly. "I'm really just here for the food and to dance."

Carlex halted, eyeing me down with a humored crook in his smile. "Is that so? Then how do you explain the first place ranking you currently hold?"

Sheer luck...

"Pure skill." I removed my arms from his to place both fists atop my hips. "Just because I'm here for the food, doesn't mean I don't want to showcase my outrageous talent." I flicked my hair, attempting to channel my inner Jezebel with a proud puff.

"Talent, indeed." He chuckled, folding his arms with a bemused smirk. "I've never seen a lady with the skill of falling asleep so efficiently in a chair before."

My mouth fell open in offense, and I narrowed my eyes. "I'll have you know that napping is a well-practiced, and well-respected, art amongst the Palleep family," I said tartly. "You should be ashamed for insulting my skills."

Carlex took a long stride forward, closing the distance between us with ease. "I'm terribly sorry, Miss Evie." He stopped only inches away from me, his face a breath from mine. "I hope my attitude hasn't offended you too drastically." He reached out for my hand, picking it up with a gentle touch that sent a bolt of energy through me. "Because I think I know the answer to your earlier question."

My breath hitched. *Oh no... Was I too friendly again?* Butterflies rippled through my chest, sticking tightly into the layers of webbing that had tangled my complicated heart. "What question would that be?"

He smiled, a real one this time. "What am I looking for...? I'm looking for someone who is talented in ways I'm not." He brushed his thumb against the back of my hand, sending a sparking shudder up my arm. "I'm not as good as I would like to be at making others smile. Perhaps one day you can enlighten me with a lesson on how you do it so seamlessly." His warm eyes softened me, causing me to reflect his infectious smile with a nervous one of my own.

Wait a moment… Is the prince actually…

"I'd be happy to teach you." I gulped.

What am I doing!? I can't teach the prince anything! He's not even supposed to like me!

My nervous gaze tore away from the prince, fixating on an intricate spider web that glittered with dewdrops on a tree branch. My breath hitched as my attention narrowed in on the small spider as it rapidly began twisting its silk around its captured prey. The tightness in my chest heightened as I recognized the similarities between the spider's delicate weaving and my chaotic mess of lies.

Ever since I stepped foot in the palace, I thought I was the one trapped in the web, waiting to become prey…

Carlex's face brightened, and he offered his arm out to me once again. "Wonderful." He beamed sweetly. "I greatly look forward to it."

But maybe I'm the one spinning the web after all…

chapter eleven

"He really said that!?" Evie gasped dramatically, nearly dropping the gown she was half-finished lacing me into. "Lacey, that's wonderful! But mostly terrible... It sounds like he's starting to fancy you."

I groaned, burrowing my face into my hands as I felt Evie tug the laces as snuggly as they could go. "Wonderful, indeed..."

Evie flitted around in front of me, inspecting the baby-pink ballgown with a curious squint. The dress was fairly simplistic compared to others I had packed for Evie, with only a few dainty ruffles along the hem and lace-capped sleeves.

"Well, hopefully, this dress helps dull his interest in you. Don't get me wrong, you still look beautiful, but the dress code for the event was ballroom attire. The other girls shouldn't have any trouble outshining you." She gave the dress a nod of approval before turning back to the drawer set to select a few simple jewels. "I couldn't get much information out of the staff about tonight's event—everyone is exceptionally tight-lipped about it—but I did overhear that it has something to do with strategy."

"Strategy?" My throat tightened as my nails clawed at the soft satin skirt. "I studied *lots* of strategy in the library..."

Evie gave me a reassuring smile, quickly picking up on my meaning. She'd been getting better at deciphering my lies over the last few days. "Don't worry. Most ladies don't study much strategy, anyway... that's more of a royalty thing. It should be perfectly fine if you fail this event, but you should probably still try to do a little better than the rest so you don't go from first to last. That would be a sure-fire way to get my family's attention, especially since I'm sure they've already told the entire town about how their incredible daughter swept the first event."

A nervous lump formed in my throat, and I swallowed hard. "So, I need to lose, but not fail? Sounds easy enough," I said meekly.

Evie gave me a sympathetic look, opening her mouth to likely spout more encouragement, but was cut off by a knock on the door. It was still too early for me to be summoned for dinner, so we both shared a perplexed look before Evie straightened her apron and opened the door with a perfect curtsy. To both of our surprise, a young woman with strawberry blonde curls and a polite smile greeted us.

"Good evening, I'm just here to drop off a delivery from the palace cobbler." She gave her own curtsy, then motioned to the gentleman just beyond the doorway, who held a blinding stack of boxes.

"Ah, yes. The royal cobbler..." Evie eyed the stack of boxes, risking a quick glance back at me for an explanation I wasn't sure how to give. *The shoe Carlex had kept... He couldn't possibly have...* "Just set them inside. I'll sort through them after my mistress leaves for dinner." Evie widened the door for the servants to step through, and I felt my jaw drop to the floor as yet *another* man with an armload of boxes passed through the door.

Evie's eyes widened at me, and when the servant's backs were turned, she mouthed two deafening words at me, "*The prince?*"

The blood drained from my face as I watched the maid open one of the boxes, displaying the most stunning jeweled dancing slippers. I bit my lip and nodded at Evie. She blinked back at me with almost the same amount of shock that coursed through me.

I mouthed back at her, thankful that my curse didn't prevent me from simply orienting my lips, "*I'm in trouble.*"

• •

The dining room was far livelier this time than it had been upon everyone's initial arrival. As I entered the room, the steward announced my falsified name and kindly guided me to my new assigned seat for the night, which was thankfully, much farther from Jezebel than before. One by one, the other girls trickled into the dining room, each dressed in even finer gowns and adornments than before. I placed my napkin on my lap, mentally congratulating myself for successfully completing the first test of etiquette this time.

Not long after I was seated, Lady Sasha was escorted to the seat on my right. I celebrated internally when she took her seat. Lady Sasha was polite, and she wasn't much of a talker, therefore this dinner was already looking to be easier than the first. It was already hard enough to pretend that I knew everything a proper lady was supposed to, but having to pretend I was properly educated *while* lying should have earned me the title of most intelligent on its own.

As the seats slowly filled, the one on my left remained empty. I watched curiously as the stewards announced and escorted each of the ladies, wondering who would be my other seat neighbor. Jezebel had already been seated when I arrived, placed at the head of the table next to another empty seat, where I presumed Carlex would join us. No matter who was placed next to me, it couldn't possibly be as bad as...

"Now entering, Amirah of Sarnold."

The blood princess...

My stomach knotted as I darted my gaze around the table, looking for any other empty seats. The steward's gaze instantly locked on the final chair next to me, casually escorting Princess Amirah to the empty seat. Nerves twisted in my chest as I centered my gaze on my empty plate.

Just relax. She may have a creepy backstory and a terrifying nickname, but that doesn't mean she's dangerous or anything, right?

The sound of the steward scraping the chair legs against the floor sent a shudder through me as he pulled out the seat for the princess. Amirah accepted the seat silently, elegantly crossing her legs before allowing the servant to push her up to the table.

I risked a quick glance at her, my focus instantly latching onto the ugly scar that marred her beautiful face. *What could have possibly caused such a deformation?* To my relief, she seemed just as interested in making conversation with me as Sasha had. Without even looking down, she carefully took her napkin from her setting and gracefully unfolded it onto her lap. She seemed completely at ease, yet for some reason, the panic in my chest was still growing.

It must be the nerves. I just need to relax.

Any chance I had at relaxing vanished when the steward stepped forward again with a strong clear of his throat. "Now entering, His Royal Highness, Prince Carlex of Reclusia."

In a lightning-fast moment, every girl

flicked their hair and fluttered their lashes in near perfect unison just before Carlex strolled through the door. Smiles lit up across the room as Carlex gave a dapper bow to his guests.

"Good evening, ladies," he greeted warmly. "As promised, I will be dining with you before the remaining events of the competition. While I intend to engage all of you, the seating arrangements will change each night to ensure I can spend equal time getting to know everyone. So, with that said, let's all enjoy our first proper dinner together." Carlex made his way to his seat, settling into his chair with the briefest grimace when he caught sight of Jezebel.

Normally, I would have found his reaction amusing, but for some reason, I couldn't shake the growing sensation of panic. Princess Amirah seemed just as uninterested in me as before, but whenever I looked at her, my chest tightened with a sensation of suffocation.

Why does she seem so intimidating?

Jezebel instantly sank her teeth into Carlex the moment he sat down. Her raspy giggles and obsessive hair twirling made me squirm uncomfortably, even from where I sat. The other girls weren't much better, but at least they had the decency to keep their hands to themselves. I watched with tense breaths as Jezebel stroked Carlex's sleeve, gushing over how strong his arms felt. I'd held his arms a few times now, and while he wasn't by any means puny, he definitely wasn't as burly as she was implying. Carlex was doing an impressive job of being polite to her, despite her unnecessary touches, but I could tell he was feeling slightly unenthusiastic about his seating arrangement for the evening. For the briefest moment, his eyes met mine from across the table. I startled for a moment, noticing my heart rate elevate as he twitched the smallest smile at me. Sweat pooled in my palms and under my hair, trickling down my neck with an unpleasant glide.

Is it always so hot in here?

Heat burned inside me, radiating from within my chest and spanning outward to the ends of my fingers. Carlex's expression furrowed as I dabbed my napkin at my beading forehead, a look of concern dousing his cheerful eyes. Alongside the growing heat, the tension in my chest began to wind tighter, crushing my organs with suffocating pressure and nauseating pain.

What's happening to me? Am I growing ill?

The first course of soup presented a welcomed distraction from the imploring glances from the prince and the unexplained riling within me. I turned my attention to the savory lamb broth, but instantly, I felt my stomach seize when I even considered taking a bite. The panic I'd felt before had escalated into nearly a full attack on myself. Pain dug into my skull, festering even more pressurized heat with each passing second.

I d-don't understand... What's the matter with me?

I set my spoon down with shaking movements, pressing a hand to my slickened forehead with a sharp breath. The pain was growing worse, fighting with my mind to retain the ability to think or even consider speaking. A tight constriction clamped around my lungs, threatening to rob me of my breath entirely.

This is horrible. The last time I felt like this I —

I bit back a gasp, my eyes widening as I slowly turned my eyes back onto Princess Amirah.

My ailments didn't begin until she sat beside me...

My heart pounded rapidly in my ears as I slowly scanned her attire with blurring eyes. First, my attention landed on her ring, and then her necklace, and then her earrings...

Magic stones...

The pain in my head heightened, sending me a strong warning. The unrefined power of my curse was conflicting with whatever magic was in Princess Amirah's jewelry. If I didn't move away from her soon, the conflicting powers might even combust. The nausea that was festering within me twisted at the thought. I needed to move seats, and quickly. It may be bad table manners, but it sure beat imploding.

I looked back up across the table, where

my eyes instantly locked onto Carlex's—seeming as if he had never looked away from me at all. I bit my lip, scraping up all the courage I could to offend the blood princess of Sarnold.

Maybe combusting internally would be an easier way to go...

Carlex's face was twisted with worry, his attention completely enveloped by my flushed cheeks and heavy breaths. I took in a wavering gasp, steadying myself for what may very well be my last words.

"Excuse me, Your Highness, but would it be alright if I requested to move seats?"

A stunned hush swept over the room, causing the roiling in my gut to burn even fiercer. I didn't look, but I could feel the eyes of the blood princess skewering me relentlessly, likely already considering my murder.

Carlex's brows knitted together, the worry in his eyes still present. "I s-suppose that would be alright. Is there any reason why you need to move?" He gave me an imploring look, clearly seeking further explanation to my frazzled state.

I bit my lip but couldn't feel any of the pain with the throbbing in my head numbing every other feeling.

What do I do? If I insult the blood princess, then who knows what she'll do.

"I-I can't sit next to Sasha," I wheezed, deflating my lungs of the rest of their harbored air. Black spots began to dot my vision, and the swirling heat inside me felt on the verge of bursting. I pushed back from my chair with the rest of my strength, stumbling toward the wall as offended gasps echoed throughout the guests.

"You can't sit next to *Sasha*?" Jezebel's sneer barely crept into my brain through the ringing in my ears. "Why in the kingdoms not? She's the calmest person here, for goodness sakes."

I leaned back against the wall, barely even listening to Jezebel's scolds. The first gasp of air filled my burning lungs, and I took in long, laboring breaths as I leaned my hands on my knees, slowly sensing the decrease in building pressure.

The scrape of another chair caught my attention and I glanced up from my bent-over crouch to see Carlex toss his napkin atop the table and hurry in my direction. The pain was beginning to settle, but the lingering ghost of it left me too numb and dazed to move. I pressed my back against the cool stone wall, relishing in the icy bliss it brought my core. A strong arm laced around my waist, sending another chorus of gasps and whispers across the table. Now that my body temperature was beginning to return to normal, embarrassment crept over me, returning my cheeks to a feverish crimson.

Prince Carlex's face was almost as white as mine was red as he tightened his steadying grip around me. "Evie, what's the matter? You're looking terribly flushed; are you ill?" He placed a hand over my burning cheek, cradling my face with a gentle touch that I'm certain sent the other girls squirming.

"I-I'm fine," I huffed.

"No, you're most certainly not," he said firmly. "Your breathing is short." He searched my eyes with a desperate look, gripping me with a fear I hadn't expected him to have.

Is he really that worried about me?

"Oh, please... She's obviously faking." Jezebel snorted, leaning back in her chair with a clenched frown. "She just wants your attention, Your Highness. Why else would she make up something as silly as needing to get away from poor, sweet Sasha?" She gestured over to the quiet girl who had now half-shrunk into her chair.

Guilt flooded me as I recognized the humiliation that dotted her pretty face. I hadn't meant to embarrass her. I needed to think of an explanation to save face for us both...

"I-it's her perfume!" I blurted out a little louder than intended. "I'm afraid I have some sort of allergy toward it... The smell was constricting my throat and raising my temperature." I gave Sasha an apologetic look, hoping to have at least eased her humiliation a bit.

"Her perfume?" Carlex raised a brow, looking between Sasha and me. "Are you sure it was an allergy, you looked very—"

"Yes, I'm certain," I cut him off, forcing the conversation to halt before any more deductive reasoning could occur.

A few of the girls shot me dirty looks, clearly offended in the prince's honor that I had dared to cut him off. I half-expected him to grow stern with me after such a rude reply, but he merely released his grip on me and took a ginger step back.

"Very well then," he said wearily. "If you believe that was all it was, then we shall have you trade seats with Miss Lydia for the evening and carry on with the event." He gestured toward the gawking Lady Lydia, who remained frozen in bewilderment for a moment before rising from her seat.

I let out a relieved breath, bowing my head graciously at Carlex before turning to the new seat. "Thank you, Your Highness. I promise, I'll be more cautious around allergens at our next meal." Every eye seared into me as we all made our way back to our seats, but the heat of their stares was nothing compared to the molten singe in my chest that had nearly destroyed me moments ago.

I decided to skip the first course entirely to ensure my stomach had settled before testing a bite of bread. Carlex's eyes still swept over to me from time to time, studying me for any further progression of my ailments... or perhaps he was questioning if I had truly faked it after all.

Jezebel and a few of her closer companions eyed me down as well, sticking their powdered noses high in the air whenever I caught them glaring. My new seat neighbor, Lady Gabrielle from Sarnold, continued to give me particularly icy stares throughout the main course. I took a small bite of my porkchop, trying to remain focused on my settling stomach before Gabrielle interrupted my bite with a light nudge in my ribs.

"Just so you know, causing drama won't earn you any favor with the prince," she hissed between her polished smile, her eyes never losing contact with the prince and Jezebel.

I swallowed my bite stiffly, my fingers clenching around my fork. "Like I said, it was merely an allergy attack," I whispered back, aggravation clenching my jaw. The last thing I wanted was to get flagged as the drama stirrer—that title could only belong to Jezebel.

"Don't take us for fools," Gabrielle growled back, her smile fading briefly. "My sister suffered from a dangerous allergy and *never* reacted like that."

My breath caught, sending a ripple of anxiety through me at Gabrielle's words. *Did it really look that fake?*

Gabrielle glanced at my ashen face, sneering softly in victory. "It's just pathetic, really. I mean, everyone knows the prince doesn't get to choose his bride based on his personal tastes... You have to actually *win* the competition, not just earn his favor. It's almost as if you're expecting to fail the next event and are trying to gain his sympathies ahead of time." She took a long sip of wine, a small smile tugging at the edges of her glass.

"Is there something you're getting at?" I asked coldly, my fingers growing numb from my increased clenching around my cutlery.

"Oh, just the obvious," she said coyly, lowering her glass with a charming smile in Carlex's direction. "You're falling for the prince, and now you're desperate to do anything you can to maintain his attention."

What!? That's ridiculous. I don't like the prince at all.

I nearly dropped the fork, but instead, I barely managed to set it atop the place setting to avoid snapping it in two. "Gabrielle, what are you talking about? I don't even like the prince—" I sucked in a sharp breath, my hand flying to my lips in surprise.

I just said I don't like the prince... so it was a lie. But that would mean—

"Alright, ladies." Prince Carlex rose from his seat, rubbing his hands together with an eager smile as his gaze drifted across all the faces at the table before landing on mine. "It's time to begin tonight's event."

chapter twelve

We all filed into the ballroom in a loose cluster behind Carlex. Tension twisted inside me like a grinding gear, filling me with anxiety about the possibilities that lingered behind this new contest. After such an eventful dinner, I wasn't sure I was mentally prepared for the stress of another competition.

Evie said it's about strategy. All I have to do is rank somewhere in the middle.

It sounded like a simple plan, but that was what I thought during the last event when I accidentally became the only winner. Why did nobility have to be so... dumb?

When I stepped through the familiar doors of the ballroom, I instantly found myself disoriented by the space. It looked almost nothing like it had before, aside from the unmovable walls, floor, and windows.

Where there had once been an open dance floor, dozens of decorative wood pillars had been sporadically placed, littering the floor with vertical obstacles. There were no fake princes to sift through this time, but along the walls were poised servants, each spaced equally apart with what appeared to be a spool of colored fabric in their arms. It was all rather bizarre, but despite the odd décor and statuesque servants, there was still something that caught every girl's eye far more instantaneously.

"Good evening, ladies, and welcome to my son's second event." King Aldrich stood proudly in the center of the room, with his gorgeous wife Queen Viviana at his side. "We hope you all have been enjoying your time at the palace these last few days, and we wish to apologize for our absence until now. Our business in the kingdom of Bellatring proved to be more time consuming than we had initially intended, but we are present now and wish to enjoy celebrating all your victories in the remainder of the events." He smiled warmly at us, glossing his gaze over each one of us as if picking out who would become his future daughter-in-law.

"I'm so glad you've returned, Mother, Father." Carlex parted from us to approach his parents, greeting them each with a friendly hug that sent a pleasantly sweet feeling through me. "You're just in time for me to explain the rules to our guests." He turned his attention back toward us, all of us fighting to conceal our fidgeting curiosity. "While the last event was focused on showcasing one's perceptive qualities, this one is centered around highlighting one's ability to strategize."

I let out a quiet breath, reminding myself to thank Evie later for gathering accurate information. *At least there won't be any more surprises for tonight.* I snuck a quick glance over in Princess Amirah's direction, making certain she was a safe distance away from me at all times.

"The goal of this event is to be the first lady to reach your target, which, in this case, is me." He flashed us his signature grin, bowing slightly at the waist with a charming wink. "For the challenge, I will remain here, in the center of the ballroom."

He stepped in between his parents, giving a slight spin underneath the glow of the centered chandelier. "Each of you will start at an equal distance away from me, at the edges of the ballroom with a dance partner."

I looked back at the servants who dotted the walls, only now noticing they weren't servants at all, but the same men who had attended the first event, only now they were wearing uniformed suits.

The prince nodded to the men. "Each lady will receive a spool of colored silk fabric, which will be attached at their hip. The spools unwind as you move, so you'll need to be wary of twisting your silk around the pillars. The silk will also act as obstacles, therefore if any lady crosses in front of you and leaves a trail of her fabric, you may not cross it. Sabotage is permitted and welcomed in this competition, so you may choose to use your silk to barricade other competitors. Just keep in mind that your spool has a limited amount of silk, and if you run out, you'll have to backtrack in order to reach your objective."

My mind stirred to life as I glanced between the awaiting dancers and the collection of pillars, imagining the twisted strands of colored silks that would soon spiral around the ballroom.

I see... So you have to select which strategy you believe will help reach your goal the fastest— cutting off your enemies and risking running short on silk, or racing straight for the end but having to dodge the trails of the others.

"This is a test of strategy, not speed, so you will be required to move in count to the music, no slower, no faster," Prince Carlex continued. "If you are caught exceeding the tempo of the song or passing through another player's silk, then you will be disqualified. Other than that, you may use any plan you choose to reach your target first. Are there any questions?" Prince Carlex briefly scanned over the collection of puzzled and determined looks before smiling in satisfaction. "Very well then. Please, find a partner."

It took a few minutes before we were all situated with our spools of silk and chosen partners. I made certain to hang back a few feet while Princess Amirah chose her starting point, making certain I chose a partner on the opposite side of the ballroom so we wouldn't risk clashing again. Unfortunately, that left me next to my other dreaded competitor, Jezebel.

Jezebel's bright yellow silk flashed like a warning in the corner of my eyes, threatening to cut me off at the earliest opportunity. I looked over to my other side and felt my stomach plummet, noticing Lady Gabrielle already eyeing the closest pillar that would cut me off.

If they corner me from both sides, I'll be completely trapped.

I nervously fiddled with my tail of purple silk, trying to measure the distance between the nearest pillar and my rivals. While I certainly didn't want to win the event, Evie was right about me not being able to afford to lose. It would be suspicious if the unmatched champion received the lowest score on the second event. Evie's parents would most definitely have an uproar about it and assume she was trying to tank her scores.

I need to score, at least a little bit.

Carlex waited patiently in the center of the room, casually spinning in a slow circle to take in each of the competitors. When he turned toward me, I could have sworn he tilted his head a touch, as if challenging me to catch him. I turned back to look at the spool that rested above my bustle, eyeing the swirled spiral of silks with a contemplative glare.

Wait a minute... is this even enough to reach him?

The game was laid out similar to a giant circular loom weave, except with multiple threads going at once. Having spent hundreds of hours crouched over my loom, I knew approximately how much wool or thread it took to complete a design. While the strips of silk were far larger than the scale of my usual thread, it still struck me as an insufficient amount for all the sabotaging the prince had welcomed.

Perhaps that is the point?

A thought flicked to life in my brain as I mentally began to guess the amount of time it would take for Jezebel or Gabrielle to cut off my path. If I waltzed directly toward Carlex, then theoretically, I should be able to pass the pillars before they could cross their silks in front of me, right? If I tried to cut off one of them first, then the other would box me in, so my best strategy would be to ignore them both and hope they don't have a more detailed plan in mind for cornering me.

If I can get past Jezebel and Gabrielle, then I'll have more maneuverability in the center of the room to avoid other silks. I have to reach the prince, even if I'm the last one to do it.

The first bell of the music chimed, signaling for us to take our positions with our partners. My partner, Sir Gavin, kindly bowed before taking my hand and slipping his other arm around my waist. He made certain to keep his grip lose, signaling I would be the one to lead the direction of the dance. I flicked one more glance in Jezebel's direction, earning a prudish grimace that did little to improve her appearance.

"Ladies and gentlemen," Prince Carlex announced over the first notes of the harp, "let the dance of strategy... begin."

Perfectly on cue, every foot stepped off into the dance floor with a synchronized echo. The music was painfully slow, forcing us all to glide at a snail's pace in the direction of our goal. The spool instantly began to unravel behind me, purring with a soft *whirling* sound as the tension of its pin on the wall tugged the fabric free. I hadn't ever really danced before, but fortunately, my partner seemed to expect my nervous and uncoordinated movements, considering that most ladies had never had to lead before. Wordlessly, we waltzed toward the center of the room, my eyes locked nervously on the first scattering of pillars that could quickly become overrun with barricading silks.

Focus, Lacey, it's just like the loom at home...

A stream of Jezebel's yellow trail flicked in the corner of my eyes, sending a tense throb through my chest. Her beady gaze was fixated on me, her frustrations from dinner clearly motivating her to ensure I failed. My legs twitched to move faster, but I forced myself to submit to the flow of the music. I couldn't allow her to override my focus. She shouldn't be able to cross in front of me before I pass... right?

Anxiety twisted in my chest as a flicker of Gabrielle's blue silk caught the other end of my vision. Just as I'd suspected, they were narrowing in on me, both trying to cut me off from different angles. My limbs urged me to veer in their direction, sparking a race to see who could imprison the other in their web first, but I restrained. That wasn't the strategy I'd decided on, and I needed to stick with something that would ensure I scored.

My hammering heart refused to quiet, so I shut my eyes, allowing my feet to move straight toward the center. With the flash of blue and yellow cleared from my brain, I managed to recenter my spiraling mind, envisioning myself as one singular thread on my loom that was casually making the first lace. It felt oddly natural, as if I didn't even need to open my eyes to know where I needed to lead my partner. The lull of the music calmly cascaded my steps, easing my scattered mind until I heard the aggravated huff of Jezebel only a breath behind me.

I opened my eyes a touch, gaping in relief as I watched Jezebel and Gabrielle nearly collide with each other, with me only a half-step in front of where Jezebel would have trapped me. Jezebel quickly readjusted her sights and led her partner in Gabrielle's direction, trapping her behind her silk before looping around a pillar to pin Gabrielle in place. Gabrielle let out a frustrated squeal, leading her partner backward to seek an alternative route to the center.

A relieved breath pressed out of me, though it was still constricted with all the tension. The path ahead of me was mostly cleared, but I could see Princess Lyra beginning to stretch another line of silk across my path. A few feet beyond her, Lady Lydia was creating a blockade around another route I would have chosen. It quickly became clear to me that it wasn't just my behavior at dinner that had made me a target—I was in first place, and the others needed me to fall. *But I still need to score.* I glanced around the room with rapid movements, envisioning a tangle in the loom.

There. They left an opening. Lady Sasha can block me off if she notices it in time, but it looks like she's fixated on dodging Lady Ellen.

I redirected my partner's feet, guiding him toward the opening. In what felt like the blink of an eye, a rainbow of silks laced throughout the ballroom, filling the open space with an elegant web of color. I continued to guide Sir Gavin past the vibrant stretches of silk, twirling across the floor with simple movements that crafted a complicated plan. We casually waltzed through the gap in silks beside Sasha, earning a few uneasy glances from the other girls.

Yes, that's it. Now it should be a straight shot to the prince.

I looked up and felt a flood of excitement fill me as I glanced at the clear path in front of me. Carlex's attention was already locked onto me, folding his arms with an impressed light streaming through his gaze. Coming from another angle, Jezebel was nearly in front of him as well. I glanced back at the yellow trail she'd left, noticing that after her initial cut off for Gabrielle, she hadn't endured any other obstacles. She was perhaps a half-step ahead of me now, with a few other girls not far behind.

Perfect.

I shortened my steps the smallest amount, while still remaining in time with the music. If a couple of the girls could get ahead of me, then I would score in fourth or fifth place. That would give me plenty of wiggle room to fall behind in the next events without raising any suspicion with the Palleeps. Just as I'd hoped, the other girls took the lead over me, reaching closer and closer to where Carlex stood waiting. Jezebel was only a few feet away from him now, but Carlex's smile remained latched to me.

Why is he smiling at me? It's already clear that I won't win—

Jezebel stopped abruptly, desperately stretching her hand out to Carlex with only mere inches to go. My mouth fell open as I glanced at the tension pulling at her waist, the spool entirely empty of silk.

She's run out... So, I was right about there not being much for sabotaging. But wait...

Jezebel hastily turned her partner around, quickly undoing her latest tangle to gain the last needed inches. The other girls quickly moved in, but as I followed their colored trails, I felt my stomach drop as I noticed the number of twists they had collected as well. One by one, the girls snagged the end of their leash, each only a few feet from their prince. I looked back at my trail and compared it to the remnants on my spool.

I never sabotaged... I can still reach the prince.

My face paled with nerves as I looked back up at the smiling prince, my steps shortening even more. Once again, I had accidently outwitted an entire ballroom full of nobles. I probably should have been proud of myself, but in this moment, only terror ripped through me.

If I win again... will anyone be able to overtake me?

The choke of an invisible noose seized my breath, causing my features to scrunch up in fear. Carlex's beaming smile faltered, his face dropping into a disheartened frown at my reaction. I glanced back at Jezebel, who had now successfully undone her last tangle, but was still far behind my lead. Even with my shortened steps I was still bound to reach Carlex first.

I need to do something, quick.

An idea washed over my mind and before I could even consider thinking it through, I snagged my foot behind my partner's ankle and tripped us both, sending us crashing to the floor. An audible gasp echoed from where the king and queen had been observing us, and I felt a twinge of shame for forcing us to tumble in front of our rulers.

"Ow! Could you watch your step please?" Sir Gavin huffed, scrambling back to his feet with a displeased scowl.

"My apologies... It was an accident." I accepted his outstretched hand but turned my head to observe Jezebel's progress.

She's almost caught up.

Sir Gavin aided me to my feet, but I didn't hurry back into his arms; instead, I paused for a moment to dust off my skirt, delaying my return to the dance for as long as possible without appearing suspicious. Once I had collected myself, I returned to the dance, breathing a sigh of relief when I noticed Jezebel was once again a step ahead of me. Her ice-blue eyes were greedily latched onto Carlex, with her and her partner now only steps away from her prize. I looked back at the prince, and once again, I found him looking at me, but this time there wasn't a trace of a smile on his lips. He looked almost... heartbroken.

Had he wanted me to win...?

A moment later, Jezebel threw herself into Carlex's arms, squealing with excitement as the first bell chimed signaling the first winner. Despite my blunder, I was still ahead of the other women who had gotten twisted, reaching Carlex only a few moments after Jezebel. She turned her smug expression to me, her arm still hooked around Carlex, as if gloating with her new trophy.

"You were so close, Evie... Better luck next time." She smiled with a sickly sweetness, stirring up a round of anger in me that was better left undisturbed in such a formal setting.

I managed a gritted smile. "You did well, Jezebel. It was a fair win." Carlex's face twinged at my words, flinching from a wound I was beginning to fear I'd inflicted.

One by one, the other girls reached Carlex, with only Gabrielle, Fallon, and Sasha left trapped and unable to score. Once the scores had all been recorded, our partners aided us in removing our silk leashes and began gathering up the kaleidoscope of fabrics. The king and queen rejoined Carlex at the center of the room, and we all gathered to listen.

"Congratulations to Jezebel for being the first to reach her target," Carlex announced, earning a stiff round of polite applause. "This game was designed to test your ability to strategize, but also test your approach to formulating a plan. As I'm sure you all came to notice, the silks were only long enough for you to reach your target with only enough excess to dodge the obstacles. Anyone who used their silk to block off an opponent ran short at the finish. The intention was to see how well you reacted when your plans were shifted, or if you were able to notice the deficiency in advance and plan accordingly." He glanced over at me, his eyes knowing and still loaded with sorrow. "Nonetheless, you all performed exceptionally well, and we look forward to announcing the current rankings first thing in the morning."

King Aldrich stepped forward, placing a hand on his son's shoulder. "To celebrate the end of the second event, and our return to the kingdom, we would like to invite you all to an evening of *real* dancing so my queen and I may have the opportunity to socialize with the extraordinary young ladies of our fellow kingdoms." The king motioned to the musicians, who instantly strung up the start of another song. He gave Carlex a squeeze on the shoulder, gazing out into the collection of anticipating ladies. "Son, who will you select for your first dance?"

The king's face was full of mischief, with Queen Viviana's curiosity burning behind them as well. It was obvious this was the king's way of asking which girl he fancied, but Carlex's heavy expression didn't seem interested in seeking out a beautiful partner. Instead, he looked hungry for answers—answers he was hungering from me.

I bit my lip, giving my head the subtlest shake in hopes he would take my hint, but his hollow eyes remained set on me.

No, no, no...

Calmly, he approached me, his posture sullen and dragging as he reached out a hand to me. "Evie, may I have this dance?"

chapter thirteen

If looks could kill, my body would have flopped lifelessly to the floor right then and there. Fifteen pairs of blazing eyes skewered me from all angles. I didn't dare risk a glance at Jezebel, but I felt more than certain I could imagine the fury that was undoubtedly coursing through her. Behind Carlex, Queen Viviana latched onto her husband's arm, giggling girlishly as she whispered something to the king. My stomach roiled with unease as Carlex's question sat unanswered in the air.

Why me...? Out of all the girls, why ask me to dance first?

"I'd love to dance, thank you." I didn't even bother to smile this time; instead, I dipped my head low with my curtsy.

I accepted Carlex's outstretched hand and nearly jolted when I noticed how cold he was. My skin burned with festering energy, anxious to make the dance quick, but he was cool to the touch, with a far less energetic presence. As Carlex led me into the first steps of the dance, the other ladies slowly snagged their own partners, while a few approached the king and queen to schmooze.

The music was slow and lingering, much like the awkward silence that lingered between the prince and me. The quiet was insufferable and rang in my ears louder than an off-tune harp string. For the first few moments of the dance, he refused to look at me entirely, his eyes fixated on either our hands or the floor.

Why did he ask me to dance if he didn't want to talk to me?

The suffocating silence snagged at my chest until finally, I couldn't bear it any longer. "Is something troubling you, Your Highness?" I tilted my head toward his eyes, trying to catch his attention in some fashion.

He finally looked up to me, but the moment he did, I understood why he had tried to avoid my gaze. His eyes were sunken and full of distress, rimmed in a soft red that accented a shadow formulating under his lower eyelid. "Yes, Miss Evie, I'm afraid so." He sighed, twirling me into a half-hearted spin across the floor.

My whole body jolted when I landed back in his arms. Did he know that I tripped on purpose? Was he upset with me for my blunder?

"Would you care to share your woes with me?" I asked softly, a snag of guilt tugging within me.

A sad smile pulled at his lip, and for a moment, he gravitated closer to me. I took in a soft breath at the fresh contact as he wrapped his arm tighter around my waist. We were so close now that I could almost read the words on his lips before they were spoken.

"You see... that's the problem, Miss Evie." He breathed. "There's no one else in this ballroom I feel like I can share my woes with. You're the only one I crave to speak with." His hold on me deepened, his arm snaking further around my waist with a longing, yet withheld grasp.

My heart beat wildly, stretching against the entanglement of fears and worries that had built up a firm wall within me. The tempo of the music began to build, but Carlex only swayed us slow. His broken eyes remained as latched onto me as his arms. I knew the other girls were staring and that I would be forced to endure their envy for the next few days, but that all paled in comparison to the more pressing trouble I was facing now.

I'm the prince's favorite... but how?

My toes wiggled inside the comfortable new dancing slippers he had gifted me, reminding me that I had seen the signs of his affection all along. For some reason, the prince had taken a shine to me out of all the other girls, though I couldn't possibly imagine why. I wasn't nearly as poised, privileged, or pretty as the other ladies, and that wasn't even including the secrets I harbored.

"Is that your woe, then? That there's no one else you wish to speak with?" I glanced up at him through my lashes, trying to blink back the discomfort in my clenching throat from my lack of straight lies.

He let out a soft, humored huff. "Is it that obvious?" He spun us gently across the floor, blurring the world around us as if trying to fade out all the other distractions.

"Yes." I smiled, frankly surprised that the answer had been as simple as that.

So, he is upset that I am his favorite? Is that why he's disappointed in my loss?

"You truly are a clever one, aren't you?" He smiled, his face still tinged with sorrow. "It would seem this competition is suited for someone with your wits, which is why I now *fear* that you might become my victor."

My breath hitched, my fingers tensing around Carlex's arms.

"Do you not wish for me to be your victor?" I breathed. My tongue was growing dry and cottony after my overuse of questions, but I wasn't interested in appeasing the curse just yet. I had so much more to ask him...

He didn't answer me at first, but instead, he lingered in the moment of our dance, his cozy brown eyes gripping me as if they were afraid to let go. "I may have to tell you a lie to answer that question," he whispered, sending a feverish jolt through my chest. "No, I don't want you to win;

I would much rather you lose like you clearly desire to."

My steps fumbled for a brief moment, but his firm hold prevented me from falling. I gaped at him in shock, my eyes widening as his sad but knowing smile returned.

He knew I was trying to lose?

"But, Your Highness, I-I don't want to fail the competition," I stuttered, my mind replaying the last event in terror, wondering if anyone else had noticed my intentional failure.

If word gets back to the Palleeps that Evie tried to lose...

"Don't worry, I'm not going to alert your family or anything," he reassured me quietly.

I let out a tight breath, still biting my tongue to channel the nerves swirling within.

"I'm sure you only participated because your family urged you to. It only makes sense considering your lack of interest in spending time with me, not to mention your *accidental* fumble this evening." He gave me a knowing look, tilting his brow in a rather adorable manner despite his solemn expression.

"I-I don't know what you mean." I looked guiltily toward the floor. My gaze focused on the beautiful slippers he had given me, sending another ripple of shame through me for lying so directly.

He released my arm, hooking his finger under my chin to raise my gaze to his. "You don't have to lie to me, Evie. Not anymore." He smiled kindly, his voice silky and honest, to the point where it physically pained me to know that I couldn't honor his request, at least not as Evie. "It's clear to me now that you don't want to win this competition and become my wife, and as much as it disheartens me..." he released my chin, returning his hand to my arm where he gently eased our close proximity apart, "I don't want you to become my queen if it's not what you want as well."

So many bottled up emotions broke free from the web in my chest, sending an overpowering wave of relief and numbed pain through my core, spreading out to my fingers and toes.

"Are you alright with that?" I implored. My eyes dug into his distanced look, seeking out the last signs of confirmation I needed that Evie wasn't going to be in trouble for this.

"I'll manage," he breathed with a defeated smile.

Despite my growing relief, I couldn't feel any joy when I looked into the dullness that had swept over the prince's once warm eyes.

"Frankly, I understand how you feel... being forced to compete due to your parent's desires." His grip softened on me a touch, his body leaning away another few inches to distance himself. I don't know why, but I wasn't ready for him to completely cut me off, so I squeezed his arm the smallest amount, pulling him back in to urge him to continue. His eyes widened the softest amount, but he accepted my pull without argument. "You see, I never wanted to hold a bride competition. In fact, I found the idea rather barbaric, but my father insisted that I uphold the tradition." He sighed, and for the first time since we had met, I was starting to understand the reasoning behind his unspoken sorrow.

He didn't just want a queen; he wanted a wife.

Pity enveloped me as I continued to gaze into his despairing eyes. This was essentially the equivalent of an arranged marriage for him, except he had to endure the pain of waiting to see if the girl he desired would actually become his. At some point during our dance, the music had stopped and a new song had begun, but neither one of us seemed interested in pulling away just yet.

"You didn't believe that you could find love in a competition, did you?" I asked boldly.

His face twisted with pent-up emotions, but he quickly silenced them with that fake smile I knew all too well. "I was hopeful." His fingers pressed into my arm with almost a longing, as if he wasn't ready to let go of the possibility of a connection between us. "I've tried to get to know the other girls, but they only seem interested in my crown or are like you... only here for the sake of their families." His body shifted a step closer to me, causing my heart to flutter with unexplained anticipation. "Plus, they don't invade my thoughts the way you do."

My blood froze in my veins as I melted under the yearning eyes of the crown prince. He thought about me... but he couldn't. The name he desired wasn't even mine; he was attracted to a lie, an imposter.

His hand trailed up my arm, catching my breath once more, until he rested his cool touch on my cheek. "I'll help you lose the competition, Evie. But before I do, can you just put my mind to rest and tell me if there was any connection for you? Did you ever actually want to be my queen?"

We stopped moving, our feet frozen in the center of the ballroom as his tender hand remained cradled against my face. Never in my life did I expect the prince of Reclusia to pine for me—the mere thought felt entirely intangible, even while he was caressing me. But no matter how dearly he cared for me, I couldn't possibly form a connection with him.

How could I?

We were from two completely different worlds, and I was nothing more than a dolled-up imposter, a pretty spider who had accidentally ensnared him in my web. He was sweet, and handsome, and thoughtful, but I could never be his queen. I was a cold-blooded liar.

"No," I breathed, tears burning in the

corner of my eyes. "There was never any connection for me."

My lie... I was afraid of that.

He took in a fortifying breath, giving me an understanding nod as he took in a hard swallow. "Thank you, Evie," he said in a gravelly voice, "for being honest with me."

Please, don't tell me that... anything but that.

"Of course," I said quietly, my heart cracking as I spoke the words.

He slowly guided us back into the steps of the dance, taking a moment to collect himself before reinforcing his plastered false smile. "Now that I know for certain you don't want to be my queen, I would like to help ensure that you don't score any further points so another candidate can pull ahead of you."

My shattered heart slowly pulled itself back together, focusing on the fact that I at least had a new solution for my competition problem. "What did you have in mind?"

His smile grew mischievous, displaying the small dimple on the side of his cheek. "As the host of the competition, I have the honor of selecting and organizing each event. So, if there are any areas in which your remarkable talents don't stretch, I would be more than happy to center the next event on them." He winked at me, and I felt a rush of relief pour over me.

If he selects a challenge I'm unskilled at, then

I won't have to fear winning on accident anymore.

My face lit up the slightest amount as an idea sprouted in my mind. "So, for instance, could you make the next competition about art?" My eyes twinkled at him eagerly, earning a bemused furrow of his brows.

"Art? You mean like painting and drawing?" He asked.

I nodded, dizzying myself a touch in the midst of a spin. "I'm *fabulous* at painting," I said airily. "If you have any hope of me becoming your queen, Your Highness," he twirled me back into his arms, catching me only a breath away from his face, "then you'll want to see me paint."

He nodded softly, still holding me close to him, despite the end of the song. "Very well then, Miss Evie..." He smiled slyly. "I'll begin the arrangements tomorrow morning."

Despite his collected expression, I could still feel his heart hammering against where our chests pressed against each other. A soft fluttering sensation pulsed through me, making me wonder if he could feel my racing heart as well. Our breaths were both soft and heavy from two dances in a row, and his forehead glistened from a slight bead of sweat. I was certain I looked equally worn, but I would have never thought I looked anything other than flawless by the way his gaze burned at me.

If only he knew he is falling for a lie...

"May I cut in?"

We both jumped back, separating our close embrace to a far more appropriate hold when Jezebel's shrill voice sliced through the tender moment like a sharpened butcher's blade. She fluttered her lashes so intensely at Carlex that, for a moment, I wondered if a speck of dust ailed her. She avoided eye contact with me entirely, which was probably wise in the presence of the prince considering how ugly her glares could get.

I took an awkward step back from Carlex, my hands feeling cold and empty after leaving his touch. "Please do."

I curtsied to Carlex, giving a gentle gesture to him for Jezebel to swoop in with a twirl of her hair. My heart seized with an aching throb as I calmly made my way to the corner of the ballroom.

As much as I despised Jezebel, and everything her family had done to mine, I knew she would be a better match for the prince than I would. She was educated, poised, and trained in diplomacy, while I only knew the proper way to fold a bedsheet or weave a loom. I'd gotten too close, and now both the prince and I were facing the sting from it.

But it doesn't matter... We never could have worked, anyway. Eventually, it would have been made clear that I'm not the real Lady Genevieve.

A small crack split through my heart as I watched Carlex's false smile radiate in front of

Jezebel as she laughed playfully. A pained smile touched my lips as I leaned back against the cool stone wall of the ballroom, watching his perfectly faked chivalry.

Perhaps that's why we have a connection. He's a practiced liar, too.

chapter fourteen

The next morning came with a painful blare of light through a crack in the curtains. After a long night of dancing, competing, and breaking the prince's heart, I wasn't feeling up to my normal early waking. Evie groaned in her bunk, showcasing the same amount of appreciation for the morning sun as I had.

Despite the late hour, Evie had been awake when I returned to the suite last night, though she hadn't seemed too thrilled about it. She'd already heard through the grapevine of servants about the competition, so she was aware of my failed attempt at scoring poorly. By the time I had trudged back to the room, it was far past the midnight hour, so she had essentially helped me unlace my dress and then collapsed in her bed.

I rolled over with a groan, still wearing my petticoat and dress slip after being too tired to hunt down a nightgown. My feet throbbed from my elongated dance with Carlex, causing me to mentally thank him for gifting me shoes that hadn't carved my feet into blisters. Memories of our dance haunted my mind like the mixture of a nightmare and a blissful fantasy.

He had wanted me to win... but now he knows I can't.

A squeaky yawn emitted from the corner of the room as Evie stretched to life, her long dark lashes still clinging together with her slow blinks. "Good morning, Lace." She yawned, smacking her lips indelicately.

I sat up the slightest amount, propping my tired body up against my mountain of pillows. "How did you sleep?" I yawned back, snuggling back into the pillows.

She sat up with another yawn, unveiling her wild hair that clung to her cheek in clumps. "Terribly," she groaned. "I could hardly sleep because I couldn't stop thinking about your scores from last night."

She snagged her cotton blanket off the top of her bunk, wrapping it over her head like an over-sized shawl before climbing down to join me on my bed. I creaked off my pillows the slightest amount, wiggling over to make room for her swallowed form to vanish into the mattress beside me. She quickly cozied up against the pillows, adjusting her sleepy blue eyes to face me with a pondering look.

"I've been running the numbers," she blinked sleepily, "and no matter how they divvied up the scores last night, I'm certain you'll still be ranking first today. You're the *only* person who scored in the first event and now you've claimed second place in round two. I hate to break it to you, Lace, but you might be too smart to avoid becoming queen."

I sat up groggily, stretching my arms out to the bed's canopy with a final yawn. In all my exhaustion, I hadn't told Evie anything about my new arrangement with the prince.

"Don't worry, Evie, I'll definitely become queen at this rate." I lifted my brow perceptively, watching slowly as her half-awake face blinked with understanding.

She propped her chin up on her palm, narrowing her eyes at me thoughtfully. "You think so, huh?" She tilted her head, slowly allowing her clouded thoughts to reawaken. "Why is that? Did something happen?"

I nodded. "No, nothing at all."

Her expression brightened with new curiosity, leaning forward with sparkling eyes. "So, something *did* happen. What was it? Did the prince say something? Did he notice you wore his shoes?"

"Did you hear about how I lost the competition?" I asked, shifting into a more upright position to face her.

She remained low to the mattress, her face still cradled in her palm. "I heard that you got second to Jezebel." She gagged on the name, earning a slight snicker from me. "And that you would have won if you hadn't tripped at the end. I'm guessing that fumble was intentional, though."

"It wasn't," I confirmed.

A mischievous smile tickled her voice. "Thought so, but don't worry, no one else seemed to think it was odd." She took in a sharp breath, scrambling to sit up with widening eyes. "Did the prince see you fall? Did he think it was intentional?"

I smiled victoriously. "No, not at all."

Evie pressed her hands to her lips. "Oh, my kingdoms! What is he going to do about it now? If he caught you cheating, he might report it to the king... or even worse, my parents." Her face darkened for a brief moment, lowering her voice to a hush. "Do you want me to... you know, *get involved*?" She winked. "I'm sure even Prince Carlex has some dirt on him I can dig up. If I do a little snooping around his chambers today, then maybe I can find something juicy enough to blackmail him with, and then I'll—"

"Evie!" I cut her off, gaping at her while biting back a laugh. She gave me an unapologetic shrug and I pressed a hand to my forehead. "The prince will tell people about my fumble, I'm certain."

She opened her mouth to say something but left it hanging for a moment before collecting her words. "So... no blackmailing then?"

"Evie!"

"What!? I'm only trying to help." She

raised her arms in defense. "So why won't the prince tell? Did he confess his love to you or something?" She pressed her hands together romantically, leaning forward with a dramatic flutter of her lashes.

I shifted uncomfortably against the pillows, recalling our dance. "N-no..." My voice came out soft and weak, uncertain of whether or not the words were permissible by the curse.

"Lacey!?" she gasped. "He confessed!?"

"N-no, Y-yes, I mean—" I groaned, turning around to shove my face into the fluffy pillows as Evie poked the back of my neck impatiently.

"Well, which is it!?" she pestered.

I sighed against the silk pillow shams. "He essentially said I'm his *least* favorite candidate."

Evie swooned dramatically, collapsing onto the pillows beside me with a puff. "Oh, my kingdoms, he's got a little crush on you, doesn't he!" She rolled over, pushing my shoulder up with her so I was facing her. "So, was he pretty upset when he saw you fail on purpose? I can only imagine how heartbroken he must have been."

I winced at the reminder of his pitiful smile at last night's dance. *I didn't actually break his heart; I just... disappointed him.*

"He seemed okay," I said solemnly, earning a soft frown from Evie. "Anyway, he knows I'm *really* trying to become his queen now, so he offered to select an event I'm *spectacularly* skilled at so I'll have the best chance of winning."

Evie chewed her lip, carefully untwining the truth behind my lies. "I get it now. He doesn't want a queen who doesn't want him too, so he's bending the rules to ensure you don't become his queen." I gave her a nod of confirmation and her face drooped. "How tragic. The poor man now has to watch the woman he's pining for fall to the bottom of the ranks. Geez, Lacey, you really are a viperous one, aren't you?" She popped a hand on her hip, giving me an accusing glare.

"Who got me into this whole mess again?" I matched her glare, watching in satisfaction as she slowly backed down.

"Okay, you made your point," she huffed. "So, what did you tell him? About what you wanted the next event to be, I mean. Hopefully you picked something that snotty ole Jezebel is terrible at, too."

I held back a slight laugh, sitting up with one final stretch of my back. "I told him I love painting."

Ever since I was little, I had been completely uncoordinated when it came to art. Anything outside of weaving was horrendous for me, and Evie once discovered it when she asked me to paint her mother a birthday present when she was too busy. Needless to say, her mother didn't receive a proper gift that year.

I glanced back over at Evie, expecting to see a touch of amusement wash over her face from the same memory, but when I looked over, she had gone completely ashen. Her paled face was stiff with what looked like panic, sending a wave of uncertainty through me.

"Evie...? Is everything alright?" I asked anxiously.

She didn't say anything at first, but instead, she sat up from the pillows with a stark expression. "Lacey... you can't paint," she said coolly, biting her lip in between breaths. "But I, Lady Genevieve, *can*. Rather well. In fact, my parents have sent my work all across the kingdom as gifts to the nobility." Her eyes latched onto mine as the seriousness behind her meaning slowly donned on me.

Evie is a painter... and most of the girls probably already knew that.

A pit formed in my stomach, shattering the ease I had blindly accepted ever since my dance with the prince. "I-I'm in trouble, aren't I?" I sputtered, my fingers now twisting at the sheets.

"If the prince was being honest about letting you pick the next event..." her face went grim, "then, yes."

• •

I wandered anxiously through the palace halls, chewing my nails in an unladylike manner as I trudged toward the dining room for lunch. I'd been such a fool. I've watched

Evie attend painting lessons for years, yet it never once crossed my mind that her talents would be recognizable from across the kingdom. My stomach knotted, bundling together like a tangled cord of thread. Why hadn't I considered the *real* Evie's talents when answering the prince? I bit hard on my nail, knowing perfectly well why I hadn't given it any consideration.

I just wanted to be Lacey when I was with the prince, not Evie.

As I climbed down the palace steps to the lower floor, a few of the other girls began to trickle in from other corners of the castle, all directed for the dining room like me. I tried to blend in alongside them, while simultaneously remaining a half-step behind to ensure I wasn't going to get roped into any conversations. My tactic worked well for the first quarter of the walk, until Jezebel swooped up from behind me and hooked her arm into mine.

I jolted at the uninvited touch, my head whipping in her direction with a quizzical stare. Her over-powdered face was stained with an overly-polite smile that sullied my appetite even further.

What is she up to?

"Evie, dear," she said brightly through clenched teeth, "I've been looking all over for you." She tightened her hold on my arm, slowing my walk with her until the other girls gained a fair amount of distance ahead of us.

My heartbeat accelerated, warning me that I was dangerously close to a ferocious predator. "Whatever for?" I asked tightly, my throat squeezing in discomfort. There wasn't a bone in my body that felt at ease with Jezebel wanting to find me.

She laughed playfully, pressing her free hand to the edge of her lips with a posh flick of her manicured nails. "Oh Evie, dear, isn't it obvious?" She giggled. My chest tightened as I watched her ice-blue eyes flick back in the direction of the other girls, measuring the distance between us and any other witnesses. "I'm here to let you know that I'm on to you." Her smile dropped instantly, surging a rush of ice through my veins. Her friendly grip on my arm fastened threateningly, digging her polished nails into my bare arm. "I know about your little secrets and soon, I'll dig up enough evidence to expose you."

My breath caught painfully in my throat, nearly causing me to choke on the air. *My secrets...* Memories flashed through my mind, clouding my vision with images of Jezebel's younger self, her devilish glare searing into me with a resentful grimace.

"Eww! Get away from here, Lacey. Relatives of a criminal like you and your mother shouldn't stand so close to nobility. Someday you'll probably join your father in jail, anyway. You're just a sleazy little liar."

I flinched, jumping back into reality as I gazed back into the aged face of my tormentor. "W-what are you talking about?" I mumbled and my legs wobbled unsteadily as we continued our painfully slow walk down the corridor.

"Don't play dumb," she hissed impatiently, digging her nails in with another squeeze. "You know perfectly well that it's long since time that you be expelled from this competition."

My heart rammed furiously against my ribs, distracting me from the tight sting of Jezebel's razor nails. "Expelled? Whatever for?" I gulped, my last strands of hope for survival slowly snaking around my throat like the start of a noose.

If she finally remembers me, then I'm as good as dead...

"For cheating, you twit."

She yanked my arm, pulling me into an adjacent corridor before pushing me toward the wall. My back smacked into the stone, knocking the air out of my lungs from the unexpected show of force. My face flushed with stunned confusion, but her raging eyes didn't seem interested in showing any sympathy.

"You've been seducing the prince into helping you win the events, haven't you!?" She jeered her finger an inch from my eyes, shrouding me in the stench of her floral perfume.

Seducing the prince?

I gaped at her as both relief and shock settled through me. *So, she doesn't remember me after all.*

"J-Jezebel, what are you talking about?" I sputtered, my throat closing up on the question as the anger in her face deepened.

"So that's how you're going to play it, huh?" she seethed and took a step back with a murderous glint in her iced-over gaze. "You're not fooling anyone, you know. I might have believed that the first event was a fluke, but after watching you *fall* yesterday, I'm plenty convinced you've been cheating. It was obvious that you were trying not to look too suspicious for winning again." Another cluster of girls passed our hallway, causing Jezebel to snag me by the arm again and tug us back into a shadow. "I don't know what you told the prince to convince him to help you win, but I'm going to find out. And when I do, I'll tell the king and get you banished from the capital for good."

I blinked at her in astonishment, my words lost on my lead tongue. *She thinks Carlex and I are working together? I mean... I suppose we are, but not in the way she has imagined.*

"Jezebel, the prince isn't helping me cheat," I said firmly, yanking my arm away from her ensnaring grip. "I don't know any more about the upcoming competitions than you do, and my fumble at last night's event was simply that, a fumble. I had no intentions of losing the event to the likes of *you*." I narrowed my eyes at her, taking a bold step forward that was met with pure resistance.

She stood, undeterred by my words, her presence fighting to overpower mine in the castle shadows. "You're a pretty liar," she rasped through a locked jaw. "I wonder if that's how you got the prince to favor you."

An icy chill ran down my spine, forcing me to tense in order to hold back the shiver. Jezebel's perceptive gaze caught my miniscule flinch, her eyes slitting thoughtfully as she looked back into my face with a more searching expression.

I swallowed back the growing lump in my throat, attempting not to gag on her noxious perfume. I straightened my spine, staring down at the woman who stole my tongue as a child and whose father broke my family.

"Jezebel," I took in a sturdy breath, my voice steel, "I am *not* a liar. I'm playing this game as fairly as everyone else, and if you don't like it, then that's because you clearly don't want to win badly enough."

Her face flushed with heated red. She balled her polished nails into fists, nearly quaking with pent-up anger.

"Who are you to judge how badly I want to win!?" Her voice elevated, echoing down the hall enough that I secretly pleaded someone would hear her tantrum. "You know nothing! You're just a sleazy little liar—"

She stopped, anger still staining her paralyzed face. My straining heartbeats vanished entirely, leaving a soft growing burn in its place. Her mouth remained open, still hooked on the last word that lingered on her lips.

Liar.

"It can't be..." she whispered as her eyes carefully narrowed onto mine.

Panic shot through my core as her lingering gaze grew hungrier by the second. I averted my face from her, tearing away from her scrutinizing glare with a quick flick of my skirts.

"You should really focus on your own game, Jezebel, because you really know nothing about me," I said sharply as I faced the hallway. My heart resumed beating, jolting up to a lethal speed as only deafening silence echoed behind me.

She doesn't know anything... How could she? She probably doesn't even remember me from back then, anyway.

"I'm not so sure of that..." she mused quietly, a dark light lacing her pondering voice. "Maybe I know more than I thought..."

chapter fifteen

I hurried to my usual seat at the lunch table —one that was fortunately far from Jezebel. Churning pain sifted through my stomach as I looked down at my meal with an absent appetite. The freshly peppered salad looked completely picturesque, but I couldn't even imagine eating with Jezebel's incredulous glare. She had taken her usual seat, but I could sense her watchful presence from across the table, eyeing me down like a starving vulture.

She doesn't know... She can't know...

Once all the ladies were seated, we began to eat our meals with the same polite conversation that had become routine over the last week. My fingers trembled horrifically as I reached for my fork, causing me to accidently clatter the tines of the utensil against the edge of my goblet. A soft *clink* echoed throughout the dining room, darting every eye in my direction with a curious or annoyed look. My face went white as my sights locked onto Jezebel, who was narrowing her gaze on me.

I cleared my throat and turned my

attention to the unappealing salad, attempting to ignore the clatter of dishware entirely. I skewered a small bite of undressed lettuce, gingerly raising it to my lips while secretly hoping it wouldn't rile my stomach more. The moment I crunched down on the fresh green, the dining room doors sprang open, thankfully shifting even Jezebel's attention. Soft murmurs and giddy gasps filtered throughout the table the moment Prince Carlex stepped into the room. The single green leaf I'd attempted to ingest remained flat on my tongue; my jaw locked shut at the sight of the prince.

What is he doing here? He never attends our meals unless it's before an event—

I swallowed back the bite of lettuce with a stiff gulp.

No... Not now, Carlex, please...

"Good afternoon, ladies." The prince beamed brightly, flicking his polished smile across the dining room with a well-practiced radiance. "I'm sorry to intrude on your meal, but I'm actually here to share some exciting news."

The room went silent as every girl covertly tucked their half-chewed bites into their cheeks to smile with enthusiasm. His eyes flicked to mine for a brief moment with unspoken excitement. My stomach rebelled against the bite of lettuce, tensing in my gut with a tunneling terror.

"The third event will not be occurring at

the end of the week as scheduled, but will instead be occurring directly after lunch."

Soft, dainty gasps peppered the room as the prince absorbed their astonishment. I nearly dropped my fork as I felt the gravity of my predicament crush me from all angles. My grave expression lowered to the barely-touched salad, wondering now if it might be my last meal. If Carlex had truly chosen an event based on my suggestion, then it was only a matter of hours before I was discovered...

"I'm also here for another reason," Carlex continued. "Normally, the event's rules are not given until just before it begins, but today is going to be a little different. For today's event, you will be instructed to paint a portrait of me in an allotted amount of time. The catch is that I will not be present in the room while you all are painting; therefore, you will only have until the end of this meal to study me and commit my attributes to memory before the event."

His lips tugged into a soft smirk, barely drifting his eyes toward me with an expectant gleam.

I clawed at my skirts, feeling the weight of my conviction press down on me until I feared my chair would splinter. All at once, a cluster of eyes shot accusingly in my direction. My body urged me to flinch away from their stares, but I couldn't even muster up the courage to breathe.

They knew about my supposed talents...

"Painting, huh?" Gabrielle spoke up first, a soft fire flickering behind her doll-like eyes. "Isn't that interesting..." She slipped Jezebel a side-glance, looking for support to her building claim, but Jezebel's expression remained twisted and lost.

Jezebel tapped a nail against her pursed lips, studying me with renewed interest. "Yes, yes, it certainly is..."

I took in a wavering breath, my chest harboring enough pressure to combust, even without the presence of a magic stone. Jezebel looked entirely thrown off. If she was still suspicious of me cheating the rules with Carlex, then this event would have been undeniable proof. But that wasn't what had left her speechless... She no longer believed I was Evie, and a painting competition wouldn't benefit Lacey.

So, who does she believe I am now?

"Is there a problem, Miss Gabrielle?" Carlex interrupted my thoughts, his intrigued gaze centered on the blushing Gabrielle.

"Why actually, yes, Your Highness." She cleared her throat, then set aside her napkin to stand from the table and meet his gaze head-on. "You see, Jezebel and I were merely discussing how convenient it was that Genevieve has an intensive background in painting. I don't mean to speak out of turn, but it almost seems unfair that the next event is catered to her talents while she's already in the lead." No one spoke, but a few soft nods followed Gabrielle's declaration, forcing me to shrink back even further into my chair.

Carlex blinked in disbelief, turning to look at my shrouded form. It was nearly unbearable to look at him. His face was entirely contorted in confusion, shock, and even a slight touch of pain.

"Evie, is this true?" he muttered with baffled eyes. "Are you a talented painter?"

The burning eyes that pinned me in my chair left me feeling cornered and exposed. *What am I supposed to do?* If I play the role of Evie and admit that I'm a painter, what would Carlex believe? He might think I was trying to play him from the start... But if I try to state that I'm not a painter at all, then I'll have to combat all the witnesses of Evie's skill.

I'm completely trapped... Twisted in the web I so foolishly built.

"Yes," I breathed through a hollow voice, "I'm a practiced painter."

Flustered whispers circled around the table as I felt angry stares prickle my face. Despite their prodding looks, I could only feel the lost gaze of the prince clinging to me with a mountain of unspoken questions.

"You see?" Gabrielle interjected over the building chatter. "She's already got an advantage over the rest of us."

Carlex shook off his shock momentarily,

still latching his eyes to me. "Allow me to assure you all, I had absolutely no knowledge of Miss Evie's talents." I expected him to look hurt after catching me in a blatant lie, but for some reason, he looked almost... pleased? "These events are designed to reveal the most intelligent and well-rounded candidate for Reclusia's future queen. If this event is suited to her talents, then it must simply be fated."

A soft smile twitched at his lips, straining me with nauseous guilt.

Oh no, Carlex, don't say that... anything but that.

The prickling glares transformed into penetrating daggers, and each punctured one of my vital organs. I could hardly bear the intensity of their envy, nor could I blame them for despising me in this moment. It couldn't have appeared more obvious that the events were rigged in my favor, and everyone seemed to take notice of it except for the prince, who was rigging it. Perhaps that was the solution to this mess; I needed to get him to see that his twist in the rules was more harmful than he realized.

"Perhaps, we can request a change in the event?" I asked meekly, my fingers burrowed into my satin skirts, twisting wildly as I felt the tension in the room thicken. "I can assure you all that I had no influence in the prince's decision of this event, but if it makes you all uncomfortable, then maybe the prince will reconsider?" I turned my pleading gaze to Carlex, who in turn, seemed at a complete loss.

He must believe me a fool who forgot her own talents when selecting an event to fail.

He opened his mouth to speak but didn't form any sound as he fought desperately to understand all the things I was trying to convey with a single unspoken look. "Well... I suppose if everyone is in agreeance—"

"We're not," Jezebel interrupted, shattering the last remnant of hope within me. A devilish grin trailed up her reddened lips, sending a fearful chill down my spine as she snuck a knowing glance in my direction. "Forgive my rudeness, Your Highness, but I don't believe it to be fair for the event to change after the rules have already been announced."

My blood thickened in my veins, slowing my heartbeat to a meager crawl as I processed what she was planning. *She is trying to catch me in my lie...* She fluttered her lashes, sweetening her smile as she turned cordially to me.

"Besides, I would be honored to compete against the spectacular talents of the infamous Genevieve Palleep. It will really give me and the other ladies a proper challenge to showcase our gifts. Don't you all agree?" She glanced around the rest of the table, where the girls remained silent.

"Very well then..." Carlex's eyes tried to catch mine, but I looked away, staring down at my fistfuls of fabric with nauseating breaths. "The competition shall remain unchanged. To ensure each of you has ample opportunity to study my features, I'll be moving around the room so you'll all have a proper view. Please, enjoy your meal."

He gestured to our plates, but hardly anyone seemed interested in staring at their chopped carrots now that there was an open invitation to gawk at the prince's face. I put my fork down, sipping my tea to help calm my churning nerves. Jezebel's snakelike eyes darted between studying the prince and glowering at me with a victorious smile. Even if she wasn't certain that I was an imposter, she would be receiving her answer by the end of the event, and I would be receiving a notice of my scheduled execution...

"Is everything alright, Miss Evie?"

I nearly fell out of my seat from Carlex's hushed words. I had been too busy following Jezebel's glares to even notice that the prince had circled around to the back of the table. He was still being eyed by the rest of the girls, but when I turned to look back at him, I saw he had spoken to me through smiling teeth. Although his smile maintained the perfection of royalty, his eyes were shadowed, heavy with concern.

"I'm doing fine, thank you," I said quietly, ensuring my face was turned away from the onlookers.

His smile faltered for the briefest moment. "Evie," he breathed, "I already told you, you don't have to lie to me." His fingers curled around the hem of his coat, much like the way I grabbed at my skirts whenever I was distressed. "Why did you lie about your painting skills? Did you secretly want to win the event after all?" His eyes tore away from the table to me, flooding my cracking heart with a terrified hopefulness.

My heart strained under his brown-eyed stare. I couldn't trap his heart in my lies again; he deserved better than that. How many times would the curse force me to drag his emotions through the dirt?

And how many times would it drag mine?

My chest swirled with aches and a burning warmth that itched to be exposed. I wanted to tell the prince that I didn't want to hurt him any further, that the things I wished to tell him were locked inside my throat with no way of escaping. He had cared for me once, and now I cared enough for him to know that leading him on again was the last thing I wanted to do. I would never be his queen, but the magic trapped inside my soul would never let me tell him.

"I'm trying to win," I whispered in a hollow voice. The sting that pierced through my heart nearly tore me in two. Carlex let out a soft sigh—one I couldn't quite interpret while staring defeatedly at my hands.

"This is a competition of intelligence, so

I suppose I shouldn't be surprised that you played me." His voice was tight and heavy, surely hurting from the betrayal I had imposed upon his heart. "Though I admit, I wish you'd been honest with me. You're not the only one who desires a certain conclusion to this competition... Please, just tell me what you really want, because I know what I want, and I'm willing to seek ways to achieve it."

He took in a shallow breath, sending a throb through my chest.

He moved away from my seat, both of us leaving shattered remains of ourselves at our feet. His question lingered in my mind as he strolled around to the other girls, flicking his falsified smile at all angles. *What do I really want?* The answer had seemed obvious at first —I wanted to return home to my mother like none of this had ever happened—yet I couldn't pretend it never happened. I couldn't pretend that I never met Carlex, and now that I'd captured his attention once again, I doubted he could simply forget about me, either.

But he will have to...

The lunch carried on with little conversation since most of the girls were busy silently committing the curves of the prince's jaw and the angle of his nose to memory. I didn't feel the need to study him nearly as intensely, because the memory of his face was entirely locked in my mind. I shut my eyes, picturing his warm almond-shaped eyes, the sway in his dark hair, and the dimple that dotted his cheek only when he presented a real smile. If only I could actually paint... Maybe I could win this event as well...

But winning will only push me farther up in the scores.

I let out a half-strangled breath, reminding myself that it didn't matter how well I scored or not. I wasn't Evie, and that was going to become utterly apparent within the next few hours.

"Alright, ladies." Carlex returned to the center of the room as the doors swung open behind him. "It's time for the third event to begin, so if you would please follow me to the drawing room... your canvases await."

I stood shakily from my seat, sensing Jezebel's knowing gaze chewing into the side of me as I made my way to the doors.

If I wanted to survive as Evie, I needed to paint better than I ever had before. But if I wanted to survive as Lacey, then I needed to fail so I wouldn't score well. And if I thought I could survive this event *at all*, then I was a better liar than I realized.

chapter sixteen

My head dizzied with stress as I stepped into the sunlit drawing room. Long, sparkling windows covered two of the walls, bathing the room in natural light that would have likely been excellent for a true artist. Fifteen uniform canvases sat in a perfect circle, facing outward, designed so none of the participants could see the others' work when seated. My gaze drifted toward the collection of brushes and paints that lined the base of each easel, recognizing the line up from Evie's easel back home.

"Please select a seat, but don't pick up a brush just yet," Carlex instructed, the warm sunlight glittering against his shiny dark hair, catching the attention of a few girls who appeared to make some final mental notes. "Your instructions are simple. You will have ninety minutes to complete your best interpretation of my portrait. You shall receive time warnings once every fifteen minutes. During the allotted time, you may not rise from your seat to ensure that no one views anyone else's work. Once time is up, your portraits will be presented to the king and queen for judging."

I gulped. *The king and queen are judging...? Oh, can things get any worse?*

"I will be permitted to have an influence on their decision, but overall, the scores will be determined by them." He paused, checking to ensure we were all appropriately seated on our stools.

When his eyes glazed over me, I sensed a slight linger in his gaze—one that expressed the need for further conversation. I bit the inside of my cheek, trying to suppress the biting sob that threatened to tear from my stress. *After this event, we'll likely never speak again.* Carlex nodded at the two servants who stood at the front of the room as acting moderators.

"I believe we're ready. Your time will start once I exit the room." He flashed us one final smile, sealing it into everyone's memory before leaving us blind. "Good luck."

As soon as the door shut behind him, the first moderator gave us a soft nod. "You may begin. You have ninety minutes until brushes must be put down."

No sooner than he had said the words, every jar of brushes rattled from grabbing hands. I reached for the first brush handle I saw, then lifted the fine bristles to my eyes, trying to determine if they were too wide or too narrow.

Do I need to outline his face first? Or should I do all the big features, then fill in the little details after?

I returned the first brush to the jar, selecting a wider one with a more satisfied grip. There was no doubt I was in over my head, but I couldn't give up yet. If I could create something with even the slightest resemblance to Evie's work, then perhaps I could convince everyone that the stress impacted my performance.

Except, the stress is already impacting me...

I picked up the wooden pallet, inspecting the different colors in search of a light tan that would match Carlex's skin. There was blue, red, green, yellow, black, white, and an odd brown color, but nothing close to resembling a proper skin tone. Sweat collected in my palms, slickening my grip on the brush as I chewed my bottom lip.

Do I have to blend the skin tone myself? Oh dear...

I picked up the jar of brownish-red paint, tipping a small amount onto my pallet with shaking hands before selecting the yellow and then the white. I carefully blended the three colors together, creating a sickly dark yellow that mirrored the shade of a spoiling banana.

I can't possibly use that for his face. If anything, I need to get the skin tone correct. Evie would at least know how to do that much.

I dipped my brush into the jar of turpentine, dissolving the paint off the wide bristles before trying a new combination of colors to blend. Again and again, I failed to create a skin tone that wouldn't pose the prince as a dying leper.

"Seventy-five minutes remaining," the moderator announced stiffly.

My heart pattered rapidly, warming my blood that was already overheated from the blanket of sunlight pouring in behind me. I looked down at my array of failed skin tones and selected the one that looked the least likely to send a man to the physician before turning back to the canvas. I held my breath as I took in the blank canvas, terrified to dot it with even so much as a blemish of paint.

You can do this... You know what the prince looks like, just recreate him here.

I shut my eyes, imagining his hidden smile and joy-crinkled eyes. The image of him was flawless, leaving nothing forgotten from his warm features. I took in a fortifying breath, steadying my heart rate as I dabbed a fresh glob of paint onto my brush.

Let's do this.

• •

"Time's up. Put your brushes down and please rise from your stools." The moderator's voice struck me like the call of the grim reaper.

I dropped my brush back into the dark jar of turpentine, now thick from all the globs of paint I'd stripped from my brushes. I rose from my seat, feeling my legs wobble with a lack of blood flow from being stationary for so long. My spine ached from the backless, stiff stool, but the pain was nothing compared to the agony that filled me when I looked at my completed canvas.

"Now entering, Their Royal Highnesses, King Aldrich, Queen Viviana, and Prince Carlex." The doors pulled open, revealing the smiling and eager faces of the royal family.

My posture stiffened the instant the prince's eyes turned to me, my body rebelling to even breathe as he looked curiously toward my hidden canvas. I clutched my hands in front of my dress, digging my nails deep into my skin in search of relief from my suffocating nerves. The sting of Jezebel's sinister gaze chewed at me from the corner of my eye and sent a sickening ripple through my stomach.

Please let someone's portrait be worse than mine...

"Congratulations on completing the third challenge." Prince Carlex's voice illuminated the faces of every girl in the room, while simultaneously shadowing mine. "We are all eagerly awaiting to see what you have created for us. To keep comparisons fair, you will all reveal your canvases at the same time."

I squeezed my hands tighter until my fingers turned numb. If my canvas was as bad as I had imagined, then it might stand out instantly. Or maybe turning them all at once would help it blend in with the other less skillful paintings. A soft scoff from Jezebel caught my attention, and I noticed her eying my clenched hands.

"Mother, would you care to do the honors?" Carlex gestured toward the smiling queen, who eagerly stepped forward to gain a full view of the hidden canvases.

"Of course, dear." She beamed. "Ladies, you may now reveal your portraits."

I couldn't look. Instead, I placed my trembling hands on the frame of the canvas and flipped it around with clenched eyes. I raised the canvas in front of my face in an attempt to hide my growing shame. A horrible silence followed the unveiling and tormented me with each passing breath. The lingering quiet felt dismal and grim, leaving me wondering if the canvas I was raising had become the official declaration of my death.

"Fascinating..." The queen's soft voice nearly caused my knees to buckle after breaking the tense silence. "Such an interesting array of talents, wouldn't you say, dear?"

A nervous cold saturated my veins, causing me to shiver. The king hummed a contemplative sigh.

"Yes, an interesting array indeed..." His voice dipped low and the chill in my blood deepened.

I couldn't handle the anticipation any longer. With miniscule movements, I peeled open my scrunched eyes and gently lowered the canvas from my face until I could see the eyes of the royal family. The moment I caught sight of Carlex's ashen face, I felt my entire body freeze over. The king and queen were both staring directly at my canvas, along with all the other girls.

Horror swept through me as my eyes darted to the other girls' portraits. Only a few of them actually held any real resemblance to Carlex, while the rest were a touch more abstract, but none of them were quite as sloppy as the disaster I had concocted.

My breath caught as I glanced down at my atrocious smudges of paint. His skin ended up being a murky yellow-brown, and his head appeared to mimic the shape of an avocado. I'd made the mistake of using a brush that was too wide, so his nose was disproportionately large and one of his eyes was higher than the other. It was absolutely laughable.

As if reading my thoughts, Jezebel let out a muffled snort as she eyed my canvas. My cheeks burned red-hot, which only worsened when I saw the elegant portrait that filled her canvas. She had somehow blended a perfect skin tone and managed to shape his eyes symmetrically, but his smile was all wrong. It wasn't his real smile; it was his falsified political grin that lacked the light in his eyes and the dimple on his cheek.

I glanced back at the real Carlex, whose face was still paled in utter disbelief. I couldn't even imagine what was going through his mind now. Once again, he had caught me in the center of a catastrophic lie.

"What are your initial thoughts, son?" King Aldrich turned to address the prince but stiffened when he saw Carlex's pained look.

A sick guilt seeped through me as I felt the burden of his pained heart blare at me through his eyes. He looked between me and my painting, over and over, as if trying to deduct a reason as to why, once again, my words didn't line up with my actions.

"I suppose I'm at a loss for words..." Carlex breathed. His perfected posture slumped, making him look as broken as I felt.

I'm sorry, Carlex... I really tried.

"I'm sure Your Majesties are dreadfully confused at this moment..." Jezebel's shrill voice cut through the quiet like a piercing rapier. My eyes widened in terror as I caught the edge of a sinister grin tugging at her lips. "But perhaps I can help shed some light on a few things." She returned her canvas to her easel to perform a low curtsy.

Jezebel, don't do this... Do you really want to see me dead?

"Shed some light?" King Aldrich's brows knitted together with a grumpy frown. "What are you getting at?"

Jezebel rose from her graceful dip, posing eloquently as she met the king's eyes with a twisted smile. "I believe I understand the reasoning behind poor Prince Carlex's confusion." She batted her eyes in Carlex's direction. "I apologize for not bringing it to your attention sooner, but I had to be certain my suspicions were correct. It would appear that the prince and the rest of the royal family have been deceived."

No...

My heart stopped as stunned whispers echoed around the room. It didn't take more than a second for eyes to drift in my direction. My fingers weakened, nearly dropping the canvas from my hands, as if it were a sign that had *imposter* etched across the top. My lungs constricted and forced me to take shallow breaths that I had to fight to mask as Carlex's eyes widened at Jezebel.

"Deceived?" He gaped, mirroring the same look as his parents. "By what, exactly?"

Jezebel turned her beady gaze onto me. My legs trembled violently beneath my skirts as I fought to stay upright from beyond the point of her accusing finger.

"By Lady Genevieve."

My mind numbed the sound of everyone's gasps as my petrified gaze locked onto my tormentor. She took a challenging step forward, her devilish smile perfectly suiting her red lips.

"Or is your name actually Lacey? Lacey Arachne. The daughter of the imprisoned thief and traitorous liar, Merritt Arachne."

The canvas dropped from my hands, clattering to the floor with a splatter of undried globs of paint. The terror that gripped me was all too familiar. I blinked and for a moment, I saw Jezebel as a child again, donning the same malicious smile that absorbed her now. The memories flashed before my eyes with a jarring blur.

"Oh, look, there's the little liar." Jezebel snatched the loom from my hands, holding it just out of my reach as I tried to grab it back.

"Give it back, Jezebel! I need to finish the weave by today so I can sell it before Mother meets with the Fredor family." I tried reaching out again for the loom, but she took another step back, her eyes filled with a searing hatred.

"There you go lying again. Yesterday you said your mother was meeting with the Yolan family," she snapped as she dug her claws into the delicate weave I'd been slaving over, proceeding to tear out and snap the cords of thread.

"Wait!"

"Be quiet!" She pushed her arm into my shoulder, knocking me off my feet with a hard gasp. "I don't ever want to hear you speak again. Stop hanging around so close to my house already. We aren't friends anymore, and we never will be again. Not after your father tried to blame mine for

stealing those stones."

I gaped at her, tears clustering in my eyes. "T-the gems weren't stolen—"

"Liar!" she hissed, tossing the shredded loom at my feet. "Of course, the gems were stolen! Why else would your father be in jail?" She stepped forward, looming over me as she crushed her foot down onto the remnants of my weave. "I bet your father is cursed, just like you! That would explain why he tried to sully my father's good name. People like you don't even belong on the streets of the capital. When I get home, I'm going to tell my father to warn all the nobles in the capital about you and your mother, that way no one will get saddled with a lying servant."

My mind snapped back into reality as the present-day Jezebel crossed her arms with an expectant glare. Her tongue has always been her mightiest weapon, starting from when she spread rumors about how my mother and I were in league with my father's crimes, and that the curse I possessed was shared by him, too. She did everything she could to elevate her family's reputation at the cost of mine, and now she was wielding her tongue once again to take away the little I had left to live for. I swallowed hard, pushing back the festering tears that urged me to surrender.

I can't let her destroy me... not again. I already had to disappear once to protect what little reputation my father had left, and I'm not going to let her make me disappear for good. She's not the only one who can wield their tongue as a weapon.

"Y-you're wrong." I straightened my spine, attempting to force every ounce of confidence I had remaining into my tone. "My name is Genevie—"

"Oh, enough of that," Jezebel cut me off with a rude wave of her hand, stepping in front of me to pick up my fallen canvas. "Tell me... does this look like the talents of the *real* Genevieve Palleep?" She flashed my horrid painting to every eye in the room.

Thoughtful whispers erupted amongst the girls, tightening my chest. "I-I was merely nervous."

"Nervous?" Jezebel snorted. "I would certainly imagine so. It must have been difficult to juggle so many lies at once." Her victorious smile weakened me, sending me back to the streets of the capital and the shredded loom.

"Jezebel, are you implying that Lady Genevieve is an imposter?" King Aldrich's face was saturated in anger. I winced as his furious glare flicked to me and found myself instinctually averting my gaze to Carlex, which also seemed to be a mistake.

There were no words to describe the pain that gripped his silent features. Remorse swallowed me as I cast my gaze to where my new slippers hid beneath my skirts. I wished he had never noticed my blisters that night, that he never developed any sympathy toward me at all. Then maybe things wouldn't be so painful.

"Yes, Your Majesty." Jezebel nodded promptly. "It is my suspicion that this girl is a commoner, a lowly street urchin I once knew in youth. I didn't recognize her at first, but she has one characteristic that has swayed me, and I am certain it's undeniably her." Her eyes darkened, crippling me before she even said the words.

After so much climbing... this is how I finally fall.

"She's cursed, Your Highnesses, to only tell lies."

chapter seventeen

"Evie?" Carlex's voice cracked, breaking through my numbed defenses with a fresh sting. "Is… is this true?"

Bewildered silence permeated the room. The anger that had enveloped King Aldrich continued to silently burn red in his face, and Queen Viviana had turned as pale as a blank canvas. Any strands of dignity I had left were now crumpled at my feet. I bit my lip, unable to face the prince as I softly nodded my head in answer to his question.

"You see?" Jezebel puffed. "She can't say it. She was cursed by an unrefined magic stone her father had tried to steal. Due to his negligence with the magic, he accidentally cursed Lacey and himself, which is why he always tried to blame my father—the duke, no less—for his crimes."

The pain that left me crumbled rebuilt into fury as Jezebel's rumors unfolded. *Is that what she told everyone in the capital?*

"No! That's *t-true.*" The lie caught in my throat as I desperately tried to fight the curse on my tongue. "No, it's true. It's true, it's true…"

Tears welled up in my eyes as I pressed a defeated hand against my lying lips.

Carlex's eyes grew wide beyond my blurred vision. He stumbled back a step, eyeing me like a deranged monster at war with my own words. I couldn't bear to look at his scathing eyes any longer. He was no longer looking at Evie, the quirky noble who snagged his heart, but instead, he was glaring at Lacey, the cursed peasant who had been tricking him since they met. I turned my attention toward the king, who looked entirely appalled. He curled his hands into fists, veins bulging along his arms and forehead.

"The daughter of a common thief?" The king's voice sunk into a low growl, causing even the onlookers to sink back. "And a cursed one at that. Never within the generations of this sacred competition has a mere commoner slipped through the cracks. How dare you sully the good name of the Reclusian crown with your tainted presence here?"

The king swung his fist against the air, taking a commanding step forward that nearly sent me crumbling to the ground.

I clasped my hands in front of my chest to maintain their quaking. Terror coursed through my blood with a paralyzing effect, leaving my already useless tongue tied and limp. "I-I—"

"Don't listen to her, Your Majesty," Jezebel snipped. "She can only lie. Therefore, you can't trust a single word that comes out of her mouth.

That's likely why she managed to have us all fooled for so long." She turned her monstrous smirk to me, basking in the shadow of my horror. "She only knows how to be fake... just like her father."

It felt as if the castle walls were crashing down around me, crushing me beneath the weight of their stone and mortar. I opened my mouth to try to speak once again, but all I could do was stare mutely at Carlex as the first tear slid down my cheek. He watched it trickle from my face with nearly no emotion at all, still clearly in shock from the unveiling of my true identity. I couldn't blame him for hating me, not after everything I'd done...

"I'm *not* sorry." I sobbed, pressing my hands to my reddening eyes. "I *meant* to do it, I really *meant* to. Please understand that I truly meant to fool you, and that I'm not sorry."

"Are you really so foolish as to admit that you're proud of your crimes in front of your king!?" King Aldrich's temper snapped, causing me to jolt my hands up from my eyes just in time to see Carlex pull him back by the arm.

"Wait, Father! She's lying, remember?" He tugged on his father's arm, forcing him back a step before he could approach me in his fit of rage. I stared up at Carlex in disbelief, unsure of whether or not he was an ally. His eyes searched mine, loaded with questions that I knew I would never get a chance to answer. "You were trying to say that you *are* sorry, weren't you?"

I nodded shakily. "No."

Queen Viviana gasped, lacing her arm around her husband's for support. "Oh, my kingdoms, it's true... She really is cursed."

The king's anger eased the slimmest amount once he recognized I wasn't gloating about my deception to his face, though his face remained hardened.

"If you're not the real Lady Genevieve, then where is she?" He folded his arms, shaking off his wife's hold with a stiff tense.

I bit my lip. *I don't want to get Evie in trouble, too...* "I-I don't know."

Jezebel rolled her eyes. "That's a lie as well, Your Majesties," she huffed. "As I said, you can't trust a single thing she says. You're better off talking to a wall."

I winced at her painfully true words. There was nothing I could say to help clear mine or Evie's name in this situation, especially since we were both immensely guilty. My throat tightened as I watched the king's eyes darken, the anger still festering behind his glare.

"I see..." His words were like ice, rushing a chill across my neck. "Then there is no need for me to question her any further. It seems clear to me that this girl is indeed not who she claims to be, and has therefore broken the laws of our kingdom by impersonating a person above their rank, infiltrating the royal palace, and insulting the crown through deception."

I stumbled back a step as all the blood drained from my skin. My skin went cold and numb, paling from the fear that tightened my heart in a web that no sword could tear through. Everything I had feared, every lie I had told, was all being unveiled, leaving me trapped and exposed.

"The sentence for these crimes is severe." The king flicked his wrist, and two guards burst out from their statuesque positions to approach me from either side.

I braced myself for their ruthless grabs of my wrists and arms, trying to bite back the rest of the tears that remained barricaded behind my heavy blinks. The king measured his eyes up to mine, showcasing the full fury my deception had crafted.

"Lacey Arachne, I hereby sentence you to the gallows."

Everything went quiet.

I stared blankly at the chaotic room swirling around me, but I couldn't hear a single sound anymore. My mind blurred out the sound of the gasping competitors, Jezebel's victorious chuckle, and even the queen's attempt to soothe her husband's anger. I couldn't hear any of it anymore, for it was all too quiet to interpret beneath the piercing cry of defeat that split my mind.

I failed... Even after an entire life of lying,

I couldn't even uphold the one lie my life had depended on.

My broken gaze drifted upward to where Prince Carlex gaped with a paling face. He hadn't moved an inch since his father's decree, but his expression was gradually changing. At first, he had been overwhelmed by shock, but slowly, his eyes began to fade into an almost sympathetic stare, and then one furrowed in panic. I let my eyes remain fixated on his as the guards pushed me toward the door in slow motion. He knew the truth behind my lies now, but I would never get to explain how I never meant to use them to deceive both his mind and his heart.

It is a shame I'll carry that to my grave.

My slippers dragged across the floor since my legs were too shaken to take proper steps. My shoe snagged on the floor, knocking loose the beautiful slipper Carlex had requested be crafted for me. My skirt slid over the top of the fallen shoe, catching Carlex's eyes with a pained look of reminiscence. He approached the forgotten slipper, allowing his eyes to linger on it with a thoughtful look before he shot his widened gaze up to the guards.

"Wait!" Carlex's voice cut through the numbed quiet of my mind, jerking my head back into reality. "You can't execute her."

Carlex? What are you doing?

The guards froze but didn't make any move to release me. I stared blankly at Carlex's newly determined expression as he reached down and picked up my slipper from the floor. The king's face returned to his vibrant red as he approached his son and whirled him around by the shoulder.

"Carlex, I understand that this woman had your favor, but I cannot ignore the law, especially with such an atrocious crime against the crown." The king shot me a spiteful look, earning a startled flinch from me.

"Exactly," Carlex said blatantly. "You cannot ignore the law, and the law states that all the competition's rules must be upheld until the crown prince is betrothed."

The girls who had been silently observing the altercation began to whisper with nervous breaths.

The king glanced at their chittering for a moment with a lost expression before turning his attention back to his son. "Exactly, and the rules don't allow commoners to participate. She has sullied your honor by her mere presence; therefore, she must receive the punishment for her crimes."

My stomach tumbled into thick knots. Never in my life had I expected to watch two men quarrel over the value of my life. The intense pressure that squeezed my chest was utterly suffocating. Carlex flicked his eyes in my direction for the briefest of moments, and to my surprise, I saw a touch of reassurance in them.

What is he planning?

"But, Father, if you remove Evi— I mean, Lacey from the competition, then the entire event will be voided by a breach in the rules." Carlex straightened his spine, squaring up to his father with the confidence of a future king. "The rules clearly state that once the competition has begun, each participant must commit to the entire tournament. Lacey has already been competing; therefore, she may not be permitted to withdraw from the competition until the last event has concluded and my betrothed has been selected."

Bewilderment overtook me as I slowly absorbed the prince's words. *I still have to finish the competition... So I can't be executed.* A harsh reality crashed through the slight touch of relief that brushed me as I recognized the flaw in this rule. *What about after the competition, though? Will my execution only be delayed...?*

"That rule will only postpone the inevitable," the king huffed, glowering at me over the prince's shoulder. "Even if the girl carries out her commitment to the competition, she will still be at fault for her crimes. Her execution shall take place either way."

My stomach seized, threatening to hurl the miniscule amount of lunch I had managed to stomach. It was kind of Carlex to try to preserve my life for a few more weeks, but admittedly, the longer walk toward death sounded almost more agonizing.

Carlex took in a fortifying breath, turning away from his father to look directly at me. "Not if she wins..."

My breath hitched. Every eye went wide in disbelief as the prince stood firm with his back against his steaming father.

"Win!?" the king bellowed. "The girl is a *commoner*; she's the cursed daughter of a criminal! She couldn't possibly win in a competition designed to measure intelligence."

"Yet she has already won, twice actually." Carlex snapped his head back to his father. "She was the only one to solve the riddle in the first event, and the only reason she fell in round two was because she knew winning would risk her exposure." My mouth fell agape as I watched his understanding of my actions slowly unfold. His warm eyes turned to me, full of fresh understanding and heartfelt remorse. "And if she continues to win, she will become my crown princess, a *true* noble."

I gasped, allowing his words to wash over me with a dizzying effect.

If I win the competition... I will become a noble, which will mean—

"If Lacey wins the competition, she will no longer be guilty of the crime of rank impersonation," Carlex announced over the gawking crowd of competitors and servants. "The crime for imposing as a noble is indeed death, but if Lacey becomes my betrothed, then the crime will cease to exist because she will then *be* a noble, and she will be free of all charges."

I couldn't believe what I was hearing, even as I watched the words spill from the prince's mouth. Carlex was trying to save me, even after all the times I'd lied to him. Why would he care now that he knew who I truly was?

"Carlex," the king hardened his eyes on the prince, his face full of frightening disapproval, "I know what you're trying to do, and I must say that I certainly do not approve."

Carlex didn't waver. "What do you mean, Father?" he asked calmly, his voice steel. "I'm only trying to ensure that Reclusia receives the most intelligent queen possible, and right now, I'm not letting go of the best possible candidate."

My chest tightened, surging my heart with an unsteady beat.

Carlex turned to the guards still gripping me, his face stone. "Release Miss Lacey at once. Until the end of this competition, she is a guest of this castle and is not to be harmed."

The guards removed their clamped grasps from my arms, leaving red imprints from where they had tunneled their nails into my skin. I nearly fell as I fought to regain balance on my wavering legs. Carlex instantly reached out a hand to steady me, still holding my slipper in his hand. He caught me by the waist, snagging my breath for the briefest moment before he let go and stretched out my forgotten slipper to me.

"Here," he said softly. "You'll need shoes if you're going to keep competing."

I don't remember taking the shoe from him as the shock continued to work its course through my veins. It wasn't until he had turned back to his father that I realized I had been left clutching the slipper.

The king's anger enveloped the whole room, forcing even Jezebel to disappear into the crowd of petrified girls.

"The law will be upheld," he said grimly. "But the rules don't require that the crown prince select the events; therefore, I shall take on the task of arranging the final two challenges."

A lump formed in my throat as I noticed Carlex's face turn a shade whiter. "Very well then. But until the competition ceases, Lacey will be under the same protection as any other guest."

The king didn't look at me, but I could tell he desired to add another layer to my curse. He gave the prince an unenthusiastic nod, then turned to leave the room with a scuff of his boots.

"We'll announce today's scores in the morning," he called out to the room, then stopped in the doorway to meet his son's eyes one final time. "We'll let the peasant compete. And if by some miracle she wins, she can be your queen, but if she falls even a point behind..."

He turned his foreboding gaze toward me, robbing me of any strength I had previously salvaged.

"She'll be visiting the gallows during your betrothal feast."

chapter eighteen

"Lacey... I-I'm so sorry." Evie's face swelled with guilt, causing her lip to quiver as she blinked back tears with her heavy lashes. "I'll find a way to fix this. This ridiculous plan was my idea anyway, so if someone has to go to the gallows, then it should be me, not you."

The unrelenting sickness that had lingered within me all day surged at the thought of Evie hanging by a rope. I shook my head profusely.

"Do you really want us *both* to get sent to the gallows?" My breath caught around the word, as if it itself was the first knot in my noose.

"Of course not, but I'm not going to simply sit by and let you take the fall for my crime."

She paced the floors of the suite, her face furrowed in fretful thought. Her servant's bun was messy and tussled from the constant shake of her head.

After a full lap across the lavish carpet, she stopped and faced me with a rather grim look. "It seems like we have three options. Option one, I turn myself in and confess that the entire scheme was my idea and that you were forced to play along by knife point."

I sat on the settee with a heavy sigh, billowing my skirts out around me. "That will *certainly* work. They'll definitely believe that the cursed daughter of a convicted thief was the victim of a well-establish noblewoman." I slumped my shoulders in defeat, no longer caring to uphold proper posture now that the secret of my upbringing was out.

"I suppose you have a point there…" She pursed her lips, tapping them thoughtfully. "I'm sure my parents will be more than happy to twist the blame onto you and claim that I was a perfect damsel in distress." She groaned, rolling her eyes. "That brings us to option two… we string together your bedsheets and make a rope for you to climb down from the balcony and escape to the kingdom of Ebonair."

My gaze drifted to the sealed doors of our suite. Despite having promised Carlex that I would continue to be treated as a guest, the king had sent a pair of guards to monitor my movements around the palace and guard my door. This meant the only way out of the room unnoticed would be from the third-story balcony…

My knees shook a touch under my skirt at the thought of such a treacherous climb. "What's option three?" I gulped, my mouth dry.

Evie let out a heavy breath, sinking into

one of the armchairs that cozied up to the unlit hearth. "Option three is you win the competition and become queen." She gave me a pitied look, and I could instantly tell what she was thinking.

It is impossible.

Before this afternoon, I had still been in first place based on my results from the first two events. But after what transpired in the art room, I had no doubt I scored zero points from the king and queen, which would have easily dropped me behind some of the other girls. There were still two events left, so technically, there was still a chance for me to reclaim my lead. However, the king decided that *he* would be choosing the final two events, and based on the amount of hatred he held toward me, I couldn't imagine he would pick challenges suited for lying handmaidens.

My gaze shifted back toward the glass balcony doors. The last rays of sun were sinking behind the horizon, bathing the glass in soft tones of orange, pink, and yellow. I imagined slinging the bedsheets off the edge, jumping into the sunset, and fleeing from the castle without looking back. As badly as I wanted to escape with my life, I wasn't sure I could run from the web I'd lain. The king still had my father in the royal dungeons. If I chose to run, he would never be permitted to see the light of day again…

Could I really trade his chance of freedom for my life?

A soft knock disrupted my thoughts and

jolted Evie out of her chair. She flicked me a curious look, and I returned it with a shrug as she approached the door. Fear swirled inside me as I wondered if it was the king or one of his knights.

Has he changed his mind about letting me compete?

I sank down against the cushions of the settee, failing to camouflage myself in my gaudy blue gown. Evie straightened her posture, then cleared her throat before opening the door, wide enough where we could both gawk at the shocking visitor.

"Y-your Highness?" Evie bumbled, her eyes wide for a moment before she blinked them back into focus on Carlex. "What can I do for you?"

I sat up from my crouch, knitting my brows together as I watched Carlex stand in the door with a shameful expression saturating his features. He rubbed his hands together with uncomfortable tension, glancing up at the two guards who stood stiff on either side of the door.

"I would like to have a word with Miss Lacey," he said quietly.

I rose from my seat, finally catching his eye as Evie motioned for him to enter. His face softened when he caught my gaze. Carlex hesitantly entered the room, still fiddling with his fingers as he approached.

"What are you doing here?" I asked. My

eyes darted back to the door as Evie pressed it closed, wondering if the guards would report Carlex's visit to the king.

He didn't answer me at first; instead, his eyes simply searched mine, as if he was looking for the honesty that wasn't there. He took in a long breath. "I came to get some answers... and also to apologize."

I nearly choked on my breath. "Apologize?"

Why would the prince be apologizing to me of all people?

Evie swept up behind me, folding her arms with a quizzical glare at the prince. "What for? Did you do something to my Lacey that I wasn't aware of?" Her protective glower earned a puzzled startle from Carlex.

I pulled Evie back a half-step. "Sorry, Carlex, this is the real Lacey. Wait, I mean—"

"Evie," she finished for me, holding out her hand toward the prince. "She means Evie. I'm Lady Genevieve, who got poor Lace into this mess."

Carlex snapped his mouth shut, raking his eyes over Evie with a new wash of understanding. "I see. Well, that answers one of my questions at least." He accepted Evie's hand with a cordial bow. "It's a pleasure to finally meet you, Lady Genevieve."

She allowed him to complete the bow, then pulled her hand away with a fierce flick of her wrist. "Now, what's this about apologizing?

Did you do something to cause her to get exposed?" A deadly aura radiated off her, causing even Carlex to flinch back a step.

"No, of course not. Well, not intentionally." He sighed, pressing a thumb to his forehead. "I came to apologize for trapping you in the competition."

He settled his gaze on me, and a soft pang tore through my chest as his eyes bore into mine. Evie uncrossed her arms, appearing somewhat appeased, but still kept a suspicious glare on him.

"I believe my father's judgment is far too harsh. I now understand that you didn't want to win the competition so you could avoid being found out. But now that your secret has been blown, I'm afraid the only way you'll be able to avoid execution is by fleeing the castle or... becoming my queen." He paused, searching my eyes once again for the answer to his unspoken question.

What do I want to do?

"We've already considered escaping out the window," Evie said nonchalantly. "But Lacey didn't seem too keen on the idea."

Carlex's shoulders turned toward me with a soft light burning behind his eyes. "You don't want to leave?" Maybe it was just my imagination, but it almost felt like there was a touch of longing buried beneath his question.

I sighed, sinking my chin down as the thought of my father weighed upon me. "I will escape," I breathed.

Carlex's shoulders dropped. "Oh, I see. If that's what you wish, then I'll—"

"No, that means she *can't* escape," Evie interrupted, giving me a *"can you believe this guy?"* kind of look. "She can only lie, remember? You have to reverse her words."

A bright red flushed up Carlex's neck. "Oh yes, that's right. My apologies."

His embarrassed blush threatened to rile a giggle up in me, and I noticed Evie biting her lip as well.

Carlex cleared his throat. "Why can't you escape? If you're worried about getting past the guards, I can offer you my aid to bypass them."

A quick jolt pulsed within my heart. *He wants to help me escape? Would he really go above his father's wishes to help save me? Perhaps he simply doesn't want his betrothal feast sullied by an execution...* I fought back a shiver at the thought, refocusing on Carlex's question.

"My *mother* only has two and a half years left of her fifteen-year sentence for being framed for theft. It's a retrial, so if I sully our family's reputation any further, she might not be released."

Evie gasped. "Oh, my kingdoms, I nearly forgot about your father! No wonder you didn't want to jump out the window." She pressed a touching hand to my arm, giving me a soft squeeze. "If you leave, you'll become a fugitive.

Your father may not even be permitted a retrial if that were to occur..."

My heart sank at the thought. Ever since Jezebel threatened to expose my curse as children, I'd been on my best behavior to ensure his chances of release weren't tarnished by my curse. But here we are... so close to the finish line and I've fallen hard.

"Wait a moment, did you say that your mothe— I mean, your *father* was framed?" He leaned forward, intrigue swallowing his expression.

I nodded, then turned to Evie. "Can you help me explain?"

Evie didn't even hesitate, and instantly unloaded the entire story I had only recently shared with her. She didn't leave out a single detail, starting with how Duke Byron had framed my father and how his daughter had gotten us shunned from the capital only a few years after. She then concluded with how Jezebel had sniffed me out due to my curse, being certain to add in only a slightly excessive number of eye rolls. It was nice having a non-cursed friend handy to explain a story in a manner that wasn't like solving a jigsaw puzzle.

Carlex paced the room, his face dizzy from the litany of information. "So that's why you got ill during dinner... And why you always asked so many questions... And why Jezebel clearly has it out for you."

Evie snorted. "Perhaps we should find another unrefined stone to curse Jezebel with. Oops, that wouldn't work; she's already a ruthless liar." Evie pressed a hand to her lips with feigned apology.

I barely noticed her antics as I fixated my gaze on Carlex, trying to dissect his thoughts after hearing my full tale. The question I'd been withholding burned in my throat, until I couldn't suppress it any longer. "Why are you trying to help me?"

I winced, half-expecting him to suddenly remember all my crimes and drag me to the gallows himself. But he didn't react; instead, he slipped his hands into his pockets, bunching his fingers into fists beneath the fabric. Evie flicked her gaze between the two of us, taking note of his quiet demeanor. Without waiting for either of us to request it, she wordlessly slipped out toward the balcony to give us some privacy. A touch of me grew uneasy as Evie left my side, but a bigger portion was grateful she'd given us a moment alone. We both watched quietly as she stepped out into the sunlit balcony and Carlex turned his focus back to me.

"I don't want you to die," he said solemnly. He took a half-step forward, jeering my heart into full throttle as his broad shoulders towered over mine. "But I don't want to force you into becoming my princess, either."

My breath caught. The dark shade of his

eyes felt both looming and protective as he gazed down at me. I'd never realized how tall he was until now... "Force me?"

"Well, if you refuse to escape, becoming my betrothed is the only chance you have at survival." His gaze shied away from mine with a pink tinge in his cheeks. He slipped one of his hands out of his pocket to run his fingers through his dark locks before looking back at me. "I keep thinking back to what you said the night we danced. I asked if you had ever felt a connection between us, and you said *no*..."

This time it was my cheeks that burned. *He remembers that?* My heart pattered relentlessly within my chest, recreating the warmth that had burned in me that night.

His lips twitched but didn't break into a smile just yet. "So, if that was a lie..."

He took another step closer, forcing me to lift my chin to match his heightened gaze.

"That leaves only one final question I have." His right hand remained buried in his pocket, but with his free hand, he gently picked up mine, lifting it up with a tender hold. A soft ripple flowed up my arm from his tender touch, warming my skin underneath his calloused fingers. "I'm not going to let you die for a crime you didn't intend to commit. It may be selfish of me, but I refuse to let something so terrible happen to you. So... how would you like to survive? Do you want to leave? Or do you want to stay and try to win?"

The fluttering in my chest overwhelmed my thoughts, drowning me in the comforting presence his words filled me with. *He won't let me die...* I looked up at him through my lashes, not trusting my eyes not to betray my swirling emotions.

If I leave, Father may never see the sun again. If I stay, I'll have to win; otherwise, Father's reputation will still be sullied after my death. The only way to help us both is if...

I met Carlex's gaze with full vulnerability, trying to imagine a world where I lived by his side as a queen. *Is such a thing even possible?* I tensed my fingers around where he still held my hand.

"Do you even think I can win?" I asked through shallow breaths.

His lips turned upward the slightest amount, hinting at the dimple I knew was hiding. "I think there's a good chance."

He removed the hand that had been burrowed in his pocket and opened up his closed palm for me to see what was inside. I gasped as I recognized the glittering radiance of a necklace set with a magic stone.

I attempted to pull back from him, but he tightened his grip on my hand to keep me close. "Hold on, it won't hurt you."

I froze, focusing on the absence of heat in my chest. I blinked at the stone, studying its glistening shine with a perplexed look. "Is it a fake?"

He shook his head and his smile broadened. "Not at all. It's actually a purification stone—one of the rarest in all the kingdoms. It doesn't react to unrefined stones the same way others do."

My breath caught in my throat, and I took a closer look at the pea-sized stone. It was embedded in a dainty silver chain and looked similar to a clear diamond, aside from the sparking magic that radiated beneath it.

"If I understand your curse correctly, it's caused by the tainted residual magic of an unrefined truth stone," Carlex explained, holding the stone up to glisten in the dwindling rays of light. "I spent the afternoon searching for this in the royal treasury. Purification stones are capable of absorbing tainted magic, which leads me to believe that this stone might be able to nullify the effects of your curse. Well, at least until the stone grows oversaturated with the tainted magic. They sort of work like a sponge, except you can't wring them out after they get too full."

I could barely believe what I was hearing. *Is he saying that my curse could be lifted? Even just temporarily?*

My gaze followed the shifting light of the stone in disbelief. "Do you think wearing a purification stone will be enough to help me win?"

Carlex's smile grew into a soft smirk. "I do," he breathed. "You've already proven that you're capable of winning, even while restrained by lies. I'm not supposed to know this, but the next event will revolve around another riddle. I have no information what the riddle is based upon, only that a riddle will be involved. Without the burden of your curse, I fully believe you could win." He paused, holding out the necklace to me with a heavy look. "But is that what you want?"

My head spun wildly in attempt to keep up with my hammering heart. My blood burned like fire in my veins, urging me to sit and process the prince's words, even though I knew sitting wouldn't help. In some ways, I didn't have a choice, but at the same time, I didn't feel like I was being backed into a corner. In fact, it felt more like a sealed door had finally been opened, and for the first time in my life, I could be honest about what I truly wanted to do. My heart warmed as my gaze moved from the sparkling necklace to the longing look in Carlex's eyes.

He knows what will happen if I win... Is that what he wants, too?

I hesitantly reached out my hand, touching it to the clear stone with a trembling finger. The magic instantly swirled through my touch causing me to flinch in fear of the pain that never came. Instead, the magic sent a soothing ripple through my blood, warming me with a calming presence.

I raised my gaze to his, feeling the light of the stone reflect in my eyes. I opened my mouth to speak and for the first time in years, my tongue obeyed my wishes.

"I want to win."

Carlex beamed with joy, and he released the stone, allowing me to hold the necklace in my palm. "Then let me help you."

chapter nineteen

I slept peacefully for the first time since staying at the castle. Evie and I spent the morning eating breakfast alone since I likely wouldn't be welcomed to dine with the other girls any longer. As we ate our pastries and eggs, my gaze kept drifting over to where the purity stone necklace rested on the vanity. The clear gem had already developed a pinpoint-sized dark spot in the center from my single use of it yesterday, but its sparkle still caught the sun's glow like a ray of hope.

The relief it had given me from my curse seemed almost surreal, and I itched to touch it again, if only to remind myself that it truly worked. But I had to refrain from even going near it until the next event. The stone was powerful, but its small size didn't give it much longevity. If Carlex was correct about the next event being another riddle, then I would need to be certain my lies could be maintained long enough for me to solve it.

"It's rather pretty, isn't it?" Evie interrupted my thoughts with a smug smile from behind her teacup. She must have noticed me staring at the necklace.

"I've seen prettier..." I averted my gaze from her as the lie rushed the blood to my cheeks.

Technically, it wasn't fully a lie since I'd definitely seen grander jewels than the simple chain before. However, those jewels all paled in comparison to the beauty I found in Carlex's gift. It wasn't just any necklace that could change my life for a night...

"Is that so...?" Evie dragged out her voice with a humored tug of her brow. I pretended to be extra invested in my teacup and added another sugar cube just to watch it dissolve. Evie leaned back into her seat with a soft giggle. "Oh, just admit it, Lacey. It's not just that necklace that has you smitten..."

My heart fluttered without permission at her leading words, but I didn't look up from the dissipating sugar crystals. "I don't know what you mean." I pressed my lips together, feeling her gaze grow even giddier. I tried not to notice and dropped another sugar cube into my cup.

"Right..." She smirked, taking a long sip from her cup. "In that case, do you mind if I ask you something?" She prodded with a mischievous grin.

Oh no, that's the face she makes whenever she's plotting something...

"No."

"Perfect! Cause I was going to ask you

either way." She happily accepted my lie as a proper reply with a joyful clasp of her fingers. I finally looked up from my teacup with a displeased scowl that she didn't even bat an eye at. "So, tell me straight, yes or no… Do you have feelings for the prince?"

My cheeks flared with heat as I set my teacup down with a slosh. "Evie!" I gasped as my heart thumped wildly in my chest. "You should ask that kind of question directly!"

"I know I should, that's why I did," she said smugly, resting her chin in her hand with an evil glint in her eyes.

You smarmy little noble… You know perfectly well that I'm lying.

"Why do you need to know?" I challenged with a glare of my own.

She shrugged. "I don't, but I know you want to tell me, don't you?"

"Yes!"

"Alright, go ahead, then." She leaned forward expectantly with a wicked, yet playful grin. "Come on, Lace. I'm your best friend, who's trying to help you marry a prince to preserve your life. If you're going to try to win, then at least let me help you forge a connection with him before you tie the knot." She clasped her hands together, batting her lashes with an exaggerated pout. "*Please*… If you truly don't like him, then I can start making plans for his assassination after your wedding."

She's impossible...

I let out a defeated sigh, rubbing my throbbing temples. "Alright, fine. The answer is no!"

She gasped. "No, what!? No, you don't care for him?"

"Yes!"

"Yes, you care!?"

"No!"

"No, what?" Carlex's voice split through the air like the shatter of glass. Evie and I whipped our heads around the room in search of the sound until we found him standing by the balcony doors. "Sorry, I didn't mean to startle you. I just knew that if I wanted to visit, I couldn't keep using the main doors with the guards standing watch."

We both gawked at him in astonishment as he casually ran a hand through his hair. My blood burned with the heat of embarrassment as I found myself replaying the last bits of my conversation with Evie.

How much had he heard!? When did he come in? How did he get up to the balcony!?

"How did you get out there? We're on the third floor, for kingdom's sake." Evie's jaw dropped inelegantly as she slowly rose from her seat.

"Oh, I just vaulted from the neighboring balcony. It's attached to another guest suite and it's only a few feet to jump." He pointed nonchalantly out the window to the neighboring balcony, causing my chest to tighten with fear at the sight of the large gap he had scaled.

"Alright... I'll admit that's impressive," Evie said with a reluctant puff of her loose curls. "But next time, make sure you knock. What if we had been dressing?"

Carlex's eyes locked onto me, then widened with panicked embarrassment. His face turned red enough to shame a sunburnt rose. "Ah... I-I didn't consider— Please, forgive my intrusion." His bumbling earned a soft snort from Evie, and we shared a humored look before I looked back at him.

"Apology not accepted." I smiled warmly and the red in his cheeks slowly diluted. "Now what are you doing here?"

His shame melted after that, and he stood more assuredly as he pressed further into the room. "Well, like I said last night, I want to help you win. Rumors are still circulating that the king is going to base the next challenge around a riddle, so I want to help you prepare in any way I can." His voice was laced with determination, sending a warm pulse through my chest.

Maybe it was because of my recent confession to Evie, but for some reason I felt far more vulnerable under Carlex's warm gaze than I ever had before. *He really wants me to win, doesn't he...? Is it because he doesn't want to carry the guilt of my death?*

"I'm actually not very good at riddles." I gave him a shy smile. Evie stood a few steps away from where Carlex and I were now conversing, but I could still feel her sparkling eyes soaking in our conversation like a sappy romance book.

"You're not? Oh! That's right, lies... Got it." He cleared his throat, brushing off his mistake as I bit back a giggle. He hadn't quite picked up on translating my words as quickly as Evie had, but it was sweet to see him trying so hard. "I suppose you did win the first event after all. Perhaps my help isn't as necessary as I thought." His gaze twinkled with admiration. Why did Evie have to go make me admit the truth about my developing feelings... Now it was harder to deny that they were there.

"Oh, it's very much still necessary," Evie interjected, flicking me a private wink as she crossed in front of me. "Lacey may be talented, clever, beautiful, and an excellent hairstylist, but she will still require as much of your assistance that you can lend. Isn't that right, Lacey?"

Evie! Could you be any more obvious!?

I bit the inside of my cheek in attempt to suppress the mortification on my face. "I-I suppose I don't need that much help..."

Carlex smiled, revealing the sweet dimple on his cheek. "If you don't mind my company, then I would be more than happy to stop by whenever I can."

"As long as you knock." Evie folded her

arms with a taut glare.

Carlex rubbed an awkward hand along his neck. "Yes, of course. Again, my apologies."

I couldn't help but let out a light laugh, and Evie seemed to appear equally amused by his shame. Evie turned back to where we had left our breakfast trays and stacked them in her arms. "I'm going to return these to the kitchen. You two can go ahead and get started on your riddle lessons without me." I reached out a hand to try to stop her, but she didn't even pause long enough to slip me another mischievous smile.

My nerves flared inside me as I watched the door swing shut, leaving the prince and me alone in the massive suite. I turned back to him with shy eyes, and my heart surged the moment he gave me a casual smile.

"Shall we get started?" His voice was gentle and sweet, causing the caged emotions inside me to attempt to break free.

I nodded, then led him to the armchairs. As we sat, my gaze landed back on the glittering necklace that rested atop the vanity, sending another pleasant flutter through my chest. "Before we begin..." I paused, biting my tongue as I waited for his focus to latch onto me. "I-I just wanted to say, no thank you. For the bracelet, I mean."

His face furrowed for a moment before lighting with clarity. "Oh, of course." His eyes shifted to the floor. "It's honestly the least I can do. No citizen of mine should be forced to live with the burden of a curse. I'm sorry I can't do more for you."

"Do more?" I implored. "But, Your Highness, I deserve your apology more than anyone else. Don't you remember how *honest* I was with you throughout the first events?"

I lied so much to you... I have no right to care for you.

His expression softened as shame enveloped my face. He shifted forward in his chair as if trying to reach out to me, but our seats were spaced too far apart to form any contact.

"Lacey, I know you lied to me, but I also know why..." His voice trailed off, and I noticed his gaze lock onto my hand. I longed for him to reach for it, craving his reassurance that my curse hadn't harmed him as much as I feared. "I'll admit, it was hard at first... I thought I knew what you wanted—that you wanted nothing to do with me—and to be honest, I was willing to accept that. But now that I've gone back and picked through our conversations... I think I know where the lies were, and I must say..." His eyes warmed with an unspoken joy that could only be paired with a true smile. "I'm glad they were lies, because it showed me how badly I was craving something else to be true."

My heart swirled with a mixture of disbelief and ease. *He was glad that they were lies...* Never in my life had I expected someone to appreciate my curse. So many questions flooded my mind. I wanted to know what parts he had craved to be true, and whether that meant he still cared for me like before.

He had mentioned he was willing to accept that I wanted nothing to do with him... Had that changed?

"Anyway, are you ready to try a few riddles?" He laced his fingers together, stretching them out in front of him with a crack of his knuckles.

I wanted to laugh at the question, because right now, it felt like I was already in the middle of trying to decipher one. Lies could complicate things, but sometimes the truth was even more disorienting.

"No, I'm not ready." I nodded in approval, but deep down, I wondered if the curse had just let the truth slip...

chapter twenty

For the next two days, Carlex visited me as often as he could. The scores from the third event unveiled that I had dropped from first to third place after my pathetic painting score, so Carlex insisted I be extra prepared for the fourth event. Every morning and afternoon he stopped by my suite so he and Evie could drill me with riddles and word puzzles in preparation. I used to believe I was rather good at thinking outside the box, but after three full days of endless riddles, I felt like I might implode from so much overthinking.

Evie tugged my dress laces, forcing a breath out of me as she sealed me into the dark gray ballgown. The setting sun glittered against the silver embroidery that veined the skirt and bodice, glistening like a morning dew on a dark branch. As beautiful as the gown looked, I knew there was no chance I would impress anyone at tonight's dinner. They all knew the truth behind my identity now, and in their eyes, I was only a peasant playing dress-up.

It became impossible to spend any time around the other women after my unveiling, especially since Jezebel had taken the liberty of spinning tales of my true character. For the last three days, I hadn't even bothered to eat my meals with the other girls, and instead continued requesting they be delivered to my suite, but tonight such a request wouldn't be granted...

Tonight is the fourth event.

"You'll do great, Lace." Evie gave me a reassuring smile in the mirror as she carefully placed the purification stone necklace around my neck.

The tiny black dot starkly contrasted with the rest of the clear stone. I pressed my hand against where the stone touched my neck, allowing the stirring energy within the jewel to sync with my pulsating heart.

An odd sensation filled my chest as the stone settled against my skin. It felt almost like a suction that pulled away at the entanglement that had knotted throughout me. I glanced back at the stone in the mirror and already noticed that the clarity had dulled the smallest amount.

How long will the stone last against my curse? Will it be able to make it through the evening?

A soft knock on the door alerted me that it was time to depart for the dining room, but I turned around to sweep Evie in a hug before she could answer the door. She startled from the sudden latch, then returned the hug with her own squeeze. My tongue loosened in my mouth, filling my mind with a dozen truths I wanted to speak while it lasted.

"I just wanted to let you know, while I still can..." I pulled away from the embrace, meeting her eyes for the first truth I had ever spoken to my best friend, "that I couldn't do this without you." My words felt almost melodic as the truth passed unrestricted through my vocal cords.

It really works. For at least tonight, I'm not cursed.

Evie's eyes welled up for a moment, and she yanked me back into the hug once more. "You shouldn't have to do this at all," she breathed solemnly. "But I'm hoping you still end up getting something out of this mess."

I blushed, knowing exactly what she was referring to. Carlex's visits had only fueled the growing feelings I had tried so desperately to avoid. Now that I'd agreed to try my hand at winning, I'd been showing him more of the *real* Lacey, but I wasn't sure what he thought of her yet...

She pulled away from the squeeze, giving me a knowing look as she turned for the door. "Here's to hoping you can win your prince."

• •

Dinner was quieter than normal, but mostly because everyone was actually quiet. Tension waded in the room like a thick slurry, silencing each girl where they sat. I was seated on the opposite end of the table from Carlex, and fortunately, a fair amount of seats away from Jezebel as well. The food was rich and savory, making it hard for my anxious stomach to handle. For the entire meal, hardly anyone spoke and only passed silent gazes between each other at the table.

Is this what it's like to be the black sheep?

It wasn't surprising that no one wanted to speak in my presence. I was an intruder, a mere commoner that none of them should have been associating with in the first place. Despite the heavy tension, I didn't mind the quiet. It made it easier for me to keep my mouth shut and preserve the energy of the stone that graced my neck.

Carlex's gaze drifted toward my neckline, eyeing the stone with a slight smile. I gave him a coy look, raising my hand over my bosom with a silent look of offense. He sucked in his cheeks at my playful tease, turning his face the brightest shade of red I had ever seen. He raised a napkin to his mouth to try to hide the blush, then averted his gaze from me entirely as I tried to swallow back a laugh.

It's nice to know I can joke with him. Because if I win...

"Good evening, everyone." King Aldrich entered the room with a flat expression, shifting every eye toward the door. The humor within me was snuffed out in an instant, suffocated under the smothering glare of the Reclusian king. "I hope you all have been enjoying yourselves these last few days, but I'm afraid the time for rest has ceased. It is now time to begin the fourth event. So, if you will please follow me to the meeting hall, I shall explain the rules upon our arrival."

The meeting hall? Perhaps that is a good place for asking riddles?

We all funneled through the door with me shifting to the back of the crowd. Carlex lingered back by pretending to hold the door open, then slid behind me to follow my steps. We fell back a few paces and he leaned over to my ear.

"Sorry for staring, but the necklace just looked a little..."

"Dull? I know, it seems to be fading faster than we expected," I whispered, relishing in the ability to speak my true thoughts.

A soft smile quirked at his lips. "Well, it at least seems to be working. You look happier."

My cheeks warmed, and I lowered my lashes with a curling smile. "I can *honestly* say that I am. I just wish it could last forever." I pressed my hand to the stone, already feeling the energy inside it fading.

Carlex's gaze followed where I clutched the necklace, his face growing worried. "Let's just hope it lasts long enough to make it through tonight."

As we neared the meeting room, Carlex split off from me to linger behind the cluster of girls. The room was large, but not quite as grand as the ballroom or warm as the drawing room. There were fifteen chairs lined up in a row along the far wall, with a podium in the center of the room. The king took his place at the front of the room and was soon followed by Carlex. They stood just beyond the podium facing it head-on.

We all filed into the room, standing in front of the line-up of chairs, but not yet sitting. I continued to glance around the room in case there would be any riddle clues in plain sight, like the blue curtain at the first ball. But aside from the podium and chairs, there was only a small table that rested beside the podium, covered by a tan sheet.

"Welcome, everyone, to the fourth event of my son's bridal competition." King Aldrich's voice boomed in the small space, resonating off the walls with a fullness that reminded me of his blistering anger only a few days prior. "For this event, you will be tested on a few different areas, including quick thinking, memory, and..." his eyes turned directly to me, "honesty."

Carlex's expression instantly turned vengeful as he shot his father an angered glare. My shoulders sank a few inches, but I tried not to look too intimidated.

Quick thinking, memory, and honesty? Those are still qualities found in riddle-solving, right?

"A true queen knows the value in truth, so tonight you will be tested on your ability to be honest and accurate in your facts." A small smirk tugged at the king's mouth as he narrowed his eyes on me.

He designed this challenge to knock me out of the competition... My heart raced with fresh adrenaline as I focused my attention on the pulsating warmth around my neck. *Let's see if his plan will actually work.*

The king continued. "This will be a turn-based challenge, where each of you will approach the podium and state a single fact to Prince Carlex. The fact must be a true statement about *only* yourself, and it cannot be something that you and the prince have in common. Once a competitor uses a statement, no one else shall be permitted to repeat it. For example, I could approach the prince and say, 'I am a king.' That is a statement that is true for me and not for him, therefore it is acceptable. However, if I were to say, 'I am a royal,' that statement is true for the *both* of us, therefore it does not count, and I would be disqualified. Each statement may only be used once, so you'll have to consider facts that are unique to you and that the other girls can't use. This test will also help you to share parts of yourself that Carlex may not have previously known, helping him to develop a better understanding of you all as individuals."

Carlex looked as if he was ready to implode. His jaw was locked tight, clenched with his veined fists that he held clasped in front of him. It was no mystery what the king was trying to do. Aside from knocking me out of the running, he was also trying to force new connections with the other girls by making them open up about themselves. The king clearly knew that Carlex had a soft spot for me, and it seemed as if he was going to do everything in his power to overshadow it.

"Lying is also not permitted," the king said brashly, stepping forward to the table that rested beside the podium. He pulled off the sheet that covered it and a sudden pain jolted through my chest as my gaze fell on the massive stone that had been hidden beneath it. "This is a truth stone." The king smiled devilishly, sending a sick chill down my spine. "When you approach the podium, you will be required to place a hand on the stone. If your statement is true, then the stone will illuminate, but if your statement is false, it will dim. This will ensure that everyone maintains integrity and doesn't share any statements we can't verify."

A magic stone...

I touched my hand to my necklace once more, clutching it like the smallest shield in existence. *Carlex said the necklace would absorb the tainted magic from my curse, but would it absorb enough to prevent my body from conflicting with the truth stone?* I eyed the glistening rock with horror, feeling my chest tighten within me at the sheer size of it. The unrefined stone I had been cursed with was a truth stone... Was this the king's version of a sick joke?

Carlex's face burned with rage. He grabbed his father by the arm, yanking him into his hissing growl. "What is this? Are you really so cruel as to risk Lacey's life to humor your ridiculous pride?" Carlex's hand clawed at his father's sleeve, threatening to tear the fabric at any moment.

The king's face remained stark as he slowly turned to match his son's steel gaze. "This is a competition, son. If the competitors can't handle the event, then they can't handle the kingdom, either." He pulled away from the prince to face us, leaving Carlex to swallow his anger.

Carlex darted his gaze over to me, his face full of concern. I looked over at the glistening stone and instantly sensed the hairs on the back of my neck prickle. The necklace left a warm spot at the base of my throat, and I tried to focus on its miniscule shield with an unspoken plea.

Please don't let the powers clash... Please, please be strong enough.

"Since each statement can only be used once, there is a bit of an advantage to whoever goes first since no statements are off limits yet. Therefore, I shall be drawing your turns at random." King Aldrich pulled a small bag from his pocket that presumably held all our names. "If you cannot state a true fact, if you state a fact that you and the prince have in common, or if you repeat a fact someone else has used, then you will be eliminated. The rounds will continue for as long as necessary until we have a winner. Now, are there any questions?"

My gut twisted into knots as I glanced between the truth stone and the king.

I just have one question... Is this game designed to be an informal execution?

"Excellent," King Aldrich interrupted my thoughts as he dug his hand into the bag of names and selected a slim piece of parchment. "First up to the podium... Lyra of Bellatring." All eyes shot to the dark-haired princess as she calmly straightened before gliding across the floor to approach the podium. The king smiled fondly at her as she stretched out her hand to gently touch the vibrant stone. "Whenever you're ready."

Lyra took in a smooth breath. "I am a woman." To no one's surprise, the stone illuminated instantly, confirming her truth.

The king looked at Carlex, who gave him an unamused glare before readdressing Lyra with a far more polite look. He stepped forward and placed his own hand on the truth stone.

"I am not a woman," he paused until the stone illuminated then pulled his hand back. "We do not have that in common. Well done, please take a seat." Carlex gestured to the first chair that lined the wall and Lyra silently made her way to it.

One by one the names were drawn, and each girl stated a fairly obvious fact to get them through the first round.

"I'm only sixteen."

"I have siblings."

"I'm wearing a dress."

"My eyes are blue."

With each passing name, my nerves spun tighter as I realized just how difficult it would be standing as the last one in the line-up. Most of the obvious statements had already been spoken, so I was going to have to get a little more creative. When the fifteenth name was called and Sasha approached the podium, I caught the slightest glint of a smirk from the king's face. Carlex must have noticed it too, based on the white knuckles that dotted his fists.

A random name drawing indeed...

Sasha's hand trembled a little nervously as she reached out and touched the stone. "I-I love birds." The stone illuminated instantly, and all eyes turned to Carlex as he touched the stone after her.

"I'm not that fond of birds." The stone lit, and he nodded to Sasha. "You may continue on; please, have a seat."

Sasha let out a heavy sigh of relief then found her seat, leaving only me standing.

All focus shifted to me as I stared anxiously at the glistening stone. A stone that large was certain to have a vast amount of power stored inside it, so how long would it take for it to overrun the protection of my tiny necklace? Would the necklace even be able to protect me at all?

"Lacey Arachne." King Aldrich's voice lost all the light it had possessed for the previous competitors as he glared at me in distaste. "Please, approach the podium."

chapter twenty-one

I approached the stone with heavy steps, gauging the pressure inside me with every inch. There was definitely some form of confliction occurring, because my chest felt more constricted the closer I got, yet there was no heat or splitting pain. When I sat next to Princess Amirah, the pain grew alongside the pressure, but this time, it only felt like I was being slowly squeezed.

Maybe the necklace is capable of protecting me after all.

I stepped up onto the podium, feeling as if my corset had been taken in another three inches. The base of my neck grew hotter underneath the burning stone, signaling that it was in active use. I itched to look down at the necklace and see if the clarity of it had faded further, but I didn't want to lose focus for even an instant.

The back of my head burned with the searing glares of my fellow competitors, but the king's gaze was far more intense. He watched me with puzzled fury as I slowly reached out and placed my hand atop the cool stone. My veins constricted at the contact, tensing my muscles and locking my arms in place as the magic rebelled against the slim armor I wore around my throat. I took in a shallow breath, then turned a firm gaze onto the king as I silently dared him to question me. He narrowed his eyes, but remained quiet, waiting for me to either combust or eliminate myself with a lie.

We'll see if he underestimates me after this...

I stared directly into the king's eyes. "I'm a commoner."

Gasps flooded the room even before the stone illuminated, proving my truth. King Aldrich's face turned as white as the radiating light as he stared at the stone in disbelief.

"No..." Jezebel sneered behind me, skewering me with her beady glare from the edge of my vision.

I looked up at Carlex, who was already grinning from ear to ear and potentially biting back a bursting laugh. I wanted to smile back, but the tension inside kept my lips pressed into a fine line. Carlex snuck his father a smug lift of his brow as he placed his hand on the stone, only an inch beside mine. "I am not a commoner." Carlex glared at his father proudly as the light radiated off the stone. "Well done, Lacey. You may proceed to the next round."

I swallowed my pressing nerves, then quickly removed my hand from the stone and hurried to my seat. Wide eyes followed me as I crossed the room, each full of confusion and wonder. Jezebel's face was red enough to shame a strawberry as she honed-in on my necklace. Her brow wrinkled together with fuming rage as she impressively held her tongue from letting out any biting insults. She hated it because I had actually played fair. There were no rules about wearing magic stones to the events—and if there had been, Princess Amirah would have lost points ages ago. For at least tonight, I was a worthy competitor. A tug of fear eclipsed my victorious mood as I watched Princess Lyra approach the podium for her second round.

I may be on an even playing field now, but that doesn't mean I have an advantage. If I want to survive, I have to win.

"I can play the harp," Lyra stated as her hand glowed atop the brightening stone.

"I cannot," Carlex replied with another confirmation.

One by one, the girls returned to the podium, but this time, they had statements that were less generic than the first round. Adrenaline stirred up inside me as I tried to consider a few good facts that I could have handy. The more I tried to reflect back on useful bits of information, the more I realized I actually possessed a rather long list of statements. My lips parted in a stunned gape as I recognized that the king had made a fatal flaw in crafting a competition to try to single me out.

He'd singled me out in a good way, too… I have far less in common with Carlex and the other girls because I'm from a completely different rank.

"I've studied cartography," Gabrielle said smoothly, causing the stone to glow once more.

Carlex's face stiffened. "So have I." The stone illuminated beneath his touch, confirming they had the fact in common. Gabrielle's shoulders shrank down, reflecting her instant disappointment. "I'm sorry, Gabrielle, but you have been eliminated."

A quiet huff left Gabrielle's lips as she pouted back to her seat. Before we got back to me, two more girls were eliminated for sharing facts they held in common with the prince, narrowing the number of competitors down to twelve.

I returned to the podium, and instantly noticed the warmth of Carlex's smile as he latched eyes with me from across the room. The pressure in my chest was a bit more constricting this time, but it was easy enough to ignore as I breathed out my next fact.

"I've slept in the streets." The stone illuminated white, and this time, only silence followed my words. I didn't even bother to look at the king, this time watching Carlex's smile drift into a dismal gape.

Maybe that one should have been left unspoken…

I blinked away from his somber eyes. I

wasn't attempting to earn his pity, only produce a fact that I was certain we wouldn't have in common. Nonetheless, his gaze lingered, tangling my heart into an emotional frenzy. I glanced up at the king, expecting him to urge Carlex into giving his response, but to my surprise, the king's face was entirely blank. He seemed to be studying me, as if he was unsure what to make of the lying girl who appeared to actually be telling the truth.

"I-I have not." Carlex finally broke the silence, his face still heavy as the light beamed under his touch. "Please return to your seat."

I didn't hesitate to remove my hand from the stone. My gaze fixated on the floor as I returned to my seat, uninterested in letting the other girls catch sight of stirring feelings.

The rounds continued, knocking a few girls out each time. I continued to use statements about my life as a commoner to push myself ahead, claiming I'd milked cows, washed laundry, and even made money selling looms. Each time I approached the podium, Carlex seemed to smile at me with more curiosity than he had prior. The king may have designed this event as a way for Carlex to learn more about the other girls, but it seemed to me that this event was just allowing us to learn more about each other. In this challenge alone I've learned that Carlex dislikes birds, can't dance ballet, and prefers muffins over pie. As the competition continued, I found myself growing eager to hear what the other girls would say so I could guess whether or not the statement was true for Carlex.

Every once in a while, Carlex would direct his answer to me instead of the other girls, but he would never smile unless I was at the podium. The event was so enjoyable, that I hardly even remembered that I was competing for my life until the heat beneath my throat began to fade. I glanced down at my necklace and bit back a gasp. The stone had become a dark gray, nearly fully saturated in the tainted magic it had been collecting. I glanced nervously up at Princess Amirah as she posed her hand above the truth stone with practiced grace.

It is just down to her, Jezebel, and me now... Will the necklace be able to last until the end?

My fingers twisted around a loose strand of my hair as I watched Amirah get eliminated. She returned to her seat with sealed lips, not giving any clues to the emotions that stirred from her loss. I risked a glance across the chairs at Jezebel, who was already glaring at me with murderous intent.

She's not going to go down easy...

Jezebel started to rise from her seat to approach for her turn, but before she could stand, the king held up a hand to pause her. "Before we continue, there is one final rule that will come into play now that we are down to our final two competitors." Something roiled inside me as I shared a nervous glance with Carlex. *A new rule?* "As you know, one of the rules of this competition is that all competitors shall be judged fairly, no matter their rank or status. I feel that this rule has been neglected in this game due to the *differences* in status, therefore I will be invoking that for the remainder of this game, no statements that are specific to your social status shall be permitted."

My hopes of winning dimmed with the light of my darkening necklace as I stared blankly at the king's unmoving lips. *I can't bring up anything relevant to my status? But what all does that include?* I chewed my lip until I tasted blood, unable to feel the pain as my terror numbed my entire body.

It's the king's rule, therefore he could deem nearly anything I say now as impermissible.

A wicked smile graced Jezebel's ruby lips as she slipped me a victorious glare. Carlex's face soured as he glared venomously at his father. He opened his mouth as if to argue, but ended up clenching his jaw as Jezebel approached the podium without waiting for him to start a dispute. She daintily placed her hand atop the sparkling stone, tapping her fingers against the top as if taunting me that she could touch it so freely. Deep-rooted frustration tunneled through my core as I grinded my teeth together with fury. My anger overwhelmed my fears to the point where I had to force myself to sit still instead of reddening her mouth even more with a bloody lip.

She slipped me a pretentious smile before turning to face the prince with fluttering eyes. "I enjoy silk painting." She projected proudly as she beamed back at the glowing stone.

Carlex's expression tightened, his hand stiffening on the stone. "So do I."

The stone beamed white.

I sucked in a breath, feeling my heart soar to life as I watched the color drain from both the king and Jezebel. Jezebel snaked her hand away from the stone, flinging her arms in the air in astonishment.

"But, Your Highness, that doesn't make any sense. How could *you* enjoy silk painting, of all things?" She pressed her hands tautly to her hips, making a far bigger scene than necessary.

Carlex's expression remained hardened as stone, showing no amusement for her complaints. "I enjoy silk painting and dying. I learned it from my mother and find it calming. I even hand-dyed all the silk cords that were used in the second event." The stone continued to blaze a soft white, illuminating the pale color that saturated Jezebel's features. "Now, please return to your seat; you've been eliminated."

"Not quite!" King Aldrich interjected, causing me to jump from my pent-up nerves. "Lacey still has to successfully complete one final round before she can be named the winner; otherwise, Jezebel will be given another attempt."

I swallowed hard, feeling the burn seep into my throat from beneath the necklace. Carlex looked ready to pummel his father into the dirt, but his face softened as he watched me rise from my seat and approach the podium with my dwindling threads of confidence. I snuck a glance down at my necklace, wondering if it would last even through another word. Already I could feel my tongue starting to tighten with the curse itching to snatch back the reigns. The burning from the purification stone reached all around my neck, encircling my throat with the reminder of the consequences that would follow my failure.

If I don't win this, my necklace will be turned into a noose.

Sweat beaded across my brow as I hesitated to touch the truth stone, wary that the moment I did, the last of my necklace's magic would be sucked away. I only had one shot at this, if even that. What was true about me that wasn't true about him? And had nothing to do with my status? I flicked my eyes up at Carlex, searching his face for any clues or support, but all I could focus on was his anxious, yet reassuring smile.

His smile!

I pressed my hand to the stone, sensing the slightest prick of pain in my chest at the touch. "I d-don't have dimples." My throat tightened on my words. The moment the stone confirmed my statement, I snaked my hand away and clutched it close to my throbbing chest.

"Neither does the prince," Jezebel scoffed, rolling her eyes in annoyance. "Now step aside. I have my next fact ready."

"Actually, I do." Carlex stepped forward, touching his hand to the stone to reveal its soft glow. "They're just hard to notice..." His gaze fixated on me with a soft surprise that seemed to touch him deeper than I could see.

The king took in a soft breath, one that actually shocked me as I glanced over to see the stunned expression tainting his hard eyes.

"It's true..." King Aldrich's voice was stark and wavering. He seemed at a loss for words, opening his mouth and closing it a number of times before finishing the thought that was trapped on his tongue. "They just only come out around certain people..."

He looked to his son with a puzzled expression, digging into Carlex's feature's as if his dimples were somehow more visible than he recalled. I caught his gaze for a brief moment, and nearly jolted as I noticed the broken denial in his crinkled eyes.

My breath caught as the king averted his gaze from me, almost ashamed to admit that I had actually won. The growing burn in my chest seemed irrelevant as the sweet feeling of victory swelled inside me.

I did it... I actually did it.

The king let out a tight breath, turning to the awe-struck competitors with a tightlipped smile. "The scores for tonight's events shall be announced in the morning. Well done, everyone; I shall see you again for the fifth and final event," his eyes dimmed, but they weren't as stern as before, "where we shall select our future queen."

chapter twenty-two

Second place...

I paced the palace gardens as the light of dawn crested over the cherry blossoms. The scores were announced before daybreak. I had earned the highest score during last night's events, but overall, I still only ranked second to Jezebel. The morning mist cooled my skin and clung to my lashes, causing my blinks to slow. The soft haze of morning burned a warm amber color, painting the blooming azalea bushes across its vibrant canvas. I stopped to admire the sunrise and attempted to allow its beauty to distract me from the terror clawing inside my heart.

This isn't over yet...

The two guards who had been assigned to me ever since my discovery lingered back a few paces, keeping their eyes glued to my movements. Despite being free to explore the palace grounds, I was still essentially a prisoner of the king until it was decided if I'd be executed.

The thought dizzied me, luring me toward a damp bench that rested beneath a willow tree.

I quickly seated myself and tried to slow my clipped breaths before I spiraled into a full-on panic.

It's going to be alright, Lacey. You just have to beat Jezebel one final time. Besides, Carlex said he won't let you die...

My breathing steadied as the image of his warm smile filtered through my pulsing mind. Without thinking, I pressed my hand to the necklace that still graced my neck. The stone had long since faded to ebony, and my curse had resumed its previous control, but I couldn't bring myself to part with the trinket just yet. It had been more than just a magic rock hidden in a chain. It was tangible proof that the prince of Reclusia found my life valuable enough to preserve. I laced my fingers around the chain, stringing my fingers up and down the metal like a cord of string.

He doesn't just want me to live... he wants me to win.

"Lacey? Is that you?"

I dropped the necklace with a flush of my cheeks as I turned toward Carlex's sudden voice. He must have spotted me through the rose bushes because I couldn't see him until he stepped out from behind their flourishing leaves.

"No," I squeaked. "Not me."

A humored grin rose up Carlex's face as he approached the bench. "Sorry to frighten you. Evie told me I might find you out here." He chuckled lightly, taking a seat on the dew-coated bench with me. He snuck the guards following me a stern glare, and the pair backed off into the garden, giving me my first true moment of freedom since they'd been assigned to me.

My face felt hot as I realized just how close he was sitting to me on the narrow bench. "Are you an early riser?" My voice cracked awkwardly, betraying the nervousness I was attempting to bury.

Carlex gazed longingly at the cresting sun, taking in a full breath of the morning air with a blissful sigh. "I prefer to be. Though there are many mornings I sleep in after long nights of ballroom schmoozing." He settled back onto the bench, admiring the sunrise with wide eyes.

As artful as the sky had become, I found my gaze drawn to the prince instead. The wonder that filled his chocolate eyes illuminated with the swirling pinks and oranges that danced across the mist. He turned his attention back to me, causing me to flinch after being caught staring. He didn't seem perturbed by my gawking, because his expression didn't change in the slightest. He continued to look at me the same way he had looked at the painted sky... as if I were some sort of treasured artwork he didn't want to lose sight of.

Does he even realize he is looking at me like that...?

His gaze caught on my necklace and his

smile lowered the smallest bit. "Goodness, the stone looks like a lump of coal now."

I reached down to brush against the blackened stone. "Yes, it would appear that my curse has little effect on it." I looked down at the tainted stone, taking in the sight of the filthy magic that had clouded such a beautiful rock. "It's fortunate it faded so quickly..."

My fingers traced up from the necklace to my throat, touching at the cage that trapped my true words. The curse somehow felt even more unbearable after having a night of freedom from it. I was in the presence of a prince for kingdom's sake... I shouldn't be lying to him with every breath I took. My eyes lowered as shame brushed against my heart, pushing away the blossoming affection I had allowed to take root.

Even if I win this, Carlex deserves better than me...

A warm touch caused my chin to lift as Carlex pulled my hand away from my cursed throat. His eyes were gentle and full of sympathy as he cradled my hand in both of his with a gentle pet. My breath caught as a calming pulse rippled out from where he stroked my skin.

"I'm sorry it didn't last past the competition," he soothed sweetly as the wind brushed his dark hair across his brow. "But it was nice to hear you, the real you, last night."

His words left me melted as I stared at him in hopeful surprise. I hadn't expected him to enjoy hearing about my life as a commoner— I had merely hoped the facts would keep me in the game. Yet, when I searched his expression for sincerity, I could tell he truly meant what he had said.

I bit my lip, suppressing a nervous smile. "I didn't enjoy the event, either. There wasn't much for me to learn about you."

Carlex's brow tilted curiously. "Oh? So, you were paying attention, were you?" He gave my hand an excited squeeze.

"Not at all." I giggled. "I learned nothing about your hatred towards birds, your love of studying, or your interest in silk painting."

His smile widened and he eagerly scooted another inch closer to me, earning another giggle. "I suppose I did expose a large amount about myself, but I hadn't expected you to commit it all to memory. Tell me, what else did you learn?" He nodded, urging me to continue.

"Well, I discovered that you and Jezebel have *lots* in common as well." I laughed playfully while rolling my eyes.

Carlex made a face, shuddering from the mention of her name. "That woman makes me want to say words a prince shouldn't even be allowed to know. Honestly, I don't know what Father was thinking when he planned that event. The only reason Jezebel made it as far as she did was because we truly have so *little* in common." He pressed a hand to his throat, forcing back a gag. "Sorry, I just recalled the scores from this morning... If Jezebel wins, I think I might steal your appointment at the gallows."

My blood went cold at the reminder of the awaiting noose. It was clear he was only making a joke, but the fear that resurfaced was no laughing matter. My face went ashen as the images of the score sheet flickered back into my mind.

1. *Jezebel Gannet*
2. *Lacey Arachne*
3. *Amirah Humphry*

Carlex must have noticed my quiet fretting, because I could hear his breath catch hard in his throat. "Lacey, I'm sorry, I wasn't trying to—"

"I'm alright," I cut him off with a wary heave of my chest, causing his hand to tighten protectively over mine. "I know I can win..."

I used my free hand to scrunch up my satin skirt. The movement was wrinkling the pressed fabric, but I'd rather wear wrinkles than allow Carlex to see the trembling that persisted in my fingers. The fear that had first shattered me after my exposure had gone dormant after Carlex's interference, but now that I was nearing the finish line, I couldn't help but fear for the worst.

If I lose... I lose it all—my life, my father's freedom... and Carlex.

Tears glassed over my vision as I blinked down at my clutched skirts. There was still time for me to run, but I just couldn't. Why couldn't I run? I knew I wanted to protect my father's name, but wasn't I still putting him at risk by possibly losing? There was something else trapping me here, something that had roped me into the web I had so skillfully twisted myself in.

And I think I know what it is...

Just as a tear dripped from my lashes, Carlex swept his other hand over to my clutched fingers. He wrapped his soothing touch around the back of my hand, tracing circles across my skin as he tilted his head to look into my tear-dotted eyes.

"I'm so sorry, Lacey. I know that nothing I say can take away your fear completely, but please know that I'll do whatever it takes to keep you safe."

His gentle voice felt like a remedy I didn't realize I was craving. A sudden lure to be closer to him shrouded my mind, and without pausing to think, I leaned into his hold. My head rested perfectly under his chin as I nuzzled into his chest. The softest thumps of his heart flooded my ears, causing my heart to sync with his. He released his squeeze from my hands, and instead, slid his touch up my arms until he had cradled me in a tender embrace. His fingers combed through my hair, sending tranquilizing flutters down my neck.

"Are you only afraid of losing?" His tone grew somber, mirroring the dark cloud that slowly combed over the morning sky. "Or are you afraid of winning, too?"

I twitched against his chest. Ever since I had been discovered, my mind had been so focused on the finish line that I'd hardly considered what was on the other side. *If I actually won, I would become the future queen. Carlex's queen.* He rested his hand against the back of my head, ceasing his petting while I deliberated on his question.

Am I afraid to marry Carlex? To become his queen?

"Yes," I gasped as soon as the word left me, shocked that it had come so easily. In a way the curse had answered the question for me by preventing me from being honest. "I-I'm afraid to win." I spoke slowly, just as curious about what I was going to say. That was the only good thing about my curse—it told me when I was lying to myself, too.

Carlex's heart pattered against my ears, and he burrowed his fingers back into my hair as he pulled me closer. "Good," he breathed. "Because I need you to win, Lacey."

My heart raced past Carlex's as I let his words wash over me. *He needs me to win...*

"Because you *want* to marry Jezebel..." I smiled weakly against his shirt. Despite my vulnerability, the tangled shield that encompassed my heart wasn't ready to believe that the prince truly needed me in the way I needed him. He needed me to win, but that didn't necessarily mean that he needed *me*... did it?

Carlex moved his hands to my shoulders, pushing me away a few inches until he was looking me square in the eye with a firm gaze. "No, because I *want* to marry you."

The first drop of rain splashed against my cheek, shocking me out of my numbed state with its cool sting. The drops continued to patter around us, gradually growing in amount, but neither of us made any motion to head inside. My heart swelled with joy and uncertainty as I reran Carlex's words over again in my mind.

Did I imagine it? Or did he really say...

As if reading the disbelief in my expression, Carlex took my hands back into his, allowing a smile to spread on his face. "I mean it, Lacey. This competition is designed to locate the most intelligent queen for Reclusia, and while I already know you're beyond clever, I feel that there's more that a queen requires."

The rain began to pick up, serenading us with its soothing patter through the trees. Water leaked down my neck and arms, but I barely felt the cold when my cheeks burned so feverishly. "Do you really think I possess those qualities?"

He released my hand to reach out and brush aside a wet clump of hair from my brow. The brief touch surged against my skin.

"I think you possess more than you know..." His fingers lined the edge of my face, then gingerly cupped my cheek. "You're not the only one who learned a lot in the last event. I learned that you're strong, brave of heart, and a fighter. Everything that happened in your past could have easily destroyed you, yet here you are, outwitting nearly every girl in the kingdom. You haven't been winning the events because you're the most educated girl in the land, but because you've already learned to navigate challenges. That's a lesson no noble will ever learn from a private tutor."

Rain flooded our vision, blurring everything except each other. His dark hair quickly saturated with rainwater, framing his adoring gaze with clusters of his soggy locks. I leaned my face into where he held my cheek, feeling the drops that had collected on my face puddle in his cradled palm.

"But will the kingdom ever accept a cursed queen?" My throat tightened, but I couldn't tell if it was from the curse or my fear of the lingering truth.

"They had better," Carlex said firmly, his face full of severity. "Your curse shouldn't define you, and if they say that it does, then I'll mine a thousand purity stones to change their minds. You may be cursed to only tell lies, but your honesty speaks for itself."

I took in a shuddering breath as the tension that had been strung across my heart snapped with a sudden burst of clarity. This is why I could never run, no matter how afraid I became. I wanted to be here, because I wanted to risk everything if it meant that I could remain with Carlex. Only he could convince a cursed commoner that she was capable of being a queen. It no longer mattered how close the scores were, or how difficult the next event might be, because right now I knew without a doubt, that I was going to win.

"I'll let you d-down." My voice cracked as I fought back against the lie, but Carlex's expression softened as he interpreted my meaning flawlessly.

"I know you won't," he said tenderly, then reluctantly pulled away to stand from the bench. "Now let's head inside. I'd hate for you to catch a cold before the last event."

I didn't want to move. I didn't care if I was soaked to the bone. All I wanted was this moment to become endless so the fear of the final event never interrupted us again. Reluctantly, I accepted his hand and rose from the soggy bench. My skirts clung awkwardly to my legs as the rain continued to shower us from all angles.

As he escorted me back inside, my eyes followed the flooding paths, watching the water stream into the drainage spouts on the edges of the garden. The dirt and debris that cluttered the walkways rinsed cleanly down the spouts, cleansing the path and making it new. In some ways, I felt that the rain was doing the same thing for me—washing away the rest of the fear and tension that had clouded my heart for so long.

I was being washed away, and my heart was beginning to fall...

chapter twenty-three

Carlex and I split off after we entered the palace. While the king hadn't actually forbidden us from spending time together, it just felt like a safe choice for us not to be seen together as much as possible. The guards still hadn't caught up with me since Carlex dismissed them outside, so I tried to enjoy the solitude while it lasted. My slippers squished uncomfortably from the sudden burst of rain, causing my stockings to chafe against my toes. It was a shame that the rain had to cut our time short. I felt as if I could sit out in the garden with Carlex for hours.

My fingers trailed up to my neck and brushed against the blackened stone. He believed I could become his queen... But could I really do it? Could I beat out Jezebel and the others without the support of the purity stone? Unlike the last event, I had no clue what was in store for the next challenge. What if it involved trivia or verbal puzzles? Would the king try to single me out again like last time?

I took a steadying breath and curled my fingers around the silver chain. My gaze drifted down to the ebony stone, imagining the moments it had been clear and effective. I couldn't let myself get carried away with the worries, not when I was so close to overcoming them. All I had to do was score better than Jezebel... and maybe Princess Amirah, too.

"Would you look at that... a half-drowned peasant."

I looked up from my necklace with a start as Jezebel and Gabrielle sneered at me from the end of the hall. My muscles stiffened, planting me in place while they approached with their clicking heels.

What do they want now?

"It's a shame she isn't fully drowned," Gabrielle snarked, eyeing down my drenched attire with a disgusted scowl. "At least we finally found her."

My stomach twisted as Gabrielle circled behind me, the two of them surrounding me like preying hawks. *Why were they trying to find me?*

"I'm actually almost glad you're not dead yet; I was hoping I would run into you." Jezebel's serpentine smile sent a sick chill across my cool skin, yet at the same time, a heat began to flare in my chest. "You see, I've been meaning to ask you something..."

She lifted her hand to the corner of her mouth, touching the edge of her lips with a devilish smile as she showcased the glittering bracelet on her wrist.

My blood froze. She was wearing magic stones... The heat that I'd felt suddenly nauseated me, forcing me to take a cautious step back until I bumped into Gabrielle. She pressed her hand into my back with a soft push, but the contact felt like I had been pierced with a flaming sword. I shrieked, stumbling forward as the burning pressure within me grew stronger. The pain blurred my vision, but I was still able to make out the sparkling blue ring that radiated on the hand Gabrielle had pushed me with.

Another magic stone...

"Huh. So it seems your little magic trick from last night already wore off," Jezebel marveled with a suspicious scowl. She took another step closer and the pain inside me instantly doubled.

"P-please, you're going to—" Another cry split through my words as Jezebel reached out to snag me by the front of my dress with her braceleted hand.

"Do what?" she spat, tightening her grip on my dress. "Do you want me to stop? If you do, then just say so." My head grew dizzy and the pressure inside me swelled with stifling heat. A bloodthirsty smile curled up Jezebel's lips. "So, what do you think, Lacey? Do you want me to leave?"

"No!" I bit my lip, fighting back the tears that wanted to burst out of my pressured head. "Please, don't stop. I beg of you." The fire inside me was far worse than it had ever been when I was beside Amirah. Jezebel's bracelet vibrated around her wrist, fighting against the power inside me with an opposing force.

"Jezebel, back off a touch..." Gabrielle said wearily, pulling away from my back. "If you push her much longer, your wrist may explode."

The pain in my spine eased the instant Gabrielle stepped back, but the pressure that fought to escape my chest lingered as Jezebel continued to grip me with a murderous glare.

"Just another minute," Jezebel hissed, ignoring the flaring gems around her skin. "She told me she doesn't want me to stop yet. What kind of future queen would I be if I don't respect my subjects' wishes?"

My knees buckled out from under me, and I fell against the ground. For a moment I thought my drop would convince Jezebel to release me, but she followed me to the floor, still holding her stones up to my bursting heart. My veins flowed with fire, infecting every inch of me with the searing pain that radiated from Jezebel's stones. I blinked up at her with a pleading glare, my eyes too dry from the heat to even cry.

She clenched her fist around the front of my dress, tightening the veins that ran up her arm with a visible fury. "The stones are hurting you, I can see it. So, why? Why didn't they hurt you last night? Why didn't you lie?" Her voice peaked with an unhinged crack, much like the snap of a branch.

I opened my mouth to try to answer, but only a dry cough came out. My throat was entirely void of air and my tongue dry and leaden. I couldn't answer her, even if I wanted to.

Jezebel's fury heightened as she interpreted my silence as defiance. Her fiery gaze searched me for answers, unwilling to give up so easily. My vision began to fade to black as the pain slowly turned into numb pressure that pushed at every inch of my skin. I blinked, my eyes slowly drifting shut as the festering energy inside prepared to snuff out my life. A sharp gasp from Jezebel and a yank at my throat halted my descent into darkness.

I fell back onto the palace floor, gasping for the blissfully cold air. It took me a moment to realize that Jezebel had fully released me. I crawled onto my knees, taking slow deep breaths of the cool air until the spots in my vision had faded.

She tried to kill me... All for what?

My breath caught as I noticed the absence of Carlex's necklace around my throat. I stumbled back to my feet, still feeling the lingering burn in my veins, along with a fresh splitting headache. Once I'd gained my bearings, I saw Jezebel and Gabrielle inspect the silver necklace that had been snatched from my throat.

"T-that's not mine." I took a half-step forward but froze in my tracks when Gabrielle held up her ringed hand in warning.

The pain that still lingered in me was nothing compared to the crushing heartache of seeing my gift from Carlex in Jezebel's hands.

Jezebel scoffed, "Of course, it's not yours, well not anymore." She turned the necklace in her hands a few times, inspecting the dried-up magic with a sharp eye. "I see. So that's how you did it... I'd say that I underestimated you, but your little hat trick is all used up, so it looks like I have nothing to worry about for the next event after all." She dangled the chain from her fingers, entangling it with the poisonous bracelet.

My heart tightened. "Exactly, I'm not a threat to you. So will you return my necklace and go?" I swallowed anxiously as I watched the playful mischief in her face darken into rage.

"What did you just say?" She clenched her teeth, wrapping her fist around the necklace with enough force to nearly shatter the stone.

"I said—" I gasped, replaying the words in slow motion.

"You said you're not a threat to me, which must have been a lie." She took a heated step forward, and I stumbled back, desperately trying to avoid her bracelet. "Do you honestly believe you stand a chance against me?"

"No, of course not!"

"You're such a liar! And if you truly believe that to be truth, then you're a fool, too!"

She raised her arm and threw the necklace

to the floor, smashing the stone into a thousand pieces. My heart shattered along with the splintered rock. My hands trembled as I crouched to pick up the broken chain, but before I could reach it, Jezebel smashed her foot atop the remnants.

"Well, isn't this a familiar scene," Jezebel sneered. "It's the same as when we were children. Only this time, I'm certain I won't be seeing you in my future."

Anger and pain clawed within me, fighting to push back or to do something other than sit shattered on the floor, but the pain flaring within me warned me not to move. Once again, the curse held me trapped. I couldn't even defend my honor without risking a horrific death.

"Don't look so glum," Jezebel scoffed, stepping off the crushed stone. "We're still fellow competitors, aren't we? Since I broke your jewelry, why don't you take mine instead?"

I barely had time to react as she tossed her bracelet at my feet. I stumbled backward across the floor, desperately trying to dodge the trinket as the two girls cackled at my efforts.

"Thanks for chatting with us, Lacey." Jezebel laughed. "We should really do it again sometime."

• •

"They did, *what*!?" Evie's face looked absolutely murderous.

I wrapped the blanket I'd stolen from the

bed tighter around my aching body, attempting to warm my shivering skin that was still cold from being drenched in the rain. Despite feeling as if my core had been replaced with a blazing inferno earlier, the chill still sank into my bones.

"I always knew Jezebel would go *that* far." I shuddered, feeling a phantom pain tug in my chest. To think she'd take advantage of my one weakness and nearly bring me to the brink of death, and all to do what? Learn why she lost? It seemed more to me that she was interested in establishing her dominance over me, just like when we were children.

"I mean it, Lace. Just say the word and I'll go to prison for murder." Evie's face was stone-cold, but her eyes blazed in fire. "I've got a few connections, so it will only take me maybe five years to get out, seven max." She leaned against the back of the other armchair, facing me with crossed arms and a look that could only be serious.

I shook my head. "Your request is tempting, but I'm going to have to say yes." Evie's brow lifted mischievously, clearly intent on accepting my lie as truth once again. I gave her a stern look. "Evie... Yes."

She slumped back against the chair with a defeated pout. "Fine... But just know that the offer still stands." She popped up from her lean to cross over to her small servant's desk. I watched her curiously as she gathered up a bundle of paperwork. She pressed the papers behind her back where I couldn't see, then walked back to me with a far calmer demeanor. "Also, there's another offer that stands... one I've been putting together ever since I realized how much danger I'd put you in."

My shivering ceased for a moment as confusion swept over my senses.

Another offer?

"What do you mean?" I let the blanket slip from my shoulders, edging forward on my seat to attempt a peek at her hidden papers.

She gave me a somber smile, and when I looked closer, I could see the mist of tears beginning to form. "I know you want to win the prince, and I fully support your decision, but..." She let out a heavy breath, then shifted the papers out from behind her back and held them out to me. "I wanted to give you a second option, as well."

I blinked at her curiously before turning my attention to the pile of documents. I took the papers with a careful touch, spreading them across my lap as I studied them with a detailed eye.

They were... identification documents. But not only that, there were also maps, a land deed, and even a banknote for a hundred gold pieces. My eyes widened as I sifted through the identification papers. There was a birth certificate, census paperwork, and

Ebonair citizenship documents, all with my exact description but with a completely different name.

Leanna Webber

"Evie, is this..."

"Everything you need to start a new life," Evie finished, her voice calm and assured. "I know a hundred gold isn't a lot to start off on, but that land deed has a small manor on the property. It should be plenty large enough for you and your mother. The land used to belong to a duke who passed away a few years ago. This specific property got lost in the squabble of financial divisions since his children each wanted his larger estates. No one will even miss it. There's a death certificate in there, too —it lists that you perished of a sudden case of tuberculosis. As long as you die of natural causes instead of by an execution, your father's name shouldn't be tarnished. I'll handle the fake funeral after you leave. As for the identification papers, I'm still working on the ones for your mother, but I can have her safely escorted over the border a few days after you. Needless to say, this is your ticket out, if you want it."

My breath hitched in my throat as I gaped down at the collection of forgeries. *Evie went through all this trouble? For me?*

"Evie... How did you even get all this?" I thumbed through the intricate papers with bewildered eyes, unable to spot even a single flaw in the documents.

She combed a finger through the end of her golden locks, averting my eyes as she swallowed stiffly. "As I said, I have connections," she said dismissively. "Either way, they're yours. If you want them. Please don't think this is me not believing that you can win or not supporting your affections for the prince. I believe in you, Lace, and I do trust you. But as the idiot who got you into this mess, I knew I could never forgive myself unless I could offer you a way out. So, it's up to you. Are we going to fashion an escape rope out of your bedsheets? Or are you going to put Jezebel in her place with one final win?" She punched her fist into her palm, putting on a fierce scowl. "Just so you know, if you decide to leave, I'll still punch Jezebel for you. So don't let revenge be your determining factor; I've got you covered there." She clicked her tongue with a jazzed point of her finger.

I let out a tight laugh, more out of disbelief than humor. Evie had already done so much to help me—even after she learned I'd been lying to her for years—yet she still did more. I swept my fingers over the pages, touching the new name tenderly.

Leanna Webber... Could such a name really become mine?

It felt ironic that this whole fiasco began with me stealing a name, and now it could be solved by me stealing another. If I took the documents and ran, this would all be over... I wouldn't have to gamble my life on any more riddles or risk Jezebel holding another magic stone to my heart. I could go back to the life I left and go back with Mother. Even Father might get to join us in a few years, and for the first time in twelve years, we could be a normal family. It was everything I had begged for when this first began, yet I wasn't certain that it was still what I wanted now...

I bit my lip as images of Carlex flashed through my mind. His warm smile burned in my memory, reminding me of his endless compassion. My heart seized at the thought of abandoning him to the fate of the bride competition. If I disappeared, then the next two likely candidates for winning were either Jezebel or the stern Princess Amirah. Would he ever be happy in a marriage like that?

Would I ever be happy if he was in a marriage like that...?

The fierce surging of my heart painted the answer clearer than my own lies. No, I wouldn't be happy. As badly as I want to protect my life, I wanted to protect his more. He had been nothing but kind and considerate to me since the moment I picked him out of the crowded ballroom. He picked me up when I fell, brought me shoes when I had none, and even offered to abandon his feelings for me when he felt they weren't reciprocated. If I left him now, Jezebel would have nothing stopping her from claiming him, and that wasn't something I could live with.

Carlex has always watched out for me, and now, it's my turn.

I took in a long breath as I cleanly arranged the paperwork in a neat stack. My fingers hooked around the edges of the papers, questioning one final time if this was the right choice. I smiled assuredly, stretching the papers back out to Evie with a firm thrust. "Thank you, Evie. I'll be needing these."

She stared at me blankly for a moment, but then an eager smile rose up her petite lips. "I was hoping you'd say that." She took the papers back from me, letting out a relieved breath. "As much as you deserve a chance at freedom, I think Jezebel deserves the pain of watching you win even more."

My face darkened with determination, and a sly smile twitched at my lips. "I'm not going to let her lose, and that's a promise from a cold-blooded liar."

chapter twenty-four

The next few days passed by in a painfully slow blur. After the incident with Jezebel and her minion, I refused to leave my suite unless absolutely necessary. The rain had persisted, showering the palace grounds on and off just enough to prevent Carlex from being able to safely vault across the slippery balconies. So Evie and I spent the hours alone, discussing potential event challenges and plotting fictional murder plans for Jezebel. Well... mostly fictional.

A crack of lightning tore my attention from the book I was reading, sending an equally aggressive spark of adrenaline through my chest. The final event was tonight, meaning that after this evening, I would be receiving either a noose or a ring.

My skin crawled at the daunting thought. I closed the book, no longer able to focus on the words. At the moment my pages snapped shut, a knock rapped against the door, causing Evie to stir from her comfortable pillow mountain on the bed.

She sat up with a jolt, her eyes full of

excited energy. "Do you think it's...?" She didn't finish her words as she scampered toward the door, only pausing for a brief moment to smooth out her skirts before pulling it open. "Hello, Your Highness, please come in." She snuck me a sly smile as she held the door open for Carlex to step inside.

My heart instantly lurched at the sight of his wary expression. I rose from my seat with the book still clutched in my fingers as his gaze softened on me. Evie flicked her eyes between our silent greeting, then took a few awkward steps backward.

"I'll just... get some air." She spun around on the heel of her shoe, flicking her unkempt curls in our direction before trotting off toward the soggy balcony.

I opened my mouth to protest her standing out in the rain, but before I could say anything, she snagged a cloak from the wardrobe and slipped out the doors with a *go get 'em* type of smile. The sound of the falling rain filled the suite for a brief moment before she closed the door, letting in the drifting scent of a brewing storm. I turned back to Carlex with a shy but pleasant sensation warming my heart.

He quirked a quick smile in Evie's direction, then turned his enchanting brown eyes onto me. "I'm sorry for barging in again... but it had been a few days since I've been able to sneak over and..." He let out a revitalizing breath, his expression brightening from the weariness that had previously enveloped him. "I just needed to see you again."

Flutters spiraled through my chest, warming my cheeks with a soft blush. I clasped my hands together in front of me, fiddling shyly with my fingers. "I'm disappointed that you came."

I glanced up at him through my lashes. I had been hoping I'd get a chance to see Carlex again before the last event. After everything that happened with Jezebel and the uncertainty of the last event, I was aching for his support.

"I'm sorry I couldn't come sooner." His voice was low and sweet. He reached out a hand to touch at my fiddling fingers, causing my skin to ripple with pleasant shivers. I relinquished my hand to him, which he gripped tenderly, stroking the back of my hand with a longing touch. "Tonight's the last event, and to be honest... I don't know what will come from it." He gave my hand a protective squeeze, locking his gaze onto me with an unspoken desperation. "I'm afraid, Lacey. I'm afraid I won't be able to protect you."

My lip quivered as I took in a wavering breath. The fears I'd tried to push away sprang out of me at full force.

Carlex is afraid, too? I can't say that I blame him... I'm probably just as terrified, but I can't let him see that. He's been the brave one for too long, and it is my turn to support him.

My chest tightened, but I sucked in another full breath to loosen the tension. I knew this was coming. I knew the results of this evening were going to be a gamble. I knew what I was signing up for when I chose to stay instead of take Evie's offer at escape. The fear that clustered around my heart couldn't be avoided, but that didn't mean I had to cave to it, either. It wasn't just my life that was at stake anymore —Carlex's was, too. If I didn't succeed, then he would be forced to spend the rest of his life bound to a woman he may very well despise.

I chose this. So, I'm going to fight for it.

"I'm not afraid," I lied confidently, forcing myself to believe that it was actually true. "I don't want to do this. I didn't choose this, so I'm not going to fight for what I want." I inched closer to him, his gaze burning into me with adoration. I squeezed his hand. "And I really don't know what I want..."

The beating of my heart overshadowed the patter of the rain against the windows, deafening my senses to everything else. I held my breath as I searched the prince's eyes for a reply, but his response didn't come in the form of words. He tugged me closer to him, wrapping his arm around my waist with an impatient desire. I blinked up at him, watching his lips twitch into his dimpled smile.

"And what is it you want?"

My skin flared with heat, but I didn't want

to miss the opportunity to tell Carlex what I was feeling. Not when there was a chance I may never get to speak with him again.

"I don't want you," I whispered. His tall stature forced me to look up in order to see the enchantment sweep over his face.

He pressed his hand to the back of my head and pulled me into a tight embrace, touching his lips to the edge of my ear before he whispered, "I don't want you, either." He pulled back a few inches, meeting my face with a coy smile. "And that's the first lie I've ever told you. I figured it was about time I told one, too."

He gave me a playful smile and I suppressed a giggle. *He truly wants me...* Being wrapped in his arms felt like a dream come true, but I knew the dream would only last if I could prove my worth to the king.

My body stiffened at the thought. "Do you think lying will pose any problems for me tonight?" I asked anxiously, pressing a hand to my deceitful lips.

Carlex's expression dimmed, and he pulled away from me a touch to reach into his pocket. "To be honest, I have no idea. Father has kept the details for the event completely under wraps, so I wasn't able to get any leads on what it might entail." He slipped his hand out of his pocket, keeping his fingers closed into an upward fist that he stretched out to me. "However, I did manage to track down these..."

I watched curiously as he opened his palm to display two dainty earrings. They were simple, with only a single clear stone attached to the hook, but on closer inspection, I could see the smallest sparks of light dancing within them.

"You found more purity stones?" I pressed my hands to my mouth, feeling my fingers tremble with excitement and relief.

This is it... I can really win with this. Maybe I can even use it to talk to Carlex for a moment without lies.

Carlex's smile faltered as he took in a shallow breath. "Yes, they're purity stones. However, they are extremely small and weak— you can tell by their clarity." He turned one of the earrings over in his hand, reflecting the clouded impurities in the light.

"So, they won't be able to stop my lying?" My heart sank, but I tried not to let the disappointment show.

"Well, at least not like before." Carlex shrugged. "The stones are too small to absorb your curse naturally, like the necklace did. Therefore, it looks like you would need to touch the stone in order to let it draw your curse away. You'd probably only have a few seconds before the power drained, so it's maybe enough for one truth each." He curled his fingers back around the stones with a defeated sigh. "I'm sorry it's not much. I tried to send out an order for more stones, but they didn't arrive in time. I'm afraid this is the best support I can give you."

The disappointed look on his face crushed me. He had done so much to help me, and it pained me to watch him look down on his efforts. He deserved to know how much I appreciated him, and just how much of a help he had truly been to me. An idea sparked in my mind, and despite knowing it was foolish, I couldn't imagine not doing it. I placed a gentle finger underneath his chin, lifting his head a touch until his warm gaze met mine. With slow movements, I pulled open his fingers, revealing the two tiny earrings that sat atop his palm. My mind cautioned me to stop and think about my actions, but I didn't pay it any mind.

I could very well die tonight. I don't want to leave this world with something so important left unsaid.

I touched one of the tiny purity stones, instantly feeling the familiar course of power through my veins.

"Thank you for everything, Carlex. It means the world to me," I whispered.

His eyes widened as he soaked in my words with an awestruck look. The power began to fade, but I wasn't done yet. There was still so much I needed to say to him, but I knew there was one thing above all that needed to be spoken. I took in a tightening breath.

"I-I love you, Carlex."

The power vanished from my skin,

snagging my tongue back into place with a twinge. The moment that passed between us couldn't be described by mere emotions or feelings. It was an indefinable break in time, where we both froze our breaths in order to absorb each other's presence.

Carlex broke the silence first, snaking his hand around the back of my head and pulling me close to him with the most blissful smile I had ever seen. "I love you too, Lacey," he murmured, and then he pulled me into a deep kiss.

I wrapped my arms around the back of his neck, drawing out the moment for as long as possible. When he finally pulled away, I could have sworn I heard both our hearts fight to hammer louder than the other. My cheeks were red and flushed, but I felt like the most beautiful girl in the kingdom under his adoring gaze. He slid his hand across my cheek, cradling the side of my face with a gentle, yet heated touch. I began to lean forward once again, fluttering my eyes shut in hopes of another enthralling kiss, but a sharp knock at the door startled us apart.

"Your Highness." The guard's coarse voice tore through the air like sifting gravel. "Your Father is requesting an audience with you."

Carlex whispered an unsavory word under his breath. I bit my lip, trying to hold back a giggle as he growled. "I'll be there in a moment," he called through the door.

My heart constricted at the thought of

him leaving so soon, but at the same time, the joy of his shared feelings overwhelmed even the fear of losing. *At least I got to see him one last time...*

I touched a hand to his arm, giving him a reassuring smile. "It's alright. I'll see you in the morning, okay?"

He took my hands into his, nodding with a determined strength in his gaze. "Yes, I'll see you in the *morning*," he repeated. He knew full well that I meant the evening, but the lie didn't dissuade his assuredness. "I *will* see you in the morning, because I'm not going to let you die tonight." He raised my hand to his soft lips, pressing a heart-pounding kiss atop the back of my hand. Before releasing me, he flipped my hand over, tucking the clear and black earrings gently into my palm.

I nodded, clutching the jewels with a painful smile. *I hope this isn't actually a lie.* "Yes, I'll see you then."

• •

"It's no wonder you wanted to stay," Evie gushed as she twisted my hair into a pile atop my head. "He loves you! And you love him! Oh, isn't it so tragically romantic?"

I gave her a questioning glare in the mirror. "Tragic?" Unease twisted within me at the word.

Evie waved her hand. "Oh, you know what I mean. It's a perfect case of forbidden love. The only tragic part is that the king isn't in support. I have no doubt you'll get your happily ever after tonight." She pulled a long ribbon off the vanity, entangling it into my hair with a dainty bow.

I swallowed stiffly in the mirror. We'd settled on a simple lilac dress with minimal details and a simplistic, yet elegant hairstyle. It was no mystery that I was from humble origins, so it felt appropriate for me to represent that humility in my attire. Since it was the final event of the competition, it seemed likely that there would be other observers outside the royal family to commemorate the event. Last thing I needed was to draw more negative attention to myself for dressing above my station.

A soft knock on the door curdled my stomach. Evie paused mid-twist, cocking her head curiously at the door as she removed the hairpins from between her lips.

"That's odd. It's far too early for you to be called to dinner." She stuffed the last pin awkwardly into my final curl of hair, latching it atop my head to keep her from losing her progress.

I kept my chin level with the floor as I turned to get a better view of the door in the mirror. Despite my slow movements, the curl still flopped in front of my eyes, blinding my view of the door when Evie pulled it open.

"I see. Thank you." Evie's voice floated across the suite as I huffed the curl out of my eyes.

When my vision had cleared, Evie had already closed the door, with a meal tray now in her arms. I stared curiously at the covered tray, wondering if I had missed some sort of scheduling change.

"Aren't the competitors supposed to have supper together?" I questioned. My eyes followed Evie's movements as she cautiously placed the tray on the small table in front of the fire, then produced an envelope from the side of the tray.

"Looks like things are moving a little differently tonight." She flashed the envelope in front of my curious eyes. "The servant said that all the competitors will be dining separately tonight, and the instructions for the final event are in here..."

My eyes bulged as I locked my frenzied gaze onto the sliver of paper.

The last event's instructions...

I scrambled out of my seat in a mad dash, racing beside Evie as she tore the letter open right as I skittered to a stop beside her shoulder. She hastily unfolded the paper, holding it over so we could both scan the contents with our hungry eyes. I held my breath as I raced through the words, fearing that the contents of this letter would end up spelling out my death.

My breath caught as I read the opening words.

This last test will be a test of lies...

Evie gasped, shaking the paper for just long enough to blur the words. I latched my eyes back onto the note as quickly as I could, absorbing the information with stiffened muscles.

A true queen must know when to be honest and when to utilize an artful untruth. For this event, each competitor shall disguise their appearances in preparation for a masquerade. Everything you need shall be provided within the hour, so instead of dining together, please take this time to prepare.

At the start of the event, you will all enter the ballroom with your altered appearances. Your goal is to be noticed as anyone other than your true self. The guests in attendance at the ball will be seeking to expose each competitor's identity, so it's in your best interest to look and act as unrecognizable as possible. Each guest will be permitted one guess for a competitor's identity, and if they are correct, you will be eliminated. The guards shall act as moderators and be informed of each guest's true identity to track any guesses. The last competitor to go unidentified will be the winner.

While there is a value to truth, there is also an intelligence behind lies. If you wish to prove yourself, then show that you can be a master at both.

Best of Luck,
King Aldrich

I gaped at the letter in disbelief, rereading

the words again and again.

It was a game of lies...

My memories rolled back to the moment of shock on King Aldrich's face when I won the last event. At the time I wasn't certain if he was only angry, or actually impressed, but either way he had seemed surprised that I had uncovered his son's true smile. Was this the king's way of apologizing? Of giving me a chance to prove my lies could be useful?

Evie placed a hand on my shoulder, still staring at the paper with an open mouth. "You're going to need a new dress."

chapter twenty-five

Nerves clamped around my strangled lungs as I took the first step into the ballroom. Dozens of curious eyes peeking through masks scattered across me in an instant, initiating the first test. *Will I even be able to make it in the door without being recognized?* My heart drummed against my ribs with a crushing force, but I fought the nerves away from my expression.

Don't show fear, Lacey... Tonight is about lying, and that's exactly what you were born to do.

With a fueling breath, I straightened my spine as Evie had taught me, then squared my shoulders with a strong, yet ladylike posture.

Slow breath in, slow breath out. You're not Lacey tonight.

I made direct eye contact with one of the guests, narrowing my eyes with a silent challenge for them to try to call out my name. A middle-aged gentleman took an uncertain step back, glancing up and down my apparel one final time before moving across the room. I let out a silent breath and stepped farther into the ballroom with wobbling legs.

So far so good... Evie did an incredible job.

The ballroom was bustling with more people than the other challenges combined. Candle chandeliers had been strung across the ceilings, illuminating the vibrant array of ballgowns and tailored suits like a sparkling jewelry box. The floral vines had been twisted alongside the cloudy windows and added a touch of life to the dreary weather outside the glass. Rain drizzled outside the balcony doors, adding a white noise to the background of the chattering chaos. It looked exactly like a proper ball should, aside from the fact that all the guests of honor were in disguise.

Guards wandered amongst the crowd, listening in on conversations in case any of the guests made a formal guess to a competitor's identity. I tugged at the gold bracelet that had been given to me before I entered, signifying that I was a competitor amongst the sea of masked faces. A few other gold bracelets caught my eye as I wandered through the clusters of people, but I couldn't get a good enough look at their faces to make my own guess of their identity.

The royal family sat at the front of the room, watching the event from their gaudy thrones. My attention instantly settled on Carlex, who was digging his nails into the arms of his seat. My heart throbbed when I couldn't seem to catch his gaze, but then I remembered he probably didn't recognize me. Sure enough, when I looked closer, I could see his eyes were darting wildly around the ballroom. His gaze brushed over me for the briefest moment, causing my breath to catch in my throat, but he barely looked at me before searching another corner of the room, and my tension eased.

Not even Carlex recognizes me like this...

I stopped in front of the glass balcony doors, admiring my reflection with a bewildered breath. The girl who looked back at me was a complete stranger—Evie had made certain of that. For the two hours leading up to the event, Evie had kept me glued to the vanity so she could smear every blush, powder, and cream on my face.

The results were astounding.

We'd swapped out my simplistic dress for the grandest ballgown in Evie's collection. I straightened my posture a touch more to avoid being swallowed by the full-skirted purple gown. The vivid color was lined with black lace that trailed up the hem and covered the bodice. Beneath my dark purple mask, Evie had layered a mountain of cosmetics that had nearly changed the shape of my face. My slightly upturned nose now appeared to be angled downward, my cheekbones looked higher, and even my lips fuller. The most dramatic change was my hair. Amongst the selection of masks and cosmetics that had been delivered to our door, there had also been a small array of jars of dye. Evie didn't even hesitate to comb the blackest ink through my hair, saturating my chestnut locks in the shade of ebony. My scalp itched from the clumps of dye that had burrowed inside my elaborate updo, but I had to admit that it looked beyond real in my reflection.

The only thing that still looked the same were my eyes, but even they were half-masked by a black birdcage veil that nestled beautifully against my twisted ringlets. I blinked back at myself in the glass, catching my gaze on the black and clear earrings that dotted my lobes.

If you need to say something true, you've got one chance.

I took in a fortifying breath, then turned back into the chattering crowd. My chest instantly seized at the sight of so many people, but I pushed the anxieties away. Lacey would be expected to hide in the corner and avoid everyone. But tonight, Lacey was dead, and if she didn't stay that way, she'd be dead in the morning as well. I lifted my chin, gazing down the crowd with the confidence of a girl who had been raised anywhere but on the streets.

It's time to lie, not only with my words, but with my entire being.

With a bold stride, I stepped into the center of the room, channeling every ounce of poise and tenacity I could muster. The lilting music cluttered my brain as I tried to listen in on conversations in search of a proper target to test my disguise on.

According to Evie, I need to establish my disposition as early as possible, so people will make early assumptions about me. But who would be good at spreading rumors...?

A collection of chattering gentlemen caught the corner of my eye, and I noticed them narrowing their gazes at me with assured looks. I recognized most of them from the first event when we were tasked with searching for the prince. If they had been invited to that event, then they would likely be well-connected. I forced my jittering feet to shift in their direction, making just enough eye contact to single out one of the men. My glance was instantly successful, drawing out a man in a tailored suit with a black mask and a dark gray ascot. He stepped away from the cluster and moved smoothly in my direction. On his way, he paused and snatched two glasses of wine off a servant's tray, while locking his eyes on me with an undeniable aim. My jaw latched shut as I watched him close the distance between us. My legs itched to turn in the opposite direction to avoid his confrontation, but I knew that would only be something that Lacey, a commoner, would do.

This game is meant to find Carlex a queen, so it's time for me to prove I have what it takes to be one.

Confidence surged through my veins as I sharply turned toward the oncoming gentleman.

His steps faltered for a brief moment from my directness, causing his relaxed smile to twitch for a moment before he continued forward. His hesitancy twinged a smile at my painted lips.

Yes, that's it... Lie with everything you've got.

My body language accepted the sway of the curse with ease, tilting my chin upward and eyes down as I pressed an impudent hand to my hip. My chest buzzed with a pleasant warmth as if the curse was thanking me for feeding its desire for control.

"Good evening, madam." The man flashed me a toothy smile, twinkling his green eyes underneath his satin mask. "You looked like you could use a refreshment." He stretched one of the glasses out to me.

My first test...

I folded my arms and turned my nose up the glass with a huff. "No, thank you. My family doesn't approve of me drinking." I tilted my shoulders back with a more relaxed sway, then rested a coy hand at the base of my cheek. "But they never said anything about dancing..." I said in an amorous tone, fluttering my eyes with a flirtatious smile.

My victim took the bait. A sly smile spread over his face as he placed the two full wine glasses back on a passing servant's tray. "Is that so...?"

He moved in a half-step closer, near enough that I could smell the tartness of a previous drink in his breath. He held out a hand for me to accept and I took it boldly, feeling my skin crawl underneath the hot touch.

"In that case, would you like to dance?" He leaned forward and whispered proudly in my ear, "Lady Gabrielle?"

Sheer triumph swelled in my chest as I pulled away with a deceptive smile. "Did you hear that?" I gave a sly look to the guard who had been hovering behind me, and he gave a silent nod.

"That's incorrect. You'll need to leave now," the guard said stiffly to the guest.

The man's face flushed white at the same moment I tore my hand away from his grasp. He blinked at me in astoundment as I watched the guards usher him out of the ballroom with a playful wave of my gloved hand. Since he approached me alone, none of his friends would have heard his incorrect guess. That's one down, so that only left... oh, about two hundred more people to fool.

My heart throbbed against my burning chest, conflicting the curse's joy with its spiraling fears. It felt so natural to let my lies consume all of me, yet at the same time, I knew it was more than just a game. I was playing with my own life, and if I allowed myself to get too tangled in my lies, then I would be paying the price in only a few hours.

Air filtered shakily through my lungs,

taking in the scent of my strong perfume and the fragrance of the powdery makeup that caked my features. The hot ballroom felt suffocating and claustrophobic, but I didn't dream of letting my discomfort show on my face. Everywhere I turned there were eyes catching onto the glint of my gold bracelet. They knew I was camouflaged, but they didn't know who was hiding underneath. I had no doubt that every guest at this event was in search of the one easy pick.

The commoner masquerading as a noble.

Lacey Arachne should have stuck out at a ball like a pig in a horse show, but since no one had found her upon entrance, the scrutiny had begun in earnest. If I slipped up even once, they would know, and I would die for it.

My gaze drifted back up to the royal family. Carlex's brow was furrowed, with his hand resting thoughtfully on his chin. His brown eyes scoured the crowds with ever-growing frustration as he tried to see through the masks. My posture straightened ever so slightly with a boost of assurance that not even the man I'd kissed earlier could recognize me.

My thoughts were disrupted by a guard ringing a bell for the crowd to silence. "The first contestant has been uncovered. Fifteen contestants now remain." Chatter resumed as I peeked through the crowd to see a dejected contestant let out a long sigh.

Even with her mask, she was rather easy to recognize as Lydia. Her dark hair had been tinged a slight red and pinned up in a tight braid, but other than that, she still looked as regally dressed as usual. The sound of another elimination bell in the corner of the room tightened my stomach, fearing that ring would soon be for me. I turned back into the crowd, feeling the nerves I'd forced away threaten to make a reappearance.

I can do this. I'll survive this night one lie at a time if I must.

My eyes caught a glimpse of my reflection in a passing tray of glasses. The quick glimpse of the ebony-haired stranger reassured me that my appearance wouldn't be my downfall. The only way I would be discovered was if I failed to lie, and that had never happened before in my life. I was a master at crafting webs of lies, so now it was time to prove they were useful. I eyed down the guests with a predatory gaze.

Who shall I snag in my web next?

chapter twenty-six

The bells continued to ring, knocking out my fellow competitors one by one. I focused my attention on the younger guests, hoping they would be less likely to notice mistakes in propriety than a more socially-practiced elder. Six more guests had made the attempt to guess my identity, with two guessing Jezebel, two more Gabrielle, one Lyra, and one Deanna. Each guess rattled me, reminding me that I was only a breath away from execution if they had classified me correctly. With each ring of the guard's bell, I found my ears muting every other sound.

I'm still in this.

My body stiffened as another bell echoed on the far side of the ballroom. "Another contestant has been discovered. Four more contestants remain."

Fear twisted in my chest as I felt the stress of the competition chip away at my confidence. I gazed through the crowds where the newest competitor had been eliminated, trying to determine if she was Lady Deanna or Princess Lyra. The only girlsI was certain were still in the game were Princess Amirah and Jezebel. Jezebel's glare was impossible not to identify, and I couldn't ignore Amirah's presence even if I wanted to.

I can't be found yet, not until Jezebel's eliminated.

My chest flared with heated pressure, and I snapped my gaze around to see Princess Amirah stride in my direction. I quickly moved away from her, putting enough distance between us until her magic-filled jewels stopped conflicting with my curse. Her disguise was rather incredible, but the magic she carried gave her away to me immediately. Unfortunately, I wasn't permitted to guess as a competitor, otherwise I could have easily eliminated her. It didn't seem like any other guests were walking around with curses that were inflamed by her presence either, so I would simply have to hope that my disguise outlasted hers.

That only left Jezebel and either Lyra or Deanna. Both remaining contestants had styled black hair, but only Lyra's would have been natural, and both wore dresses suited for a princess of Bellatring. If one was Lyra, it looked as if she had hardly concealed her identity where Jezebel had matched Lyra, and if it was actually Deanna I was at a complete loss.

I let out a frustrated breath, then turned back around to nearly collide with a tall, dark-eyed gentleman. "Oh, pardon me." He took an apologetic step backward, flashing me a brash smile.

Here we go again. You can do this, Lace.

"No pardon necessary, I'm used to shuffling through crowded ballrooms by now." I slipped a lace fan out of my pocket, flicking it open with a twitch of my wrist. I batted the fan just a touch above my mouth, attempting a displeased scowl. "I'm sorry, did you need something?"

My gaze lilted over to him, and I caught the slightest twinge of a crooked smile. "I was going to request a moment of your company, but you look a tad flushed, madam." His dark eyes followed the flutter of my fan, studying it as if it were an essential clue to my identity. I flicked a nervous glance at the lace, mentally ensuring that it was as normal as any other noble's fan. "Would you care to join me on the balcony for some air while we speak? It has gotten rather stuffy in here, and it seems like the rain has lightened."

He turned his shoulders toward the rain-dotted windows, and sure enough, the droplets that clung to the glass were only leftover from the previous pattering.

I cast a questioning glance over at the guard who had been chaperoning my conversations and he gave me a wordless nod of approval. Going out onto the balcony wouldn't be such a terrible idea. The fresh air could very well do me a world of good, and there would be less eyes outside to scrutinize my act.

I snapped the fan closed against my palm, curling my painted lips into a pleased smile. "That sounds dreadfully dull, but it's not like there's anything holding my attention inside..." My attention swayed guiltily over to Carlex's throne, my heart seizing at his white-knuckled clamp on the chair.

I won't let you down, Carlex...

Before my new acquaintance could notice my drifting gaze, I held out my hand to him expectantly with a clearing of my throat. My signal must have worked because he quickly offered up his arm to escort me, then proceeded to lead me toward the glass balcony doors.

The thick humidity in the air instantly engulfed my skin, cooling me with its lingering mist. My lungs sucked in the muggy air, tasting the flavor of fresh rain on my tongue. The clouded sky had grown even more shadowed as night encroached, leaving only the brilliant glow from the ballroom windows to light the expansive balcony.

I had never been on the ballroom balcony before, but it was absolutely breathtaking. White marble made up the twisted railings, but the flooring was a natural stone. The railings were entangled with blossoming roses and ivy. In the center of the balcony, there was a flowing fountain, one that appeared to be a natural spring that bubbled up from a cluster of mossy rocks and streamed all the way off the edge of the balcony in a narrow, rock waterfall. A few other guests lingered around the marble benches that lined the railing, and one guard followed us out into the cool night air.

I stepped around a thick puddle, feigning a disgusted look as I hiked up the hem of my skirt. "Goodness, I didn't know it would be so wet outside," I scoffed, tugging my escort along with me as I dodged another puddle. The clean scent of fresh rain revitalized my senses, helping me refocus on working with my curse.

"My apologies. I won't take up much more of your time, I promise," my escort said cordially. I snubbed my nose away from him in distaste, but still allowed him to lead me to the rocky formation in the center of the balcony. We stopped in front of the spring, and I found myself admiring the natural beauty of it and the tumbling waterfall. I peeked over the edge of the balcony railings, curious to see where the water led, and was fascinated to discover that it landed in a natural pool, maybe two stories below us.

I shook out of my distracted state, reminding myself that I was in the midst of a life-or-death competition. Now was not the time to admire architecture. I huffed out an irritated breath.

"So, did you want to ask me something or just stare at rocks?" I lifted an unimpressed brow at the fountain.

The man let out an odd chuckle, unslipping his arm from my hold. "Actually, I don't have anything to say to you." Something surged in my chest as I snapped my head back at him. His expression had darkened out of nowhere, and he took a precarious step back into the shadows. "But someone else does."

My muscles tightened around my bones, alerting me that something was clearly not right. I opened my mouth to call for the guard, but before I could mutter so much as a syllable, a crippling pain clamped around my throat at the same moment a familiar figure stepped out of the balcony shadows.

A woman with black hair, a silver dress, and a gold bracelet around her wrist stepped up alongside the man I'd foolishly allowed to lead me out here. My chest tightened once more, slowly heating from the inside out as my eyes darted in horror to the massive red stone that was cradled in both of her hands.

Jezebel...

Terror flooded my veins, mixing with the searing pain that radiated out into my nerves in response to the ginormous stone. I stepped back, preparing to run inside as quick as I could, but a sharp hiss halted me.

"Don't move." Jezebel's cold voice sent an agonizing chill through me. "This is a strength stone, probably one of the strongest in the kingdom. If I were to throw it at that lying little mouth of yours, you'd likely perish before you could even beg me to do it again."

A strength stone?

My eyes went dry as the pulsating fire stripped me of excess fluid. I blinked coarsely at the flickering stone, watching the vibrant power flare inside like a dancing inferno. My throat tightened as I took in a painfully shallow breath, warning me that the stone was far more potent than the one Jezebel had held to my heart a few days ago. I snuck a desperate glance in the direction of the guard that stood watch, but his attention was drawn by another couple who kept sneaking mischievous looks in my direction.

Were they with Jezebel, too?

"How did you recognize me?" I sputtered hoarsely, my throat already growing raw from the pressured heat.

Jezebel rolled her eyes. "Are you really that dense?" She stroked her thumb over the top of the stone, causing the power to spark beneath the scratch of her nail. "You're the only contestant in the ballroom who constantly avoided Amirah, who was easy to recognize as well, since she always wears the same magic jewelry. Once I had you spotted, I instructed my associates to lure you out to where we could... chat."

She gave the vile man at her side a pointed nod, signaling for him to join the others in distracting the guard. He gave her a sly smile, then left us to our so-called chat.

My stomach nauseated as I watched her tap against the festering stone. "W-what do you want?" The words prickled my dry throat.

Jezebel erupted into a taut laugh. "Isn't it obvious? I want to become queen." She took a daunting step forward, pushing me back a breath closer to the edge of the streaming fountain. "I didn't cut you out of my life when we were children to remain a duchess. I got rid of you and every other pest in my life to ensure I was only surrounded by people who would help me achieve my true goal." She flicked her eyes back toward the guests who were occupying the guard, allowing a twisted smile to crinkle her masked eyes. "And now I'm ready to get rid of you again. You've been nothing more than a pesky insect ever since you reentered my life, and I'm not about to let an insignificant bug tarnish my happily ever after."

She pressed forward again, spiking another white-hot flash through my vision. My veins constricted against the pressure, sending off every alarm in my body to warn me that I was in severe peril. I stumbled back another step, feeling my foot go cold when I stepped into the icy water's stream.

"Do it, Jezebel," I pleaded, clutching a hand to my burning heart. "Do you even care about the prince?"

Do you even love him?

"Of course, I care!" she snapped, thrusting out her hands to cripple me with another painful force. "He's everything I've ever needed, and once I'm queen, it won't matter what people think of my father... They'll have no choice but to accept me!"

I stared at her through my blurring eyes, hunching down lower into the rocky spring. "Y-your father? Why would people think ill of him?" The face of Duke Byron jolted through my throbbing brain with a painful twist.

"Oh, come on, Lacey..." she groaned dramatically as she casually passed the massive stone between her palms. "You've had, what? Twelve years to figure it out?" She searched my blank expression, quirking a proud smile when she realized I truly didn't understand what she meant. "Well, since you're going to die no matter what, I suppose I could enlighten you..."

My short breaths froze at her grim words, but I couldn't help but tune my attention into her voice.

"I'll have to make this quick, so don't cry or anything until the end. My father is one of the three heads of the magic stone black market. He's been covering up his deals for years by using pathetically desperate servants like your father. Unfortunately, his deals have gotten sloppier and now his enemies are threatening to spill his secrets to the crown. Obviously, I knew this was going to happen, so I made sure to make friends in the right places in anticipation of this. Once I win the competition and marry the prince, I'll have the power to cover up the rest of his crimes and scare his enemies back into hiding. Hence why I can't let you survive. If I don't win, my father might go to prison, and I certainly can't have that sullying my reputation because..." she bit back a vile snicker, "well, you know."

The world crumbled around me as the swelling inferno inside me numbed in comparison to my enraged heart. *All this time... Duke Byron hadn't just hurt my family; he'd been hurting others, too. Just how many lives had he destroyed?*

My shriveling body filled with a powerful fury, coaxing my legs into straightening to their full height. My eyes blazed at Jezebel with blinding hatred, fueling every ounce of pain I was enduring into a single piercing stare. Her face paled a touch, but she tightened her nails around the stone, using it as a crutch for her boldness.

I clenched my jaw. "My father has been *free* for over twelve years..." I took an almost mechanical step forward, ignoring the crushing pain that suffocated my lungs. Jezebel stiffened but didn't move. "Your father has been *innocent*, living a life of luxury..." I forced another foot forward, stepping out of the pooling fountain. My heart felt like it might burst, but the lifetime of pain that had been aroused from slumber eclipsed the pressure of the curse. "Do you really think I'm going to let you ruin Carlex's life, too!?"

My mind warned me to back down, but I wasn't listening to reason. I lunged for the monster before me, funneling every ounce of my agony into my strength. My legs buckled as she rushed forward with the stone raised like a shield, desperately swinging it around like a blunted sword. Her eyes looked frenzied, but I barely saw them as the excruciating torment inside me sent me falling back into the water.

No. I can't fall to her. If I fall, all of Reclusia will go with me.

"Yes, I do think you'll let me." Her voice twinged into an unhinged cackle.

Her pupils dilated wildly as she pressed the stone closer to me, forcing my limbs to scramble back another inch on instinct. My hands sifted through the gravel beneath the flowing water when suddenly I couldn't feel any ground at all. *I'm at the edge of the waterfall.*

A contorted laugh rose in Jezebel's throat as she eyed the cliff behind me. "You, see? You'll do whatever I want you to. Face it, Lacey, you never stood a chance at winning against me. Didn't anyone ever tell you that liars never prosper?"

My nerves went numb, silencing the unbearable pain as it stripped me of all my senses.

Not like this... I don't want to stop fighting, don't make me run. I'm a liar, but don't make me a coward, too.

Jezebel raised the stone once more, and my limbs betrayed me one final time. Lying about what I truly wanted to stand up against.

And then, I fell.

chapter twenty-seven

The water smacked against my spine with an icy blow. The cold pool vastly contradicted the blistering heat that had been pent-up inside me, shocking my system into a state of paralysis. I sank into the dark pool and the ache of my new bruises spread across my skin. The dark purple skirts billowed out around me, spreading through the water like a blossoming rose. A few beads of air bubbles escaped my lips as I watched the pink and tan makeup powder taint the water near my eyes, cleansing my skin of the painted mask. The magical pain that had tunneled through my veins slowly soothed against the swirling water, allowing the hurt from my fall to replace it.

I'd fallen...

Images of Jezebel's wicked smile pulsed through my mind like a fever dream. I'd been so close to winning... so close to saving Carlex from her talons. But once again, the curse refused to let me rise; instead, I could only tumble. By letting the curse envelop my whole body, I'd also allowed it to take over my free will. I wasn't ready to give up. I wanted to fight back more than I ever had before, but my desire to do so fueled the curse's ability to prevent me.

Is this how it was always meant to end?

My lungs burned for air as I watched the last bubble escape from my nose. The shock that had locked my limbs in place faded into adrenaline. I reoriented myself in the water, wincing from the fresh bruises that spanned my back. The massive ballgown acted like an anchor, drawing me closer to the bottom of the pool with each inch I moved upward. My eyes darted wildly around the shadowed water, catching onto a tiered stretch of rocks that looked climbable.

I forced the heavy skirts to move with me to the edge of the pool and snagged the rocks with my arms. My feet quickly found holds, and I used them to push all my weight upward, fighting against the pull of the saturated skirts. My arms burned as I worked muscles that hadn't been utilized in weeks. My slipper found another ledge, and I straightened my leg with all my might, pressing upward toward the glinting surface. I gasped in the night air as my head broke through the water's grasp.

My breath came short and heavy as I gradually pulled my drenched form out of the pool, stretching out on my stomach against the pebbly ground. My back throbbed with the fresh sting of the water's embrace as my head continued to spin from the shock. A roll of thunder echoed overhead, causing me to turn my eyes up to the sky just in time to feel a fresh drop of rain splatter on my nose.

I rose from the ground only a moment before the skies broke open, showering me with the bucketing storm. My elaborate hairdo lay tangled around my face in wet clumps as the black hair dye dripped around my eyes. I looked back up to the balcony's glow with a heavy heart. Somewhere mixed into the sound of the storm I could barely make out the noise of another guard bell chiming.

Three competitors left...

Everything inside me shifted after hearing the bell. I glanced down at my drenched gown, but no matter how I looked at it, my disguise had been ruined. The masterful make-up that Evie had applied had washed away and the rain was clearing out the rest of the black dye. All I had left was my mask, but even so, I was too far from the ballroom to even attempt to rejoin the game.

All girls must commit to the full tournament once the events begin... If I'm discovered missing, Jezebel will likely convince them I ran away and deserve to be disqualified.

I wiped the soggy mixture of dripping makeup and hair dye from my eyes, furrowing my brows intently as I fought to think of a way to solve this. The ballroom faced the back of the palace, so I would have to walk and climb around the entire perimeter in order to make it back to the front gate. Even if I did that, I would merely be delivering myself for execution. Jezebel would have plenty of time to spin whatever story she desired.

That won't work...

The other option was simply to give up. Evie had offered me a chance at escape earlier, so surely, I could find a way to get into contact with her again. I could easily disappear into the forest and pretend this entire fiasco never happened... But there wasn't a bone in my body that wanted to run. I wanted justice, I wanted Carlex, and I wanted to protect Reclusia from Jezebel and her viperous family.

You're right, Jezebel. I'm as pesky as an insect. Because I'm going to crawl back into your life as many times as it takes.

My blood rushed through my veins as I channeled my adrenaline into forcing out all elements of fear. I gazed up the waterfall, narrowing my eyes in on the slick rock ledges that were similar to the one I'd used to escape the pool.

If I want to get back to the ball in time, there's only one way I can go.

I kicked my slippers off, leaving them in the puddling mud as I slipped off my extra petticoats to lighten my gown. My eyes lingered on the beautiful slippers for a moment, using them as a reminder of who I was doing this for.

I took in a fortifying breath, turning my

eyes upward to the roaring waterfall that now flooded over from the pouring rain. I'd already fallen from it once, so I knew I could survive it, but even if I didn't...

I was staring death in the face either way.

I approached the wall with a determined fierceness, latching my fingers around the first notch I found and testing the slipperiness of my foothold before pushing upward.

I refuse to keep falling to you, Jezebel. I love Carlex, and I'm not going to step aside and let you ruin his life.

So, I climbed.

The rocks were thick and jagged. This made it easy to find grip points, but also easy to find sharp edges. I hissed as the ball of my foot pricked at the edge of a sharp stone. The rushing rain made it difficult to keep my eyes open, so I felt around blindly for each grab. My back screamed at me in disapproval as my injury from the fall overwhelmed my senses. I tried to push away the ache, focusing only on the sound of the rain, hoping I wouldn't hear another guard bell chime.

My progress quickened as I slowly got into a rhythm. My bare feet made it easy to find the safest holds, but every once in a while, my skin would slip against the slick stone, forcing me to pause and clamp onto the rocks until I could find another notch. My muscles burned from the climb, causing my arms to shake in rebellion at the excessive use of strength.

I puffed heavy breaths of the humid air, thankful that the rain was at least cool and refreshing. Despite shedding a few layers of petticoats, my gown still added a fair amount of weight to the climb, sapping my energy faster than I'd hoped. I risked a glance down at the fading ground and relieved at seeing that I was a little over halfway.

You're almost there... don't give up now.

Another bell chimed above the balcony, only barely reaching my ears through the growing storm. My fingers tightened around the rocks, whitening my knuckles with a petrifying fear.

That means there are only two competitors left. Is it me and Jezebel? Or had she already lost?

I didn't wait to deliberate on the thought; instead, I pushed more power into my movements and raced up the remainder of the wall with new motivation. Water dribbled down my face and neck, mixing with the remnants of makeup and sweat that had collected at my brow. I reached for another stone, then another, then another. Each time, I envisioned Jezebel smiling from an undeserved victory.

She won't win. Not while I'm still here. I may not be able to tell the truth about what she did, but I can lie... And that's far more terrifying.

My hand smacked against the top of the balcony floor with a victorious splash of water.

Every inch of me trembled violently as I smacked down atop the solid ground, heaving in the misty air with a hand clutched over my pounding heart. For a moment, my adrenaline faded, forcing my body to sink into the puddles like a leaden weight. My bare feet still dangled over the edge of the waterfall, feeling the cold water rush against my toes. I could have laid there for days, but the final chime beyond the doors bolted me upright.

"Our last contestant appears to have withdrawn from the competition," King Aldrich's voice boomed from inside the glass. I turned my frenzied eyes toward the glow of the ballroom, flinging water around from the shake of my hair. The entire balcony had emptied out when the rain began, leaving only me in the dark puddles. My eyes widened as I looked through the rain to see Jezebel stand proudly in her disguise, alongside Carlex and the king. "Our winner is... Lady Jezebel Gannet of Reclusia."

No...

I scrambled to my feet, ignoring the stinging pain of the fresh cuts and the burn of my muscles. I hurried toward the doors but stopped just before touching the brass doorknob to think through my entrance. My thoughts fluttered to the tiny purity stone that dotted my earlobe.

Remember, you can't tell the truth, except maybe once. So you better have the best lie imaginable.

I straightened my shoulders, funneling all my anger, hurt, and pain into my act. I adjusted my mask, ensuring that at least my face was somewhat concealed. My disguise may have been ruined, but appearance was only the basis of a lie, and I was ready to dig deeper.

Let's do this.

I burst through the doors, flinging water across the floor as I stormed into the ballroom with a demanding presence. Eyes flocked to me with bewilderment, but the only face I was focused on was the astounded fury that gripped my rival.

"You!" I jeered an accusing finger at Jezebel, forcing every bit of rage into my heated breath. "You're not Jezebel! She's lying! She's that blasted commoner, Lacey! She pushed me off the balcony to take my place!"

I tried to lunge for Jezebel, but a pair of guards pulled me away before I could reach her. My chest didn't flare when I approached her, sending a small touch of relief through me that she must have passed off the strength stone to one of her colleagues.

Every mouth in the room dropped as horrified gasps spread out across the crowd. King Aldrich snapped his gaze to Jezebel, studying her with a disbelieving gape. Carlex's eyes widened as he squinted at the two of us with an equal level of befuddlement.

I could almost feel the heated anger radiating off Jezebel as she balled her hands into fists. "You liar! Of course, I'm the real Jezebel! You're the one who's Lacey." She rushed forward to confront me, but Carlex snagged her by the arm before she could try to attack me again.

"Whoa, hold on!" Carlex's eyes darted between the two of us before settling on me with a bewildered gaze. "Did you really get pushed off the balcony?" He raked his eyes over my drenched and shuddering form, sucking in a concerned breath that clearly irritated his captive.

"Of course, she didn't!" Jezebel pulled away from Carlex, narrowing her murderous gaze onto me. "She's lying, just like she always does!"

"Spoken like a girl with a true curse," I spat back, fighting my arms against the grip of the guards. "Admit it, Lacey, you pushed me because you wanted to become me! You've always been jealous of everything I had!"

Her face contorted into disgust. "What!? I've never been jealous of the likes of *you*." Her pride flared in her voice, reddening her neck through the layers of powder. "I don't want to be you; I wanted to get rid of you!" The moment the words left her lips, she retracted them with a hissing gasp, mirroring the shocked exclamations from the crowd.

"So, you did push her, then?" King Aldrich bellowed, towering over Jezebel with a fierce fury.

Jezebel shrunk back beneath the king's shadow. "I-I... yes. I, *Lacey,* pushed Jezebel off the balcony."

Carlex's jaw clenched as he grabbed Jezebel by the shoulder to spin her around. "If you're truly Lacey, then you wouldn't have been able to say your own name." His eyes burned into her, causing her face to blanch.

I tugged one of my arms free from the guard and quickly latched my fingers around my earring, touching the magic stone to my skin. My tongue instantly loosened.

"Yes, because I'm the *real* Lacey, and I was sabotaged by Jezebel, which is a breach in the rules." I snapped my fingers away from the gem just before the last of the magic drained, leaving maybe one more syllable of truth left. With my hand still freed, I tore off my mask, unveiling my unpainted face to the crowd.

His face instantly brightened. "It is her. She is the real Lacey," Carlex announced to the crowd. His joyful features snapped into hatred as he turned his darkened eyes back onto Jezebel. "Which means that you just confessed to attacking a fellow competitor."

Jezebel went entirely stiff, her mouth opening and closing as only babbles came out. "I-I... N-no... That... t-that's not— H-hold on a minute, she's just a commoner! She can't win!"

"No, she's a future queen."

My breath vanished from my lungs as I watched King Aldrich step in front of Jezebel with an unmovable glower. *Did he really just say...?*

"Lacey may not be of noble birth, but she has showcased every quality Reclusia could ever need in a future ruler." The king's voice was stern, yet assured, filling me with an honor I never could have imagined coming from him. "Once I understood how truly happy this woman has made my son, I designed this competition to act as a final test of her worth. Lying can be both a danger and a skill, and if we were to have a queen tainted by a curse, I needed to ensure she could navigate it efficiently. It took me too long to see it, but now I understand why my son has chosen her out of all the others."

He tilted his head back toward me, giving me a soft look of respect. "Lacey Arachne is the winner of tonight's event. She has proven, without a doubt, that a lie can be a powerful tool when wielded wisely, for she was able to extract a confession with the twisting of her words. I greatly apologize for ever doubting her, or my son's choice." My heart pounded victoriously in my chest as my eyes latched onto the bursting joy that was seeping out of Carlex. "And with this win, Lacey Arachne is our victor. Guards, please release our future queen and arrest Lady Jezebel."

Jezebel thrashed and screamed as a group of guards surrounded her, half-guiding, half-dragging her out of the ballroom. The moment the guards released me, I practically fell into Carlex's arms. Cheers erupted from the audience in congratulations of my victory, but it all fell quiet on my ears as I felt my prince's arms wrap around my aching body. His touch pressed against my bruises, but I'd never felt so wonderful in my entire life.

I'd done it... I'd lied my way into something true.

Carlex pulled a touch away from me, resting his forehead against mine as we both soaked in the roaring celebration. "I knew you could do it," he whispered softly.

A soft giggle rose in my raw throat as I pulled him closer, resting my chin on his shoulder. "I did, too." I took in a long breath, reminding myself that I was finally safe and in the arms of the man I loved. "But I promised you I would give up."

His heart fluttered against my chest as he chuckled warmly. "That you did." He pulled away once more, taking both of my hands in his as he turned to face the crowd.

He glanced back at his father, as if looking for one final sign of reassurance before addressing the kingdom. I watched with an illuminating heart as the king gave his son an approving nod, flickering the smallest smile above his beard.

He squeezed my hand, clearing his voice as

he turned his eager eyes to me. "Lacey Arachne of Reclusia, will you do me the greatest honor and agree to become my queen, as all these citizens stand witness."

Elation swept through my veins as I stared into the longing eyes of the man I had climbed a waterfall for. He was mine now; he was truly mine. No more contests, death threats, or nobility to fight against. Carlex was going to be my prince, and I would get to keep my promise and see him in the morning after all.

Indescribable bliss poured through me as I removed one of my hands from his and touched the last drop of magic that rested in my earring. My tongue freed and I spoke the truest word in my life as loud as I possibly could. "Yes."

chapter twenty-eight

"Oh, Lacey, I'm so happy for you I can hardly stand it!" Evie squeezed me into a tight hug, then quickly pulled away to smooth out the ruffles she'd made on my gold dress. "You get to be introduced to the entire kingdom today, and they're going to love you!"

"She's right, darling." Mother stepped out from behind me, clasping her hands together gleefully as she took in my full appearance. "Oh, you look beautiful."

A tall man with a stubbled chin, dark brown eyes, and a tailored coat stepped up beside mother, slipping his hand around her waist as he blinked at me with teary eyes.

"You truly do, Lacey," Father said with a shuddering breath. "You've grown into an incredible young woman, and I couldn't be prouder."

My heart swelled with joy as I looked into the eyes of the man I had been aching to see for the last twelve years. After I had won the competition, I managed to explain everything to Carlex that Jezebel had confessed on the balcony.

It took less than a day for the royal guard to find evidence of Duke Byron's illegal gem distribution and track down all the servants who had been imprisoned on his command. As of last evening, my father was free.

I twisted my hands together nervously as I stared at the stunning glittering gown in the mirror. Webbed patterns of golden thread trailed down the cream-colored skirts and long trumpet sleeves covered up the remaining bruises on my arms from two nights ago. Today was the day I was introduced to Reclusia as the future queen... but how does one introduce herself when she can only lie?

"What if they don't like me?" I murmured, nervously biting my nail. "What if the people judge me because of the curse? Or what if—"

"Relax, Lace!" Evie snagged my hand from my mouth and twirled me across the room. "They're all going to adore you. And besides, you don't need to be nearly as worried as I do. I may not have to face an entire kingdom, but I do have to face my parents now that they know about our whole switcheroo." Her face paled for a moment as she scrunched her brows together with a sigh. "Let's hope they're in a forgiving mood..."

I bit back a laugh as I watched her pace the room fretfully. My heart hammered in my chest with nerves and excitement. Today I became known to the entire kingdom as Carlex's betrothed. Even the fear of facing an entire population dulled when I thought of the joy of becoming his wife.

A knock fluttered against the door, signaling that the time had come for me to meet the kingdom. My breath hitched and I turned back to Evie and my parents for one final look of encouragement.

"Hey, you handled Jezebel... Reclusia should be nothing." Evie winked.

"You'll be amazing, sweetheart. I don't know if you can make us any prouder, but I'll go ahead and challenge you to try." Father quirked a crooked grin at me, filling me with the last bit of assurance I needed to step through the doors.

The servants guided me through the halls, leading me to the balcony that looked into the city square. When we arrived at the doors, Carlex greeted me with a gentle kiss on the forehead. My skin warmed beneath his touch, sending a blissful ripple through me.

"You look beautiful." His gaze gripped me like a rare treasure. "Are you nervous?" he asked softly, lacing his fingers through mine.

I swallowed. "No."

He gave me a reassuring smile, brushing a gentle touch across my cheek. "You'll do great. They're going to adore you," he leaned his lips forward to whisper in my ear, "just like I do."

My cheeks flushed red at the same moment the balcony doors swung open, revealing the entire kingdom waiting below. My legs stiffened, but Carlex eased me forward with a calming pet against my hand.

We stopped at the railing of the balcony, standing alongside the king and queen, who were smiling radiantly at us. I averted my eyes from the crowds, fixing my gaze onto the one man who calmed all my fears.

Carlex smiled, then turned to address his people. "Citizens of Reclusia, it is my humblest honor to introduce your future queen, the soon-to-be crown princess, Lacey Arachne."

Warm cheers and applause broke out across the square, and I risked a glance down at the array of people. Hundreds of smiling faces warmed my heart as I watched commoners, just like me, erupt into joyous celebration.

"Now I know what some of you may be thinking," Carlex continued, "Lacey is not of noble birth, nor is she of royal blood. However, I can assure you that the bridal competition has still chosen the worthiest candidate for your queen. Lacey may not be a noble, but she has the most honest heart, filled with purity."

He turned away from the railing, facing me with an eager smile as he dug something out of his pocket. "And that's why I want to give you this."

He softened his voice, ensuring only I could hear it as he opened his palm to reveal a sparkling ring. I gasped as I instantly noticed the vibrant radiance of it. *Another purity stone.*

"It's been fortified by the most talented jewelers in the kingdom." He smiled, taking my hand into his to slide the ring onto my finger. "They believe its power should be capable of withstanding a century of unpurified magic."

My breath caught as the rock pressed against the top of my finger, instantly clearing my heart of the entanglement that the curse had left shrouded around me. I blinked up at him in disbelief.

"A century?" I gaped. "But that would mean..."

"You're free, Lacey." He pressed a kiss to the top of my hand, sending a rush of unfiltered joy through my unrestrained mind. "Now, address your kingdom with whatever words you choose. Your voice is yours now."

My voice... is mine.

I turned to the crowd with bewilderment still flowing through my veins. My heart pounded, not from nerves, but from sheer excitement to speak however I chose. I cleared my throat, relishing in the freedom that would now be mine forever.

"People of Reclusia, I may not be what you expected for a queen, but I can assure you that I'm not what I expected, either. All my life I've been called cursed, or a liar, or a peasant. I have been all of those things, but standing here today, I am so much more, and I hope I can help all of Reclusia see that we are all so much more than what we are told as well. So as your future queen, I promise I will rule with integrity, strength, and above all..." I turned to smile at Carlex and his parents, "honesty."

The crowd erupted into cheering and applause. At the same moment, the clouds parted across the sky, showering the balcony with golden sunshine that glittered off my dress. Carlex wrapped me in his arms, unashamedly showing the kingdom just how proud he was to call me his own.

"I love you, my little liar," he whispered amorously, fluttering my heart with his heated breath.

I smiled playfully, tapping his shoulder with a tease. "What do you mean? I've never told a lie in my life."

He laughed. "So I get you the most powerful purity stone in the kingdom, yet you still choose to lie to your betrothed?" He gave me a crooked smile, and I couldn't help but giggle back at him as he slowly led me back off the balcony into the privacy of the castle walls.

I stopped once we were behind the doors, giving him a giddy smile as I placed a gentle hand on his cheek. "Well, there's definitely one truth I'll never withhold from you."

He leaned in closer, pulling me in until our lips were only a breath apart. "Oh yeah? And what's that?"

I wrapped my arms around the back of his

neck, taking in a long breath before speaking the words I would repeat for the rest of my life. "I love you, Carlex."

And then, truthfully, I kissed my betrothed.

Thanks For Reading

Ready for more Once Upon A Rhyme? Keep reading for a sneak peek of book two.

Little Bo Sneak

Little Bo Sneak

Prologue

"Come along, Evie. We wouldn't want to miss your appointment," Mother said in a sing-song voice that was somewhere between proper and frustrated.

Despite my greatest efforts to delay going to the dress shop, we were still nearly there on time. I tried spilling tea on my dress, hiding Mother's gloves, and even tangling a comb in my hair, but Mother simply threw a bonnet over my head and dragged me out the door. I hated bonnets, perhaps even more than I hated dress shopping for my tenth birthday celebration after I made myself perfectly clear that I wanted to go horseback riding. Mother said ten-year-old-ladies didn't ride horses; they rode in carriages.

I told her ladies were boring, but that only earned me another lesson in etiquette.

"Ah, look! The shop is just ahead. And look at that adorable display in the window!" Mother pointed at the shiny glass storefront, filled with neat rows of mannequins and fabric displays.

I followed the direction of her finger and nearly stumbled as my jaw dropped at the horrific display she was gawking at. A bright yellow dress, just about my size, stood far too proudly in the center of the window. It had a frilly high neck, hideous rosettes down the sleeves, more ruffles than an angry duck, and worst of all... a matching bonnet.

"How adorable!" Mother awed as she dragged me toward the lacy shop of torture. "We should definitely have you try on that one."

I stared up at the sky, begging the world for a magic stone to fall from the heavens and grant me the strength to run back home until I was safely hidden in my secret blanket fort. It didn't even have to be a magic stone; even a minor distraction would do the trick since we were already almost late. I glanced around for any cracks in the ground I could trip on, or perhaps a conveniently lost child. My gaze darted wildly around the crowded street, searching as intently as I could for anything to save me from my doomed fate.

"Thief!" A shrill scream split through the air, shooting the biggest smile up my face. "Someone help! That man stole my pocketbook!"

My body buzzed with excitement as I locked on to the pocketbook thief, a dark-haired man with scary green eyes and a strange hunch in his posture.

"Oh, how terrible." Mother pressed a hand to her cheek, only pausing briefly until she noticed a few members of the royal guard spring into action. "I hope the guard can catch that man... Now, we better hurry along."

What? That's it!?

While I was grateful for the distraction, it was far too brief, but I didn't plan to keep it that way.

"Don't worry, Mother!" I yanked my hand from her grip, barely managing to pry my fingers free. "I'll go make sure the guard catches the bad man!"

I spun around, and barely felt Mother's hand graze the back of my lacy bonnet before I escaped into the crowd.

"What!? Evie, wait!" Mother reached out for me again, but I wasn't about to give up my chance at escape now. I sped up, ducking under the arms of an elderly couple as I followed the direction of the thief. "Evie, get back here!"

Mother's voice died off behind me as victory blossomed in my chest. I knew running off would earn me plenty of scoldings—and likely even another round of etiquette lessons—but if it kept me from wearing the heinous yellow cupcake, it was well worth it.

I'd only loosely been paying attention to where the thief actually went, but it was the busiest time of day in this district, which meant he'd probably try to disappear into the crowds in the marketplace. I turned the corner and found the pair of guards who'd been in hot pursuit already combing through the sea of people. They stopped a few shoppers to ask questions, and tried to funnel everyone else past them, but it seemed inefficient since the marketplace had two back alleys where a crook could hide in.

Both alleys led to dead ends, and Mother always told me not to go back there because that's where the urchins live, but that never made sense to me because my tutor always said urchins lived in the ocean. I paused in front of one of the alleys and glanced into the shadows. There definitely didn't appear to be any ocean back there, but it did smell kind of fishy, so maybe Mother was right after all.

A few people dressed in ragged clothes, camped out in empty supply crates and covered in news pamphlets lined the alleyway. I considered asking them if they'd seen any urchins, or if they would be willing to show me how they made their cool crate forts, but before I could introduce myself, a strange woman walked out from around the alley's corner.

She was blonde, wearing an oversized dress covered in patches and a bonnet, just like me. As she passed me, she gave me a brief smile, and her eyes gleamed in a wicked shade of green.

My breath caught as I recognized the color,

then again when I recognized the obscure way the woman carried herself. Her posture was leaned too far forward, her hair looked too clean for someone in a dress that old, and her bag was the perfect size to carry someone else's pocketbook.

The thief is pretending to be a lady!?

I crept through the crowd and watched closely as the thief-turned-lady approached the guards. The guards glanced at her—or him, but never truly looked, and a second later, he was let past them. My jaw dropped as I followed behind the thief as close as I dared, watching them confidently stride toward the end of the market.

"Hey you," the guard called down to me, jerking me from my thoughts. "Where are your parents? Are you lost?"

I looked at the thief, and a fresh fire stirred in my heart as I decided today was the day that I, Genevieve Rayelle Palleep, would save the world.

"Yes, I'm lost!" I smiled up at the guard. "Hurry and catch me!"

I darted between the guard's legs and sprinted back into the crowd.

"Hey! Wait—" the guard called after me, but my disappearing act was far too advanced for his meager skills.

I squeezed past crowds and pushed through clusters of shoppers until the masqueraded thief was right in front of me. I glanced back and confirmed that both guards were hot on my tail, then dashed forward and clamped my entire body around the thief's legs.

"What in the!?" the thief shouted, exposing his obviously masculine voice as he clawed at my arms. "Listen here, you little brat—"

The guards jerked to a stop in front of us, their eyes wide as the thief went silent.

"I-I mean, uh..." the thief cleared his voice, and in a mock-feminine tone, said, "what a cute little lady..."

The guard was already deadlocked on the thief's fake hair and even faker smile. "Madame, may we please see your bag?" the taller guard asked in a cold tone.

"Well, I..." The thief darted his eyes around the market, then in the blink of an eye, kicked me to the ground and made a run for it.

I fell back onto the cobblestone with a squeak, but my fluffy pink skirt padded me against any bruises. The thief only made it a few feet before the tall guard caught him, and the shorter guard bent down to help me.

"Are you alright?" he asked gently, but his eyes seemed more serious, like they were studying me somehow.

"Yes, I'm fine!" I said brightly, feeling beyond proud that I had successfully escaped the dress shop appointment and saved the world, all in the same day. "Did you find the nice lady's pocketbook?"The guard glanced back at his partner, who was currently pulling out the patterned pocketbook from the thief's bag. "We did, but it looks like you found it first."

My grin broadened. "I just noticed the lady had the same funny walk as the thief. Oh, and that his hair looked too clean to live with the sea urchins, and also that his eyes were scary."

The guard blinked at me and furrowed his brow—the same way I often saw Mother do whenever I tried to convince her I was allergic to lace.

"I see..." he said in a contemplative tone. "What's your name, dear?"

"Genevieve Palleep," I answered with a proud nod.

"You have a keen eye, Genevieve." The guard smiled, and something inside me knew it wasn't a normal smile. It was the kind of smile you saw before you received the type of news that made you even more excited than riding a horse for your birthday. "Let's get you back to your mother, but first, I want you to meet someone."

Follow me

for more updates on Once Upon A Rhyme

Abigail Manning, Author

Abby Manning Author

Abigailmanningauthor.com

Special thanks to Debbie for owning the coolest bookstore and filling it with my stories.

Printed in Great Britain
by Amazon

53609715R00209